"Have you ever fantasized about making love in the rain?" Sean whispered

"I hadn't thought about it before." Caitlin ran her hand along her arm, sliding across the droplets that left her skin smooth to the touch. "The rain is so fresh and invigorating. And I guess it would make things kind of slippery." She shivered. "There's something about having water run across your body that makes you think of..."

Her voice trailed off as the innocence of it all faded. The water might be cool, but her skin was suddenly hot and flushed. Caitlin could feel Sean's gaze on her lips, her breasts. Narrowed. Piercing. She squeezed her eyes shut and shivered.

She felt as if she'd been transported to another place. She could almost hear the sound of the rain, hushing the rest of the world and leaving her with the desperate agent who had kidnapped her and carried her away with him. She could almost feel his hot, wet kiss, his hands on her body, his mouth upon her straining breast. The heavy heat between her thighs became almost unbearable....

She wanted this. She wanted *him*.

Almost as much as she'd wanted her adventure in the first place.

Dear Reader,

When I was a kid, fairy tales and fantasy were a big part of my life. Lucky for me, they still are. After all, one of the best things about being a writer is that it gives me the chance to revisit my favorite themes. And in my opinion, you can't beat *Beauty and the Beast* for being the perfect love story. Only for Blaze, I got the chance to take that theme in a whole new, sizzling direction!

My heroine, Caitlin McCormick, is a dreamer, too. Like me, she uses her imagination and creates exciting, adventurous fantasies to compensate for the mundane lack of adventure in her life. Until adventure comes walking through her front door in the form of a bad-tempered FBI agent with a tantalizing proposition. Animal magnetism aside, Agent Sean Maddox has the heart of a prince—if only the beauty he kidnaps for the weekend can help him find it....

This isn't your average fairy tale—but I hope you'll enjoy it! Let me know what you think about Caitlin's fantasy-filled adventure. I love to hear from my readers. You may contact me at P.O. Box 5162, Grand Island, NE 68802-5162, or check out my Web site at www.juliemiller.org.

Enjoy,

Julie Miller

Books by Julie Miller

HARLEQUIN BLAZE
45—INTIMATE KNOWLEDGE

HARLEQUIN INTRIGUE
651—IN THE BLINK OF AN EYE
666—THE DUKE'S COVERT MISSION
699—THE ROOKIE

CARNAL INNOCENCE

Julie Miller

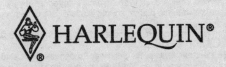

HARLEQUIN®

TORONTO • NEW YORK • LONDON
AMSTERDAM • PARIS • SYDNEY • HAMBURG
STOCKHOLM • ATHENS • TOKYO • MILAN • MADRID
PRAGUE • WARSAW • BUDAPEST • AUCKLAND

To the Fulton Public Library in Fulton, Missouri—
for having a wall full of fairy tales and fantasies
for me to read over and over again.

ISBN 0-373-79081-3

CARNAL INNOCENCE

Copyright © 2003 by Julie Miller.

Visit us at www.eHarlequin.com

Printed in U.S.A.

1

"GO HOME, Maddox. This case is washed up."

Special Agent Sean Maddox took the letter from his partner, Thomas Hall, and angrily crushed it in his fist. "Two months of an airtight investigation shot to hell because one state court judge can't keep it in his pants."

"Even the high mucky-mucks of society are entitled to a vacation now and then." Leave it to Thomas to try to reason this thing out.

"Is that what he called it? A vacation?" Sean spat out.

The whole case was slipping through his fingers, and Sean felt responsible. He'd promised Alicia Reyes he'd nail her kidnapper. She was just a kid—a sweet little thing the same age his sister had been when he'd started taking care of her all those years ago.

But the longer it took to get a judge's ruling on critical evidence, the less likely it was they'd make their case against Marquez stick. And if that sleazebag walked... "Damn!" He wanted to say worse.

Special Agent Thomas Hall pushed his glasses up the bridge of his nose, his reaction to the bad news as coolly reticent as Sean's had been hot-tempered. "There's no proof that Justice Rossini had an affair. His resignation letter states that the mere rumor of infidelity is enough to harm his family's reputation. He's resigning from the state bench effective immediately to keep the Rossini name out of the papers and go home to Roanoke to work on his marriage."

"Did he honestly think an island getaway with his secretary tagging along to take notes wouldn't raise a few eyebrows? We waited all last weekend for this guy to get back to Virginia. He's been stonewalling us since Monday." Sean shot the wad of paper onto the scattered files that littered his desktop. "He couldn't have given us a ruling on that forensic evidence *before* he went on permanent vacation?"

But the rumors sounded all too familiar. Sean knew firsthand how gossip and separations and rampant libidos could tear a family apart. He'd watched his parents' marriage go up in smoke when his British father's military career kept him away from home for months at a time. Not even the unexpected arrival of Sean's baby sister, Sabrina, could convince Admiral Roland Maddox to stay put in England.

Sean remembered encouraging his mother to move back across the Atlantic to her home in Nebraska—to be near her family while his father was abroad. He'd grown up thinking his mother was the one who was suffering. But Sean's sympathy faded the day he discovered her trips to town for a college class had been to see the professor himself. In a hotel room.

As if that wasn't enough, Sabrina had barely made it into third grade when a picture of the admiral with his female aide-de-camp had graced the *London Times*. Sean's father hadn't even bothered to deny the affair; the damage had been done. His mother had retaliated by announcing that she'd been discreet by comparison. The sparks flew. Sean had tucked Sabrina under his arm and faded into the background while their parents duked it out.

The divorce dragged on for two years. When those affairs ended, new partners quickly filled the empty spaces in their parents' lives, but commitment was never part of the scenario. And the children were never more than an afterthought.

With that stellar example to learn from, Sean planned to do better. He'd found his most enduring relationship to be with the Bureau. But women were another matter altogether. Other than his relationship with his sister, whom he still called once a week at college, his longest relationship with a woman had been eight months, two weeks and a day.

It had taken him that long to notice Elise's roving eye.

Elise had initially been turned on by the badge and the gun. She'd gotten a thrill from dating a real-life hero. But after the fun had worn off—about the time Sean was thinking about getting serious—he'd found her recent correspondence with her old college sweetheart. When he'd seen Elise and Frat Boy meet for dinner and had caught them kissing, Sean had known it was over with her.

Thank God he'd had the Bureau to return to the next morning. For eight years now, the job had never let him down.

Letting his shoulders expand and settle with a weary sigh, Sean picked up the goofy card that had come in the mail from his sister at Stanford University, and smiled. Sabrina might be the one woman he could count on in this world. Count on without question. Even if she did have the balls to razz him about his single status.

He had nothing against women, nothing against marriage.

He just wasn't going to put his faith in either one of them.

"Something you want to share?" Thomas's pointed question brought Sean back to the glassed-in confines of their tiny office.

"Nah. It's just a note from Bree." Sean smiled again, easily picturing Sabrina's long wavy curls and mischievous grin. "Checking on me before she leaves the country for her next graduate studies project."

Thomas adjusted his glasses. "You're okay with that?"

Sean shrugged. He'd had a lot of years to get used to

taking care of his little sister. He hadn't had enough to get used to her being all grown up and gallivanting around the world to dig up buried treasures in pursuit of her Ph.D. in archaeology.

Another image, of a little girl with equally long hair—black instead of blond—filled his mind and pushed aside his sentimental thoughts. A simmering frustration tensed his muscles and pulled his mouth into a taut line. He tucked Sabrina's card into his top drawer and looked across the desks to Thomas. "One thing I know I'm not okay with is Alicia Reyes's kidnapper walking away because of a legal technicality."

Sean swiped a hand over his jaw and scratched at his scraggly beard. He hadn't shaved since yesterday morning. He and Thomas had been too busy piecing together the facts of the young girl's kidnapping. Alicia was home safe now, but her kidnapper would never stand trial if they couldn't come up with more than circumstantial evidence to warrant an arraignment.

"We were that close to nailing Marquez. So what if we entered that house without a warrant?" Sean thumped his finger on the desk. "We had the warrant in our hands before we opened the closet and found the ropes with the hair samples."

"You're preaching to the choir, Maddox." Thomas stood and straightened his tie. By this time of the afternoon, Sean had no idea where he'd discarded his. "But without Rossini to give us the go-ahead on using that rope, Marquez is just a creepy guy who lives in the neighborhood."

Thomas adjusted the holster he wore strapped around his shoulder, and picked up his suit coat from the rack beside their office door. Then he reached into his pocket and pulled out a small package. He tossed it to Sean. "Here. Do you even know it's May 29?"

With easy reflexes, Sean caught the package. Closer inspection showed it to be a present.

"Happy birthday," Thomas added.

Sabrina's card had come early, before she took off for parts unknown. Since then, Sean had lost track of the days. Thomas, of course, never missed such details. "You shouldn't have." Sean dredged up a sly grin and ripped into the ribbon and paper. "What's this supposed to be?" Thomas had given him a tiny, black, leather-bound book. He thumbed through the pages. Inside he found an assortment of names and phone numbers. "Noelle. Kris. Cassie. Sue. Sherry. Mary Ann."

"Since Elise left, you don't seem to have a little black book of your own, nor would you take the time to use one. So I thought I'd share some friends of mine." Thomas walked over and tapped the book. "I put the names of six very nice ladies in there. They're smart, they're sexy, they're available. And they're willing to meet you, which is no small accomplishment on my part, I might add. Why don't you call one of them and go celebrate your birthday tonight?" Thomas shoved aside a stack of files and sat on the corner of Sean's desk. "What are you now? Thirty?"

"Thirty-two."

"That's almost over the hill, buddy. You're good at your job, Sean. No one would ever argue that. But this stack of paperwork and that badge aren't going to keep you warm at night." Thomas shrugged, indicating the logic of his argument was irrefutable. "It's not as if women don't like you. You're not bad-looking, you work out, you have that James Bond accent you inherited from your dad going for you."

Sean leaned back in his chair and listened. As much as he might not want to hear it, he trusted Thomas's opinion. No one could have predicted the two men would become such good friends. First of all, they were polar opposites in looks and personality. Thomas was tall and lanky. With his bookish demeanor and dark hair, he'd always reminded Sean of Gregory Peck playing Atticus Finch in *To Kill a Mockingbird*. Sean wasn't quite as tall, and he was more likely to be cast as Schwarzenegger's stand-in in some action flick. His blond hair always seemed to be out of place while Thomas was neat as a pin. Thomas was a thinker. Sean trusted his gut.

But they understood each other. Inside. Where it counted. A woman could never do that.

"I notice you're not wearing a ring either, buddy," Sean stated. "You're thirty-two also."

Thomas rose and headed for the door. "True. But I've got plans tonight. I can get the job done *and* keep the ladies happy." He turned in the open doorway. "There's not another thing we can do on the Marquez case except hope that legal gets a postponement until we can get a ruling from another judge on that rope."

Sean refused to give up hope. Alicia Reyes had never given up hope while she'd been held hostage. He reached for the nearest file and opened it. "There's got to be another angle we can work here."

Thomas shook his head. "Go home. Get laid. Get some sleep, if that's how you want to celebrate. But do something for yourself. The case will still be here in the morning."

Reluctantly, Sean agreed to the logic of Thomas's argument. He was battle weary. But the thought of going home to his empty apartment wasn't making him feel any peppier. He tossed the file back onto his desk and stood. "You're right. We can finish saving the world tomorrow."

"If you want, I'll take you out for a beer," Thomas offered.

"I thought you had plans tonight."

"I do. But I can give her a call."

Sean wouldn't be such a spoilsport. "Forget it. I'm a big boy. I'll find some entertainment on my own."

"Okay, hotshot." Thomas put two fingers to his brow and saluted him. "I hope your mission goes well tonight. See you in the morning. I'll be expecting a full report."

"Get out of here." Once his partner had left, Sean reached behind his neck and rubbed at the tension that seemed to hang like a perpetual burden across his shoulders.

He really should take Thomas's advice. Spend some time with a pretty lady. Share a few laughs. Do some serious catching-up on his involuntary celibacy of the past months.

At the very least he could call one of those names in Thomas's black book and introduce himself. Maybe he could convince one of them to share some birthday cake with him.

His sex-deprived body jumped at a hazy image of a sexy naked lady licking frosting off his fingers. But as he squeezed his eyes shut and tried to bring the image into sharp focus, it faded in a puff of smoke. His eyes shot open and focused on the mounds of paperwork instead. Damn, his imagination stunk.

Maybe he'd do better to buy a six-pack and a *Playboy* and ease his frustrations that way.

With that much of a plan made, Sean rolled down the sleeves of his shirt and buttoned the cuffs. He was crossing the room to get his jacket when the door burst open.

"Hall. Maddox."

"Chief?" The only man in the building who worked longer hours than Sean himself was Deputy Chief John Dillon. And judging by the scowl that creased his mahogany skin, his long hours were just getting started. "What's up?"

Chief Dillon scoped the office. "Hall leave already?"

"It is after five."

"Then you take a look at this." He thrust a fax into Sean's hands and started pacing. "That just came off the wire. The ambassador from San Isidro, Ramon Vargas, was found dead in his Washington, D.C., hotel suite this morning."

Sean scanned the report for pertinent facts. "The local cops suspect foul play?"

"The San Isidrans are already on the horn demanding answers. Supposedly, he drowned in his bathtub, but there are bruises on his forearms and the back of his neck that indicate a struggle."

"Isn't this a case for the locals or the embassy police to handle? Why bring it to our attention?" Then he read the last line in the second to last paragraph. "Son of a bitch. Is this information accurate?"

"From a reliable informer." Chief Dillon was shaking his head when Sean looked up. "I don't believe in coincidence, either."

"Vargas just returned from vacation on Pleasure Cove Island?"

"Sound familiar?"

With the thrill of the chase on again, Sean circled behind his desk and leafed through the scattered pile of papers. "Bingo." He pulled out Judge Rossini's itinerary for the past two weeks and compared it to the dates on Dillon's report. "They were both on Pleasure Cove Island last weekend."

He set the papers down side by side and searched for another piece of evidence. He pulled out the photocopy of a high-class, lowbrow invitation and read it out loud.

"You are cordially invited for a weekend of fun and frolic on Pleasure Cove Island. Security guaranteed.

"Meet at the New Harbor dock at 5:00 p.m. to be ferried across Muscongus Bay to my island home.

"Leave your wildest fantasies to us.

"All will be discreetly provided for you.

"Your host,

"Douglas Fairchild."

"It's a perfect setup," the chief said. "Word is, if you have the money and the power, you can go there and do the nasty however and to whomever you want. Fairchild promises anonymity. There are no telephone communications to the island. He's never allowed the press there. For medical emergencies, there's a nurse on the premises. No one goes in once the party's started. No one comes out until it's done."

"A regular playground for the rich and self-indulgent. You think Fairchild is blackmailing his guests?"

"Or maybe the guest list isn't as anonymous as Fairchild wants it to be."

Adrenaline pumped through Sean's veins. He wasn't out of the Reyes kidnapping case yet. If he could find something to prove Judge Rossini had been coerced into resigning, he'd have a whole new angle to pursue to keep Marquez behind bars. "Can I go check it out?"

Dillon grinned. "I was hoping you'd ask. Take tomorrow off. Make it a three-day weekend. The ferry to the island leaves promptly at five o'clock." He was already backing out the door. "I'll finagle you an invitation and a high-profile cover so you can go in as a guest. You get yourself the date."

The adrenaline burned out in Sean's veins. "You're not assigning a female agent?"

"You've got fewer than twenty-four hours, Maddox." Dillon talked as if he thought Sean was too thickheaded to figure out the obvious. "Take a girlfriend. Tell her you won a free vacation. Tell her you're celebrating your birthday. It'll be easier to behave as a couple with someone you're already familiar with. And since this is strictly a fact-finding mission, I don't see it as high risk. Call your girl. I'll fill in Hall tomorrow morning so he can monitor your progress. The clock is ticking."

"Yes, sir," he called out to Dillon's back, but the chief was already striding down the hallway.

Sean stood for a moment alone in the silence.

Who the hell could he call to spend a weekend at a sexual playtime resort like Pleasure Cove? Elise was out of the picture. Maybe…what was her name? Or else that blonde? "Damn."

This was a sad testament to his workaholic lifestyle.

And he couldn't exactly go to a bar or the produce aisle and try to pick up someone for more than a get-acquainted date.

Fear of failure warred with duty.

As always, duty won.

Sean snatched up the black book Thomas had given him for his birthday. He'd said these women were willing to meet him.

Maybe one of them would be willing to do a little bit more.

2

CAITLIN MCCORMICK TOOK one look inside her apartment door and knew she was in trouble.

"Cassie?" She thunked her overnight bag onto the tiled floor beside her and listened to her voice echo in the silence. "Come out, come out, wherever you are," she recited in a sing-songy voice, and then listened again. "Cass, are you all right?"

She added the last out of polite courtesy, just in case the disorder of dishes, dust bunnies and dirty clothes strewn from room to room wasn't anything more sinister than a testament to her roommate's housekeeping skills.

"Maybe aliens snatched her up." Just to be on the safe side, Caitlin quickly verified that all the rooms were empty. Leave it to Cassie to have a close encounter of the third kind while Caitlin was away. Her roomie could be off exploring brand-new worlds while she got stuck on the home planet doing housework.

Just like in one of Caitlin's *Star Trek* books, it would be Cassie's luck to get beamed aboard a starship to hang with the hunky captain while she got left on the surface to deal with a villainous Klingon.

"Hmm." Caitlin raised her eyebrows and considered the possibilities. There was a definite appeal to the idea of saving the day. "I could just tame that bad boy and take over the planet myself." She growled in her throat, imitating the imagined villain who would be at her mercy. "He'd be my consort. A warrior to serve my every need." She closed her eyes and licked her lips, savoring an imaginary kiss as the rough-edged warrior took her to his bed.

The cool air that brushed across her wet, wanting mouth brought her back to reality. Her eyes popped open. No warrior. No lover.

No roommate, either.

But a very real mess to clean up.

"You shouldn't have." She waved off the imaginary audience that was cheering her dumb luck. "I'm so thrilled you've given me something meaningful to do with my life." She'd learned to weed sarcasm out of her teaching, but the rest of her life was fair game for a loaded remark.

She shrugged out of her light-blue jacket and hung it in the closet. The reality of her life was that she had work to do. And as much as she wished she could ignore her responsibilities and just take off to indulge her latest whim the way Cassie did, someone had to clean up before ants found their way into their apartment.

Caitlin had spent the last week of May reconnecting with her father on Chesapeake Bay. She'd wanted to get away once the school year had finished, and she always enjoyed spending time with her dad. It had been relaxing—digging up crabs, sailing, chatting about the warm spring weather.

But after a couple of days of kicking back and relaxing, she'd found it boring. Not the time spent with her father. Her. *She* was boring. She'd had nothing more exciting to discuss than that she'd finally found a stylist who knew how to cut her curly hair without making it frizz like steel wool.

No wonder Retired Brigadier General Hal McCormick kept dozing off. She was reliable, sensible, boring old Caitlin. The only daughter in a long, tough tradition of rugged military men. She had no rank of distinction in front of her name like her brother Ethan's "Major." No notorious tag line to follow her name like her brother Travis's "Action Man."

She answered to the inauspicious title of *Ms.* McCormick. And her tag line went something like "Dull As Dishwater." "Same Old, Same Old." "Good Girl."

Her father probably never dozed when one of her brothers was recounting a military mission or listing the names of dignitaries he'd hobnobbed with at a diplomatic function.

Caitlin carried her suitcase into her bedroom and set it down with a heavy sigh. While she unpacked, she pulled her cellphone from her purse and punched in her father's number. She did share her brothers' dutiful habits. Being responsible meant checking in as per her father's request.

He picked up on the second ring. "McCormick." Her father's gruff voice held less bark than it had in years past, but Caitlin still found herself subconsciously anxious to please him.

"It's me."

The general's tone never softened, but she knew there'd be a smile on his face. "How's my best girl?"

Caitlin smiled at their secret code. "A-okay, Daddy."

"Was your trip uneventful?"

Caitlin's breath seeped out in a humiliated sigh. *Uneventful.* Was there any other way to describe her life?

But her father didn't need to hear her complain. "I got home just fine." Looking around her apartment, she despaired at how much work it needed, but he didn't need to hear that, either. "I really enjoyed our visit."

"Me, too." He cleared his throat. *Uh-oh. Prelude to fatherly lecture.* "Be sure you call the doctor tomorrow. I'm sorry the chemicals we used to clean the boat got to you."

"It was just an allergic reaction. A mild attack. I have an ample supply of all my meds," she assured him. "My asthma is just fine. *I'm* fine."

"Your mother used to take care of all that stuff when she was alive."

"That was when I was a little girl. I'm twenty-seven years old now, Dad. I can take care of myself."

Though straight talk and some TLC usually brought her father around to her point of view, some days—like this one—he made her feel as if she was stuck in a time warp. As if she was still that toddler who'd run out across the tarmac to welcome her daddy home from overseas, instead of an adult who still loved her daddy but who wanted the chance to make her own mistakes and earn her own triumphs without her omnipresent family waiting to oversee every choice she made.

After several more reassurances that her Memorial Day asthma attack had not been life threatening, Caitlin gave her father her love and promised to call again over the weekend.

"Unless you have a hot date…"

Caitlin laughed. She hadn't realized *hot date* was in her father's vocabulary. Without a division of troops to worry about any longer, the general focused all of his concerns on his three children. "Don't worry, Dad. When I get serious about a guy, I'll be sure you get to meet him."

"Damn straight. I don't want some sweet-talker like your brother Travis turning your head and gettin' you into trouble."

"Me? Trouble?" She wished. "I'm the most down-to-earth of all your children." Not counting her rich fantasy life—that would remain her own little secret. "Don't you trust me?"

"Of course I do. But you're my youngest." It was a needless reminder of how well her two older brothers and her father overprotected her. "You're also the one I rushed to the hospital when Travis brought home that cat and you stopped breathing."

He still thought she was that ten-year-old girl whose allergies and asthma hadn't yet been diagnosed. Caitlin tried to remember this was love, not control, talking. "Don't worry, Dad. I won't let any man tell me what to do. I won't let any man give me a cat, either."

Her father laughed as she'd intended. "Good girl."

Good girl. Responsible. Levelheaded. In other words...? Boring.

She needed to get a life. Maybe she just needed to live the one she had. She knew the one she wanted—one filled with adventure. One in which her father didn't worry about her health. One in which her brothers didn't request personal leave so they could check out her latest boyfriend to make sure he passed muster and minded his manners.

She wanted a life with the heady adrenaline rush of having her mind engaged in a creative challenge. A life filled with fascinating people. A life filled with great sex—okay, *any* sex—with a real, live, breathing man instead of one of her bad-boy fantasies. A life in which her body cooperated with her goals—where she'd push herself to her limits and then soar far beyond them.

An Olympic athlete.

A movie star.

An astronaut.

A spy.

"Yeah, right."

She didn't realize she'd muttered her frustration out loud until her father spoke. "What's that, sweetie?"

Caitlin pulled herself to attention and covered her slip. "Nothing, Dad. I'd better go. I have some things to take care of here."

"All right. Call if you need anything."

They said their goodbyes and hung up. Caitlin pushed aside her gloomy spiraling thoughts. So she wanted inde-

pendence and adventure, huh? Without alarming her father
or putting half the Marine Corps on her tail?

Fat chance.

Maybe she'd best stick to her books.

Sure, she was doing her part to keep the public schools
of Alexandria, Virginia, running smoothly. And her eighth-
grade students could reconnoiter a sentence with the best in
the country, uncovering subordinate clauses and adverbs
long before they infiltrated high school. But what was she
doing for fun and excitement in her life?

Caitlin picked up her roommate's discarded sweater from
the floor of the closet and sighed with fatigue. Today, it
seemed, she was destined for nothing more laudable or exciting than cleaning up after Cassie.

She spotted the sticky residue of fast food on the plate
beside the telephone on the entryway table and cringed. The
leather-bound book that her roommate had used for a coaster
caught her eye next. "Cassie!"

Caitlin picked up the paper cup and muttered an unlady-
like oath. The cup had been sitting there long enough to
soften up and spring a leak. The book was now marked with
a permanent circular tattoo. After trashing the cup, Caitlin
thumbed through the pages, bemoaning the damage to one
of her favorite stories.

"Sydney Carton, my hero." She opened *A Tale of Two
Cities* to the last page and read the final line. "'It is a far,
far better thing that I do, than I have ever done…'" Caitlin
closed the book and hugged it to her chest. "You got a bum
deal, Syd."

How many times had she rewritten the ending in her
imagination? In her version, Dickens's scoundrel of the
French Revolution was rescued at the guillotine by a re-
sourceful American woman. Let Charles Darnay have his
sweet, good-girl heroine. Caitlin and Sydney always ended

up in a little grass hut on the beach in Tahiti in her happy ending. Sometimes they ended up naked on the beach itself.

Caitlin returned the book to the hanging shelf above the telephone table. Being an English teacher as she was, the symbolism of closing the book on her fantasy life wasn't lost on her. Was it really asking too much for fate to break her out of her rut?

Her gaze traveled down to the table, beyond the trash and burrito remains, beyond the telephone, and lighted on the folded sheaf of flowery notepaper propped up next to a stamped business envelope that contained their rent check. Unmailed. Caitlin jabbed her fingers into the blond hair at her temples and lifted the chin-length tendrils into fluffy disarray. Typical.

A muscle-tensing sense of impending crisis zipped from the roots of Caitlin's kinky hair all the way down to her size-nine feet. "Definitely the worst of times."

Cassie Kramer had the truest heart in the world, but her impulsive approach to life had left Caitlin in the mop-up and rescue position more than once during the course of their friendship. It looked as if today would be no different. She picked up Cassie's note.

Her roommate's handwriting was as flowery as the colorful daisies on the paper, and had been punctuated by a series of smiley faces. "Sorry about the rent check." A frowny face added its own apology. Caitlin picked up the envelope she'd addressed before going to her father's. Dropping their rent into the mailbox had been a simple enough request—one her scatterbrained roommate had somehow overlooked. But Caitlin would take care of it. With the leeway granted by their landlord, she could still get it to him by the fifth of the month.

Caitlin read on.

"I know the place is a mess, too. But I got tied up, so to

speak." Smiley face. "Tim and I discovered that panty hose *will* do the trick." Another smiley face and two exclamation points.

Caitlin looked up and frowned. "Who's Tim?" Despite her roomie's diminutive height, she was generously proportioned and had a flirty, outgoing personality that men found irresistible. She was small and feminine and spontaneous, and men with sex and fun and adventure on their minds flocked to her.

Caitlin attracted a different sort. Standing nearly six feet tall in her bare feet, she found that a decent pair of heels left her towering over most men. Adding in the three bad-ass marines she called family, who loved her a little too well, didn't help set the mood for potential lovers.

And then there was the problem of being boring to contend with.

Virginia Is for Lovers.

Her home state's old tourism slogan mocked her. Maybe if she was Cassie Kramer...

Cassie could hang out until closing time at smoky bars on dance night and have her pick of the litter of available men. Caitlin could last an hour, maybe two, before her eyes stung and her lungs congested. There was nothing quite like hacking up phlegm to keep a man from asking her to dance.

Or to do anything else.

She was doomed to late nights at the library, with its purified air and rarefied patrons. While she loved her books, the fiction stacks just didn't draw the kind of men Caitlin wanted to meet. There'd been a few nice ones there—graduate students, retirees, Jimmy the bachelor librarian.

But not one of them looked the part of the disreputable beast from her favorite fairy tale. Not one bore an air that even hinted at danger. They were all charming and sweet and courteous—and stuck in the same drudgery-filled life that Caitlin was.

Lucky Cassie. Damn lucky.

Caitlin read on. Cassie's note might well be the most interesting part of her evening.

"Will you be a dear and give my note to Sean?"

She shook her head, wishing she could keep up with her roomie's love life. "Who's Sean?"

"He's coming by tonight to pick me up—he called about some sort of weekend get-together. I thought I could go, but I can't. I tried to call back but couldn't reach him. It was sort of a mercy date, anyway. He's a friend of a friend, you know?"

Caitlin chastised the piece of paper in lieu of her impulsive friend. "You could have just said no."

"I'd apologize in person, but Tim came by unannounced and surprised me with a four-day trip to D.C. We might actually leave the hotel and see some of the sights!" Three smiley faces. One of them winked.

"You'll take care of it, won't you? Thanks. See you Monday. Cassie."

At the last smiley face, Caitlin's frown deepened. "You get a weekend of adventure in the big city and I get to be the Wicked Witch of the West to your mercy date?"

She picked up the Dear John note, hoping Cassie's explanation would make everything clear to the hapless Sean, who thought he had a date tonight. Minus the smiley faces, this note was even more brief.

Sean—
    Sorry to leave you in the lurch like this, but something came up.
    Take care,
    Cassie

"That helps a lot." Caitlin's sarcasm echoed in the foyer. Cleaning house and breaking the bad news to mercy dates. Just the way she wanted to spend her Thursday night. She could feel the excitement oozing from her pores.

Resigning herself to her lackluster fate, she set the notes on the table, carried the plate to the kitchen, then went into her room to change into grubby clothes. With nothing more exciting than housework and paying the rent to look forward to, she entertained herself by making a big production of getting dressed.

Stripped to her bra and panties, she opened her closet and curtsied to the long dress hanging on the door. "Yes, my lord. I'll go with you." She pulled a hand-me-down T-shirt off a hanger and waved at the rest of the clothes. "Goodbye, Papa. I will go with this vile beast if it means keeping you and my family safe." She pulled on the shirt and bowed her head to the long dress. "Lead on, Sir Beast."

Caitlin waltzed to the bed. "Oh, no, sir, you mustn't."

She muttered the patronizing protest, then threw herself, spread-eagled, onto the bed. "My reputation, sir. I can never be yours. Well, maybe this once." In a fit of coy giggles she rolled onto her side, reaching for the full-length body pillow she slept with. She hugged it tight against her breasts and squeezed it between her thighs.

As she closed her eyes and kissed the back of her hand, the beast who was her captor took shape in her mind. A big, tawny, catlike creature. Something more than a man, something less than handsome. Virile and uncivilized, rough and rugged—the veneer of his princely rank stripped away to reveal his animalistic need. His hands and mouth would touch, kiss and stroke her into surrender.

Caitlin rolled atop the pillow, increasing the pressure to the sensitive endings of her breasts and clitoris. She arched her back above her faceless captor and stroked her fingers along her neck, purring in response to the pretend touch of her beastly lover. She clutched at his imaginary mane of golden hair and ground her hips into the pillow. A tingling sensation fluttered between her legs and she reached for the culmination of this fantasy seduction.

He was so big. So dangerous. So bad.

And he was hers.

"Take me," she begged, rolling onto her back and letting the pillow fall over her—the way her fantasy lover would fall down and consume her.

Caitlin tightened her thigh muscles and stretched her toes, urging her own release. Almost…just about…

The headboard rattled with the force of her kick. "Ow!"

An assortment of other choice words filled the air as the fantasy vanished and the throbbing pain in her little toe took over. Caitlin tossed aside the pillow and sat up to rub her foot.

"Perfect timing," she moaned, feeling cheated of her happy ending.

The pain in her toe eased along with the desire for her fantasy lover. Someday, she wanted the real thing. She wanted to know what it would be like to come when a man touched her. Her sexual encounters thus far had been remarkably limited, and had never quite lived up to her fantasies.

Maybe because she'd never run across one of those bad boys she craved.

Maybe because her father and brothers scared off anyone truly interesting.

Maybe because… "Oh, hell."

Housework was starting to look downright interesting compared to that line of thinking. Trained to do her duty, she got up and remade the bed, then finished dressing.

An hour later, the dishes were in the dishwasher, clothes were spinning in the washing machine and Caitlin was vacuuming the crumbs and dust from the carpet in the hallway. The swirling water-filter vacuum, specially designed for people with allergies like herself, roared loudly enough to drown out her imaginary duel with a dust bunny.

"Ha! Take that!" With all the style and aplomb of a musketeer, she stabbed the vacuum's hose beneath the telephone table and sucked up the dusty devil.

Her plan was a simple one. Clean up. Practice her heartfelt apology on Cassie's behalf. Then, after sending poor Sean on his way, she'd walk down to the corner to pick up some Chinese takeout and mail the rent check.

Dragging the hose and vacuum behind her like a ball and chain, Caitlin brandished the brush attachment and attacked an alien glob of refried beans that clung to the table leg. "You're next, fiend."

But before she eliminated the enemy blob from outer space, something gold and shiny caught her eye. "Ah. Hidden treasure." Judging by the scatter pattern of discarded clothes and jewelry, one of Cassie's escapades with Tim had taken place out in the hallway. Still envying the idea of casting aside decorum and seizing the moment, Caitlin bent over at the waist and plucked an earring from the wine-red carpet.

That was when she noticed the man standing in her foyer.

The beast.

Come to life.

Caitlin blinked, not trusting her eyes.

He was still there.

Framed in the open doorway, which was barely wide enough to contain his broad shoulders, he stood and stared at her. His green gaze swept her from tush to tennies. Still bent over, staring with a bit of shock herself, she noted he wore a tweed blazer that matched the tawny color of his close-cropped hair. Beneath it he sported a plain white

T-shirt that didn't look very plain at all stretched across that well-built chest. For an odd moment out of time, Caitlin wondered if it was the cut of his coat or the hug of his jeans that made him appear so big. So broad. So solid. So strong.

She licked her lips as her mouth went dry.

So hot.

"Are you real?" she whispered, unheard over the vacuum noise.

Her gaze fell on the plastic daisy key ring that dangled from his right hand. Cassie's key ring. The one she hid in the flower box outside her window and invited guests to use. Oh God. He *was* real. Very real.

Since the mysterious Tim was with Cassie in D.C., and Caitlin herself had no love life to speak of, this "guest" had to be Sean.

Great. Just great.

Even upside down and looking through her legs, Caitlin could tell this man was no mercy date.

Cassie had dumped *him?*

3

NICE BUTT.

Nice legs.

I don't get the whole upside-down thing, but...

Wow. Very nice legs.

He'd caught the woman wielding a stainless vacuum attachment as if she were dueling with a sword. Then she'd picked up something and started talking to it. Now she was studying him as if he was a rare scientific discovery.

Keeping his distance so as not to trigger any more of her apparent eccentricities, Sean cleared his throat and blinked, breaking the stunned stare that had captured both him and the woman with the endless gams.

She stood up in a flurry and faced him. Her mouth opened, but no sound came out. He squinted politely, expecting her to repeat herself. She rolled her eyes heavenward, pursed her lips and muttered something unintelligible. She was all flustered in a way that was part preteen and part prude—and disarmingly refreshing in an adult woman.

Sean resisted the urge to smile. She reached down and flipped off the switch on the canister vacuum, filling the apartment with a startling silence. If she was a housekeeper for hire, then he would seriously consider spending some time at his town house, dirtying it up so she'd have a reason to come clean it.

But she smiled and extended a hand in greeting that told

him she owned the place. His ogle-the-maid fantasy gave way to polite respect at the confidence she exuded.

"Are you Cassie?"

"I'm her roommate, Caitlin McCormick. You must be Sean."

Stepping forward, he folded his hand around hers, testing the finely boned structure of it. Despite her height and athletic build, Caitlin McCormick was still very much a woman. Certainly not a preteen and hopefully not a prude. It'd be a waste.

He nodded, once, in greeting and in silent approval. "Sean Maddox. Cassie said to let myself in. Did I interrupt something?"

"What? Oh." Her silvery gaze darted to the vacuum beside her. She glared at the inanimate object as if it were responsible for the creative housecleaning show he'd just witnessed. She snatched her hand away and brushed her palms against the hips of her cutoff denim shorts. "Just trying to make a dull job a little more interesting."

"I see." He didn't, but it was the polite thing to say.

Enough pleasantries. The clock was ticking.

"Is Cass—?"

"Cassie's not—"

They'd spoken at the same time.

He grinned, trying to ease her nervous laughter.

But she quickly recovered and started again. "Sorry. I've been out of town, ever since school got out last week."

"You're a student?"

"Teacher. Junior-high English."

Lucky kids. Why hadn't any of his teachers had a body like that? The cutoffs she wore revealed a mile of leg that even his nonadolescent libido responded to.

The delicate points of her shoulders rose and fell in a

heavy sigh that wiped away his smile and replaced his body's interest with suspicion.

"Here." She handed him a piece of flowered stationery from the hall table. "Cassie left this for you. She got called out of town unexpectedly."

Sean scanned the note. His suspicion curdled in his gut and flowed out into his veins in a frustrated temper. "Damn."

Over the phone, Cassie had sounded like the perfect woman for his plans. No strings attached. Ready for fun. But he'd expected her to keep her word about this weekend. His mistake.

He'd gotten caught at Dillon's office in Quantico and hadn't driven into Alexandria, Virginia, until nearly an hour past the time he'd arranged to pick her up. He thought his invitation had made everything clear. He was offering her a free vacation at a high-class resort in exchange for whatever she wanted to offer. As long as the other guests believed they were a couple.

He hadn't offered his heart and she hadn't asked for it. But did Cassie's easy-come, easy-go attitude mean she'd move on to the next man if one date didn't show up on time?

"I know it's a surprise." The voice of Cassie's roommate cut through his brewing temper. "She said she did try to call you."

Damn. Now what was he supposed to do? Diego Marquez might walk if Sean couldn't come up with some connection between Justice Rossini's trip to Pleasure Cove and his subsequent retirement. Sean would have a hard time dealing with Alicia Reyes's silent tears if that happened. And the San Isidrans wanted answers soon about their ambassador's murder, or they'd send up their state police looking for answers themselves. He had to infiltrate Pleasure Cove Island. Tomorrow. "Damn."

"You said that already. I'm sorry. I know Cassie left you in a bind tonight. But don't hate her. She's impulsive—not heartless." The roommate tapped the paper in his hand. "She did apologize."

"Apologize?" He glanced up and, standing nearly eye-to-eye, drilled her with the damning look he had in mind for Cassie. "What good does that do me?"

Surprisingly, the roommate stood her ground without flinching. "She told me you weren't close, that she was doing you a favor." He watched guilt play over the woman's features, overshadowing her confidence. "I know it's inconvenient, but your feelings shouldn't be hurt."

"Inconvenient isn't the half of it. I need a woman. Now." Sean gritted his teeth and swore again. Didn't that sound pathetic?

He tipped his head back and hissed an angry breath through his teeth, disgusted with himself for trusting that his plan with Cassie Kramer would work. "Women can't be trusted to go to the line on anything."

Caitlin's hands shot up in protest. "Excuse me. You got screwed out of one last-minute date. Don't blame the rest of the gender because your timing's lousy."

"She's really not here?" Sean crumpled the note in his fist and began to stalk through the apartment, searching rooms, checking to see if this was all a lie and Cassie was hiding from him.

"Hey!"

Wasn't that just like a woman? Leaving when you needed her most. This assignment was all about this weekend. She could have dumped him Monday, no problem. But tonight?

The roomie with the dynamite legs hurried after him, trying unsuccessfully to stop him from looking into the living room, the kitchen, the bathroom.

"What do you think you're doing?" she demanded, matching him stride for stride. "Could I have that key back? I don't think you'll be needing it anymore."

She tried to block his path into one pigsty of a bedroom, but he pushed past her. Empty. He crossed the hall and entered a bedroom whose soft blues and tans and wrinkle-free perfection could have come from the pages of a magazine.

He felt her hand at his elbow then. "This is *my* bedroom. Get out."

He whirled around, easily pulling free of her tugging grasp. "I had plans."

Somehow he'd cornered the woman in the doorway. She'd have to brush against him to move past. But Sean rudely held his ground, letting the soft heat of her body seep into him across the breath of space between them. The faint tang of household cleaner blended with the salt-tinged ocean scent of the woman herself. She'd been out on the water recently. He breathed the observation, in and out, her fresh scent filling his head and calming his burst of anger.

She was tall, just a few inches shorter than him—and he was six-two. Her honey-gold hair feathered across her cheeks and forehead in something like a pageboy cut. Only curlier. Sexier. Her gray eyes had darkened to the color of a battleship. And there was definitely a battle waging there. Fire. Fear, maybe. Questions, certainly. But definitely fire.

Plan B took shape in his mind.

He skimmed his gaze down the front of her gray-heather T-shirt. Her breasts were small, barely noticeable beneath the oversize cotton garment. But her hips flared nicely. And those legs... Sean swallowed hard and leaned back to scan every smooth, shapely inch. An image of those legs wrapped around his hips, binding them together in the most elemental of ways, sprang into his mind, consuming his body in a flush of instant heat. *Now* his imagination decided to kick in!

Sean squeezed his eyes shut and focused on controlling the involuntary response. It had been too long since he'd had sex. That was all. Not once during the Marquez case. Nor the case before that.

He wasn't a celibate man by nature, but he worked long, difficult hours. He kept company with equally busy fellow agents and criminal lowlifes. When he did run across a woman who charged his engines, he'd make a play for her. A few were okay with his Job Comes First motto. Elise had been. At first.

Then the hassle started. She just couldn't let him be who he needed to be. She'd bought him ties and dressed him up for dinner. At first he'd used the demands of his job as an excuse to keep things light and fun between them. But somewhere along the line, an emotional bond had formed. And suddenly he'd been rearranging appointments to catch an afternoon quickie with Elise. He'd worn her damn ties.

He'd even swallowed his fears and ventured into a jewelry store. Just to look. There were a number of rings well within his budget that looked nice. That spoke commitment.

He'd walked out with something called a tennis bracelet instead. The next day he'd gone to surprise Elise at lunch. That was when she'd kissed that old friend. In front of him and God and the entire restaurant.

The bracelet was probably still wrapped up in the back of his closet somewhere.

Now Sean understood that his job was the only thing that had never let him down. So that's where his loyalties lay. Women were for fun and nothing more—if they were agreeable. The Bureau was his full-time commitment. That way nobody got hurt.

But his lonesome body sure seemed to be paying the price for that self-imposed ideal.

He slowly opened his eyes, thinking his bitter memories had helped him conquer his body's desire. But with his head angled as it was he was staring right at this woman's breasts. Small, yes, but amazingly responsive. They rose and fell with each quick, deep breath she drew. His own chest expanded in a rhythmic response. Almost...nearly...not quite touching hers.

"What are you staring at?" The woman's croaky whisper caressed his ears, but his focus had shifted to the subtle seep of color that washed up the swanlike arc of her neck and stained her cheeks.

Despite her boyish attire and eccentric housekeeping skills, she was a long, tall drink of purely female body. South of his belt buckle, he stirred in response again.

A sexy woman was the answer his body wanted to give. But his rational mind still had control. Barely. "How tall are you?"

The question came out of nowhere, from the uncontrolled depths of his subconscious mind.

Her gaze dropped to his chest. "Five-eleven."

Then the subtle movement of her shoulders registered. She was hunching down, making herself shorter.

Suddenly, Sean had two fingers tucked beneath her softly jutting chin. "Don't."

He was lifting her up, tipping her chin up. He moved closer. She was an unexpected combination of creamy skin and steely strength. His fingertips sizzled at the contact. He wanted to sample a taste of that smooth, heated skin.

Her hands came up and splayed across his chest, halting him from coming any closer without pushing him back. It was too tender a touch to ignore, too hesitant a touch to justify the way his nerve endings jumped to greet the clutch of her fingertips. Her eyes had washed to a pale dove-gray, the rounded pupils big and black in their centers, as if she were drugged with the same hazy feeling that seemed to be clouding his own mind.

"What are you doing?" she asked.

Judging by the hypnotic effect this woman's body was having on his, he was charging his engines. He was giving vent to several months of unintended celibacy. He needed sex. Lots of it. He needed to get this fever she was igniting out of his system so he could do his job.

The idea in his mind became a living, breathing desire.

She wouldn't.

He didn't dare ask.

He had nothing to lose.

"Are you free this weekend?"

And then she did shove him. She retreated a step into her bedroom while Sean stumbled into the hallway.

Her rosy cheeks had blanched, but there was plenty of fervor left in her voice. "I don't know what game you're playing, Mr. Maddox, but you can't just come in here and take me apart with your eyes like that. Cassie stood you up, so you grab the next female who comes along? That's the most insulting pickup routine I've ever—"

"*Are* you available?" He waved aside her rightful protest before she could lambaste him again. "I know, I know." He moved into the foyer, away from the unspoken desire that had sparked between them. He needed to think clearly here. Think of the job. He glanced at his watch and swore. "I'm already late."

Unless he drove straight through the night. He couldn't risk any holdups with the airlines. But getting there in time did him no good unless he had an escort.

"Late for what?"

Bingo. Curiosity. She might have voiced a ladylike protest at his impromptu invitation, but she was interested. Despite her dating survival instincts, she was interested. Sean's libidinous radar kicked in, backed up by his professional survival instincts. She might not want to admit it, but she was interested in *him*.

He slowly turned around and studied her again, from the smooth, flushed skin of her unadorned face down to... Good God, he had to stop looking at her legs. She wasn't dressed in a particularly provocative fashion. But there was something about her. Something about the whole package of this Amazon that made him think his mission was still possible. That he hadn't blown his entire weekend. That he hadn't ruined this assignment. Yet.

She shifted nervously beneath his blatant perusal, crossing her arms at her waist, pushing the nubs of her breasts against the thin cotton of her shirt and creating twin points that tantalized him further.

"You'll do."

"I'll do what?"

This sexy, Amazon temptress was more than Cassie's odd, naive roommate. She might well be Sean's salvation.

"Caitlin, isn't it?"

"Yes?"

"Today's my thirty-second birthday."

She hesitated. "Happy birthday."

He turned on what he could salvage of his charm. "How would you like to give me the best birthday present of my life?"

CAITLIN FELT INDIGNANT anger flush through her from head to toe with a bright rosy heat. "Birthday present? How 'bout I give you a punch in the face?"

How dare he? Either Cassie's Dear John was a dangerous sex fiend or he was making fun of her.

"What?" A look of stunned surprise filled his dark green eyes an instant before an answering blush crept up his neck. Then those same eyes narrowed in an angry squint as he waved aside her prickly pride. "That wasn't a proposition. Not *that* kind, at any rate. But I do have a business proposition for you."

She arched one eyebrow in doubt. "Is it any better than your last line?" She watched as he pushed up the tweed sleeve of his jacket and looked at his watch. "And quit checking the time. It's rude. If you have to go somewhere, go. I'm not stopping you."

Caitlin stiffened in cautious anticipation as his expressive face grew still. One second he was antsy, the next completely calm. Spooky. Cool in a Terminator kind of way, but spooky.

"I don't have time to do this nice and subtle," he announced. He pulled back the front of his coat and reached inside. "I'll make it quick."

That endless expanse of taut white T-shirt gave way to a band of black leather that curved over his shoulder and hung down beneath his arm. A holster, with a gun. A big, black, deadly looking gun. *Make this quick?*

"Oh my God." Caitlin jumped back a step. Mr. Terminator was reaching for his gun! "Don't shoot me!"

She reached for the nearest thing that looked like protection and came up with the nozzle on the vacuum cleaner. She held it in front of her in both hands like a weapon.

Sean froze. He looked at the nozzle. He looked at Caitlin. He looked down to where his hand hovered beside the holster. Then he looked at her again, studying her frightened expression with a cockeyed squint that indicated he thought *she* was the crazy person here.

Their gazes held for about two seconds, just long enough for her courage to waver. Then he was moving again. All-business. He pulled a leather wallet from an inside jacket pocket. "Don't worry, McCormick. I guess I should have used a little more finesse in my invitation. But I'm afraid smooth moves just aren't my style." He inclined his head toward the nozzle she wielded in her hand. "If it's any consolation, neither is shooting a woman who could suck my brains out."

Suck? Caitlin's heart tripped an extra beat. A raw rush of heat and pressure pounded between her legs and left her lightheaded. Sex? This guy wanted her to…? Her gaze flew to his crotch. She'd never. She wanted. She wouldn't. "How dare you!"

"Here." He flipped open his wallet. Inside she saw an official-looking ID and a polished brass badge. Uh-oh. "I'm Special Agent Sean Maddox, ma'am. I'm with the FBI."

The nervous excitement that had pounded through her body flooded her neck and face with embarrassment. Sucking. The vacuum. He'd been talking about the vacuum. Of course. *Idiot.*

"FBI?"

Ignoring the aftershocks of sexual frustration and indignation that were slow to die, she gathered her wits and took the wallet in a tentative grasp. She studied it a few moments. The picture matched. He hadn't been smiling when this ID photo was taken, either. *U.S. Department of Justice. Federal Bureau of Investigation. Sean Michael Maddox. DOB 05/29/71.*

"It *is* your birthday," she murmured out loud, but read on. *New England Bureau Administrative Chief.* Though the tension eased from her posture, suspicion quickly took its place.

She handed back the wallet. "Your ID says 'Administrative Chief', not 'special agent.' And Virginia's a little out of your New England territory. Either you're a liar or that's fake.''

"I assure you, my work with the FBI is very real.'' He returned the wallet to his pocket, making a dramatic effort to show her that he wasn't going anywhere near his gun. "What I'm about to tell you can't go beyond this apartment, Miss McCormick."

Oh God. That sounded serious. Dangerous. His warning, articulated with just the barest indication of a foreign accent, sounded like a line right out of a James Bond movie.

Interesting.

The aftershocks of emotion inside her gained momentum. "You mean it's a secret?"

"Top secret."

Despite her distrust of Agent Maddox or Chief Maddox or whoever the hell this distracting hulk of male animal was, the right side of her brain kicked in, pushing logic and protestations aside. He was about to share a government secret with her. Caitlin breathed in deeply, giving her brain plenty of oxygen to fuel her imagination. She was about to become privy to some real cloak-and-dagger information.

"Is Cassie in trouble with the FBI?" she asked.

"No. But she was going to help me with a time-sensitive case. A mutual friend gave me her name. She was going to provide my cover this weekend while I conducted an undercover investigation." He paused to read Caitlin's reaction, then continued without comment. "Since she's unavailable, I'm asking you to take her place. I need you to be my mistress so I can gain access to an exclusive couples-only resort."

This man was asking *her* to take part in an investigation? To travel? To serve her country? To assume a secret role? To be a man's mistress?

Her father would have a cow.

"Me?"

"You."

She glanced down at her brother Travis's USMC T-shirt and the cutoff jeans she wore. She glanced at the vacuum nozzle she still held like a defensive weapon between them.

When she lifted her gaze back to his, his calm green eyes revealed nothing but the fact that his offer was serious. "You want me to be your mistress this weekend?"

He swiped a hand across his jaw and raised his eyes to the ceiling. Caitlin could only guess what this show of patience was costing him.

When he nailed her with those amazingly green eyes—no blue or gray to corrupt their mossy hue—she saw he was all-business again. "I need you to pretend to be my mistress. Pretend," he emphasized. "Pleasure Cove Island is a haven for rich and powerful couples to get away for the weekend without any public scrutiny. No press. No phone lines. The Bureau has given me a fake background. As a Bureau chief, I have the clout to warrant an invitation. But I can't very well go to a couples-only resort by myself without raising suspicion, and that's the last thing I want to do. I need to find answers, and I need to find them quickly."

"Answers to what?"

"Dammit, lady, I don't have time to answer all your questions." His patience snapped and he stalked down the hall to the front door. He had it open and was halfway out when he braced his hand against the open frame and stopped. His broad back rippled with a powerful shrug, and Caitlin realized the width and strength of him was all-man, and not due to the cut of the sport coat.

She held her own breath as she listened to his lungs fill and empty with cleansing breaths of air. When he finally turned around to face her, the anger was gone. But he still wasn't smiling.

"I can't give you all the details," he explained. "Suffice it to say two former guests of Pleasure Cove Island have met with...unfortunate circumstances. One just resigned at the peak of a public career. The other is dead."

"Dead?" Could the man sound any more detached from his feelings? Caitlin scooped her hair back from her temples. The more Sean Maddox talked, the more convincing his story became. She was already physically attracted to him. He gave the beast of her sexual fantasies a compelling, if not quite handsome, face.

His request for her help played into every escapist fantasy she'd ever had while trying to spice up her humdrum life. But now he was sounding as if this assignment was real. That the need for her help was real.

What should she do? What would her father do? He'd take action. If there was a problem, he'd do something about it, and deal with the consequences later. Her brothers had the same take-charge mindset. But all three would tell *her* to stay home. To stay safe. *Think of your health. Think of your reputation.* They'd tell her to take care of herself, while they tackled the problem for her.

But her father and brothers couldn't help Agent Maddox with this problem. They weren't women. They weren't available.

They weren't here. Now.

A small spark of determination lit inside her. Like a fuse traveling toward its explosive destination, it fired along her nerve endings, heating her blood and giving strength to an idea.

"Would this weekend be dangerous?" She hugged the vacuum hose to her chest, half-afraid of giving in to the burning desire that was slowly consuming her. "You said someone died."

"Not on the island itself. He was murdered in his hotel

room after returning from the island. This is strictly an in
formation-gathering mission. Otherwise, the Bureau
wouldn't consider civilian involvement. There may be some
risk involved, I suppose—the movers and shakers of the
world don't like to be deceived.''

"No one does." Her terse reply was both an agreement
and a challenge for him to be completely honest.

Sean released his grip on the door and stepped back in
side. Even though it brought him only a few inches closer,
Caitlin felt the power of his vow reaching out and touching
her as he said, ''I promise, if things do turn dangerous, I'll
give you all the protection I can. And I'll get you out of
there as soon as humanly possible.''

Caitlin imagined that his protection would be a serious
force to be reckoned with. The idea that this Terminator
would put his life on the line for hers was at once reassuring
and…stimulating. Her father and brothers served their country and protected its citizens with equal fervor. Why
couldn't she?

And pretending to be his mistress? Let's see. What was
the downside of having an extraordinarily powerful and
sexy man acting like her lover? If the other guests could
buy the fact that Sean Maddox wanted to be with her, it
wouldn't be the worst way to spend a weekend.

Sexy man.

Vacation resort.

Serving her country.

Living out a lifelong fantasy.

Hmm. Downside?

She was back to her father having that cow.

But he was still on his boat in Chesapeake Bay. Ethan
was in Washington, D.C., Travis in North Carolina. They
couldn't fret or dictate when they didn't know something
was going on.

"You said this was top secret. Does that mean I can't tell anyone where I'm going or what I'm doing? Not even my family?"

"Not a soul."

Dad and Ethan and Travis would never know what sweet little Caitlin was up to.

Caitlin was tempted. Oh, Lordy, she was tempted. But how could she be sure this wasn't really just some sick way to pick up women? Could she trust Cassie's judgment about the man? Her roommate had been willing to go. Until a better offer came along.

But this was likely to be the best—most exciting—offer Caitlin was ever going to get.

"Listen, I know you don't know if you can trust me. But you've got about two seconds to make a decision. Maine is a long way from here." Sean shifted uncomfortably on his feet, the first real sign of any emotion beyond anger and impatience. "I don't ask for favors from many people, Miss McCormick, because I don't like to be disappointed. But I'm asking you to help me now. For your country."

"*I'm* the only one who can help?" He didn't answer her. But the steely set of his jaw told her he hadn't found it easy to ask for her assistance. Caitlin finally set down the vacuum hose.

He expected her to be one of those people who disappointed him.

He expected her to say no.

She decided to act strictly on impulse. It was a liberating feeling. She didn't know if it was the McCormick in her—ready to do her patriotic duty—or the good girl in her, anxious to please those around her. Maybe it was the dreamer who had waited far too long to crash out of her sheltered life and have a real adventure.

It might even have been her woman's heart deciding. The

heart that wanted to rekindle Sean Maddox's faith in the world.

"I'll go with you on two conditions, Agent Maddox."

He rolled his shoulders back, giving the false appearance that he was relaxing his stance. His eyes still refused to show hope. "What are they?"

"That my father never finds out where I am this weekend." She shrugged, hoping she wouldn't regret this impulse, hoping Agent Maddox wouldn't regret it, either. "And that we stop by a post office somewhere on the way to Maine so I can mail my rent check."

"Done." Caitlin barely had time to grab the rent envelope and her purse before he pulled her out the door.

4

"SORRY WE COULDN'T TAKE more time, but we'll be driving straight through the night as it is just to make the ferry connection tomorrow evening at five." As Sean spoke, he steered his car down the D.C. exit out of Alexandria, Virginia, and pulled into the northeast flow of traffic on the interstate.

While he wasn't ready to admit that his luck with women had changed, his mood, at least, had improved. He had a date. It had been a long time since he'd had a date, and even though this one was on behalf of the government, he was glad to know he could still get a woman to say yes to his rusty charms.

Even if it was a woman as unpredictable as Caitlin McCormick.

According to Thomas's documentation in the little black book, Cassie was pretty much a known quantity. She'd do some flirting. Indulge in friendly chatter. She wouldn't be afraid of a few public displays of affection.

But Caitlin was an unknown factor. For some reason she'd said yes to his outlandish invitation. She was either a real patriot or a woman who took foolish chances. He'd like to think she was the former. He could appreciate that kind of dedication to a cause.

But she might be just plain crazy. After all, she talked to furniture and threatened men with vacuum cleaners.

Maybe it was a good thing he'd chosen to drive to Maine

and avoid the security checks and flight delays of air travel. He'd need the extended time together to get to know her and establish a predictable working relationship with her.

"You doing okay back there?" he asked.

Sean peeked into his rearview mirror and saw the reflection of one long female leg thrust up into the air from his back seat. The leg was long and tanned and showed off sleek curves of muscle along the calf and thigh. He was definitely enjoying this part of the getting-to-know-each-other process.

The leather interior of his Porsche 911 Targa had never been used as a dressing room before, but the idea took on a definite appeal when a second leg—equally long and curved and perfect—thrust up into the air beside the first one moments before a swatch of denim swept over them. Sean squashed down his body's responding tension and turned his focus back to the road.

She was only a couple years older than his sister. A kid in comparison to his lifetime of experience. If Sabrina had agreed to gallivant halfway across the country with a stranger she'd just met—even if he did flash a badge—Sean would have her hide. Correction. He'd have the bastard's hide.

Caitlin had hinted at having an overprotective father so, as an overprotective brother, he should be able to relate. He definitely wasn't having brotherly thoughts right now, though.

Caitlin's breathless voice came from behind him in the back seat. "I'm fine. I appreciate you running across to that discount store and buying me a dress while I was in the post office. I can't very well show up at a posh resort in my cutoffs." She grunted as she struggled with some piece of clothing. "What do I owe you for it?"

"Not a thing. The Bureau is paying for everything this

weekend.'' Sean's gaze slid back to the mirror. She wasn't making it easy to concentrate on good intentions. Her long-limbed build made it a struggle to change from her shorts into the black sundress he'd bought for her.

But it was an entertaining struggle to watch. With the car on cruise control, he tilted his head to get a better view down into the seat behind him. Caitlin was lying across the leather upholstery, scrunched down out of sight of passing motorists. She'd stripped down to her underwear, demure triangles of pink cotton that covered interesting places without really hiding them. Her small, pert nipples strained against the pink cloth as she pulled the dress over her head and shimmied it down the length of her body. Before she got things into place, he noted a wisp of darker gold hair peeking from beneath the cotton at the juncture of her thighs.

Innocent as her movements were, his body reacted as if the actions were part of a calculated seduction. In the close confines of the car, the earthy smell of the leather combined with the enticingly fresh scent of Caitlin herself. It was an erotic male-female stimulation of the senses that only intensified his imagination. He subtly tugged on the denim at his crotch and adjusted his position behind the wheel to ease the growing tightness in his groin. He could picture himself in the back seat with her, with those legs of hers high in the air and him in between them.

Get a grip, Sean. Sensing fatigue and frustration were fueling his randy thoughts, he politely turned away and changed lanes. But an inexplicable fascination soon had his gaze focused back in the mirror.

Now she was on her knees in a crouching position. Her sweet round rump bobbed up and down as she fought to work the zipper up her back. Oh man. He spread his knees a little farther apart.

"Need some help?" The offer was out of his mouth before common sense could stop his hormones.

Caitlin's head popped up in the rearview mirror. Her honey-gold hair bounced around her head in wanton disarray as if he *had* been in the back seat with her. But her cheeks were rosy pink and her eyes wide and startled. Their gazes locked in the mirror before he could look away.

But if she was embarrassed to learn he'd been watching her, she didn't say so. Instead, she tossed her white canvas deck shoes onto the floor in front of the passenger seat. "Sure. I can't get this danged zipper up. There's not much room to maneuver back here."

Bracing a hand against each bucket seat backrest, she stretched one leg between them and climbed forward. In the process the gentle swell of one breast rubbed across his upper arm.

With sight and scent already providing the tinder, the actual press of female flesh provided the spark that zapped Sean's fantasy into a reality. His fingers clenched around the wheel as his primed body jerked in response. "Watch it!"

"Sean!"

The car swerved to the left. Caitlin toppled onto him. Suddenly he was cradled from ear to cheek in the softness of her breasts. Her tangy, fresh-air scent surrounded him, and the warmth of her body pressing against his consumed him.

In the next instant, he took control of the car and his wayward reactions. He righted the wheel, steered them safely into the passing lane and pushed against Caitlin's thigh, forcing her down into her seat. She landed with a plop on her bottom, as a flush of color raced across her skin.

"Are you all right?" he asked.

"I'm fine," she answered breathlessly. Keeping her gaze

fixed on the dashboard, she dropped her feet to the floor, slipped into the shoes and buckled her seat belt. Only after she was breathing more evenly did he see her big gray eyes dart his way. "Sorry."

"No harm." He kept his gaze on the last dregs of rush-hour traffic and concentrated on his driving instead of on the gangly beauty beside him.

They'd passed the next mile marker before she angled her face toward him with a wry frown. "Not a very auspicious start to my secret-agent career."

Oh, no. Miss McCormick needed a quick reality check. "*I'm* the secret agent. *You're* on vacation."

"But I want to help."

"You are, just by coming with me."

That answer seemed to disappoint her. "What will I be doing while you're investigating the island?"

"You'll be acting as my girlfriend. My mistress. We'll have to do a little kissing and cuddling in public to justify our presence there, but otherwise it's a free day at the spa for you. Use the hot tub or whatever facilities they've got. It's on the Bureau."

Now she turned her whole body in her seat. The look she gave him must have let any number of junior-high students know they were in trouble. "You said I'd be serving my country. I agreed to do this because I wanted to see some action. How is sitting in a hot tub doing my patriotic duty?"

Sean raised a placating hand. "I'm the one who's trained in covert ops and investigation procedures. I'm the one with the gun and the experience."

"And I'm just Mr. Untouchable's moll. Yippee." She turned again and glared out the windshield. She crossed her arms with a decisive shrug, and the black strap of her sundress fell off her shoulder and caught in the crook of her elbow.

Sean narrowed his eyes on the road, but couldn't resist the urge to glance over at that long stretch of bare skin. *Too long without sex,* his mind warned. He felt equally powerless to stop himself from reaching out and lifting that strap up onto her shoulder. So what if the back of his knuckles brushed across the smooth skin there? He didn't mind.

He did mind when she flinched away from his caress. "You'll have to get used to me touching you," he warned, placing his hand safely back on the wheel. "And you can't be afraid to touch me. Not if we're going to make a convincing couple."

"I'm not afraid of you. I'm angry." She scooped her hair behind her ear, exposing a long line of naked neck for him to stew over while she lectured him. "My father is a retired Marine Corps general. He served his country proudly for over thirty-five years. My brothers are following in his footsteps. One is specializing in diplomatic security and the other works in Special Forces." Her touch-me-not glare never wavered from the endless stretch of cars and highway before them. "I've always wanted to give to our country the way they do. I've wanted to be a part of the action."

Sean wasn't sure where she was going with this, but it was his nature to play devil's advocate. "So why didn't you enlist or go through ROTC? There are plenty of women making careers in the military." Her long silence prompted him to look her way again. He saw one hand nervously picking at the hem of her dress where it rested high on her thigh. She had gone somewhere inside herself. Not for the first time, he wondered if he'd picked the wrong woman for this job. Not that he'd had much choice. "Caitie?"

"My name is Caitlin." She muttered the correction as if by rote. As if he wasn't the first person she'd set straight on not using the shortened version of her name. Just when he thought she might not say another word, she lifted her gaze to his. The energy that had thrummed through her—part anticipation, part anger—had dissipated. "I can't pass the physical."

"Oh." Sean looked back at the road and slowed the car to maneuver the twisty highway that circled around Washington, D.C. Was Caitlin ill? Flat-footed? Crazy? He brought up images of her body, already well-ingrained in his memory. Long, strong legs. Soft, flawless skin. Wild, sexy hair. To look at her, Caitlin McCormick was the picture of a healthy, fit woman.

"What's wrong with you?" he finally asked when she didn't explain further. He shook his head. An interrogation with a criminal suspect he could handle blindfolded. But this conversation wasn't going so well. Maybe his perpetual lack of charm with the ladies was partially to blame for his extended celibacy. "Sorry. I don't mean to be blunt. But if it could affect my investigation, I have a right to know. I mean, are you going to have a heart attack on me? Am I keeping you from a dialysis treatment?"

She took a deep breath that stirred the best parts of her body. "I have asthma. It's a chronic disorder that stems from lung damage I sustained when I was hospitalized with pneumonia as a child. I've outgrown the worst of the attacks. I take regular medication for it, which generally keeps it under control. But sometimes unusual stress or an allergic reaction can still trigger it. I'll cough or wheeze and have shortness of breath. Then I'll use my inhaler or, on rare occasions, take an epinephrine shot. But it isn't life threatening. It just…keeps me out of the action."

Apparently this wasn't the first time she'd been asked to explain her condition. Her speech had been glib and well-rehearsed. And alarming. "Unusual stress?"

Caitlin laughed, but her lips were pressed together too tightly for her expression to qualify as a smile. "I don't run marathons, I don't work in a coal mine or with hazardous chemicals. I don't own a cat."

"Any of those things could trigger an attack?"

She nodded. "But I do swim three times a week. I go sailing when I can. I have a teaching career. I read a lot."

"What do you read?"

"Fantasy. Action-adventure. Romance. Mysteries. Classics. Biographies—"

"A little of everything, huh?"

She nodded and sank back into that quiet place inside herself again.

He listened to the hum of the tires on the pavement for several minutes, processing everything she'd told him. She read books to find the adventures she couldn't experience herself. But she clearly wasn't an invalid. She exercised regularly—her fine, toned body was proof of that. She probably lived her life on a predictably even keel. He'd shown up at her front door and had bullied and cajoled and practically dared her to play his mistress this weekend.

What should he do? Turn the car around and drive her home? Risk an asthma attack? Take her back to her safe, sedate apartment and her books, or take her to Maine and put her in the middle of a charade that could prove very stressful?

"Why did you say yes to my proposition?" he finally asked.

"Because I thought it sounded exciting. Well, it did until you said I wouldn't be doing anything except sitting in the hot tub." Her reprimand gave way to a heavy sigh. "And because you said it was top secret. My father would never have to find out. He's a little overprotective."

Sean could definitely relate. "I'll bet he's more than a little overprotective."

"He thinks my brothers can take care of themselves. My

mother died when I was young, so I get a lot of his attention. He had a heart attack that forced him into early retirement, and I try not to aggravate his concerns. I lead a pitifully sheltered life for a twenty-seven-year-old woman. I haven't been any man's girlfriend for over a year, much less any man's mistress.'' She folded up the faded T-shirt she'd been wearing earlier and clutched it in her lap. ''I suppose you want to drop me off at the nearest bus station and send me home now.''

Sean slid his eyes across the dashboard clock and let her sad, dull tone sink into his bones. He was at twenty-one hours and counting. He wanted to do the right thing here, but he had a job to do, too.

Met with his moody silence, Caitlin rambled on. ''At least I got to change my clothes in the back seat of a sports car. I've never done that before. Heck, I've never even ridden in a car like this before. Low-slung and fast and hot.''

Heck? Was this innocent act for real? Sean's jaded sense of trust was being thrown off-kilter by her guileless confessions. She had a body made for sex, but she talked like a…well, someone very naive.

Needing some fresh air, he pushed a button on the dashboard and opened up the sunroof. Caitlin angled her head to watch the smoked Plexiglas slide back and reveal the full moon above them. The rush of cool night air lifted her hair and made it dance along that tantalizing column of bare neck.

So much for cooling off.

''Nice touch,'' she whispered.

I'll say.

Though she was still talking about going home, her voice picked up a more positive note. ''You asked me to go away with you. A decently attractive man, on the spur of the moment without knowing anything about me, asked me to go away with him for the weekend. That's something that would happen to Cassie, not me.''

"Decently attractive, hmm?''

The sudden stain of color on her cheeks made him think that had been more than a pretty decent compliment. Those big gray eyes, when she turned them on him, were full of honesty, a trace of embarrassment and something bolder that reflected her intelligence and strength. The effect was absolutely bewitching.

"That didn't come out the way I intended. You're not conventionally handsome, but—'' When her gaze dropped to his chest, Sean inhaled deeply, trying to dispel the curious warmth that suffused him. Her eyes darkened in response and the warmth refused to leave. ''—you're put together very nicely. And I love your accent. It almost sounds foreign. Even when you're all-business, I like listening to it.''

Sean narrowed his focus to the endless white lines dotting the road in front of him. Maybe *he* was the crazy one. During his relationship with Elise, she'd never once got him all hot and bothered with just an appreciative look and an ingenuous compliment. But Caitlin McCormick did.

It had to be those damn months of all work and no sex that had him wanting to teach this sheltered wannabe adventuress how to act on those longing looks. He'd never been a sucker for sad stories or quirky charms, but he half wished he and Caitlin were really going away for a weekend of sex together. Damn, what he'd love to teach the teacher.

Stick to the job, a nagging voice tried to warn him. But his brain had been working overtime for these past few weeks. Another part of his anatomy needed a workout right now. Caitlin liked him. He liked that she liked him. Probably more than he should.

"My mother's American, but my father's British. I've picked up some of his speech habits.''

Sean could tell she liked that revelation by the smile that softened her worried expression. "So you're a real James Bond."

He shook his head. "My dad was, though. You like James Bond?"

"Of course. Fast cars. Evil villains. Gadgets and intrigue and sex and adventure."

And then Sean had his answer. They both needed what the other had to give. "Do you still think you can handle this weekend? I can't promise it'll be stress free. But if you're up to it, I'll even put you in charge of distracting the other guests while I do some in-depth searching of the premises."

She perked up another notch. "You'd give me an assignment?"

He glanced across the car at her. She was quite pretty when she smiled like that. "If you're up to it. I don't really have time to find someone else," he added honestly.

Now she sat straight up. "I can do it. I have all my meds in my purse in case I have a reaction. I want to help."

Sean hoped he wasn't making a mistake here. He promised himself to keep a very careful eye on her. He promised to remember her concerns about her father. But there was something strangely seductive about granting Caitlin McCormick her wish. Something that coursed through his veins just as powerfully as his sexual attraction to her did.

"All right, then, Agent 99, prepare yourself for a weekend of adventure." He twirled his finger in the air. "Turn around."

"Why?"

At last he felt like smiling. "Because you haven't really finished dressing inside a sports car yet."

"Oh." Her cheeks flushed with color before she scooted around in her seat and offered him her back.

He squinted assessingly. He'd never really thought too much about the type of woman he liked. But right here and now he decided that tall was the way to go. The black dress opened in a V, revealing a long stretch of lightly tanned skin. The pink bra strap halfway up wasn't a barrier, but a reminder of the small, pert breasts that graced the other side of her wonderful body. He found the tongue of the zipper and slid it slowly up her back, wishing he could put *his* tongue there instead.

Maybe before the weekend was over...

When his fingers brushed against her nape, she shivered. He shivered, too. But cold was definitely not the sensation he was feeling.

Fully dressed, Caitlin settled back into her seat and turned those dove-gray eyes on him. He discreetly pulled his hand away before giving in to the urge to touch her again.

"I suppose we'll need to practice that kissing and cuddling part you mentioned. So I don't get goose bumps every time you touch me."

Her invitation was the best birthday present he could have hoped for after what had started out as a rotten, frustrating day.

"The goose bumps are a nice effect." Instead of driving as fast as he legally could, Sean was suddenly looking forward to their next stop. "But I'd be willing to put in some practice time."

After too many weeks of all work, it was high time this birthday boy enjoyed a little play.

5

SEAN EYED THE NEEDLE of the gas gauge as it teetered into the red zone. The car wasn't the only thing running on empty.

He'd driven four hours straight, following Interstate 95 north through most of the East Coast megalopolis. But with the dim glow of the endless city lights behind him now, he was starting to drag. Normally, a quick catnap could keep him going around the clock, but until he set foot on Pleasure Cove Island and his cover was in place, he had no intention of taking the time to rest.

But as he pulled into New Haven, Connecticut, he knew he needed to risk a short stop. He needed gas, caffeine and a jog around the car. Maybe even a little of that *training* time with Caitlin.

If she was up for it.

Right now, however, Caitlin was dozing peacefully, in her sleep mumbling something about a "sir" every now and then. Sean hadn't fed her dinner yet, either, but she seemed blissfully unconcerned by that fact. She leaned against the car door with his jacket curled up beneath her cheek for a pillow.

As he slowed the vehicle to merge with the smattering of late-night traffic through town, he envied her trusting nature. To her, this mission was all a game. A secret adventure that her father and brothers couldn't take away from her. She was going into this weekend ready to play, ready to risk.

He was all for the play part, but he'd protect her as best he could from any risk.

He still wondered why this undercover trip was such a big deal to her. Her father and brothers must have some good reason for keeping a tight rein on her. Did she normally take foolish chances? Was she a political zealot? Was she itching to be a bad girl because she was going through some kind of pre-midlife crisis or because some man had done her wrong?

Maybe the answer was more important than he realized. But for now, it was enough that she'd agreed to this adventure. He had the mistress he needed for the weekend, and she had her shot at unrestricted freedom.

Though he was no pro in the relationship department, he was confident that they could make this work. For three days. They could do the James Bond thing she fantasized about, and he could find the information he needed. And if they had a little fun along the way, that would be the icing on his birthday cake.

And if not?

He glanced over at the sleeping Amazon princess and heaved a sigh.

He could stand anything for three days. Even an adventure-seeking schoolmarm who was a little flaky and a whole lot naïve. His gaze traveled over her. And who had legs to die for. And miles of soft, velvety skin that just begged to be touched. All over.

"Damn." He scratched his chin and concentrated on the road signs leading to a secluded gas station. "Focus," he warned himself.

Maybe Thomas was right. Sean had neglected his personal life for way too long. His job gave him satisfaction but he also used it as an excuse to avoid any messy entanglements with women.

Caitlin McCormick had *messy* written all over her. His deprived body wanted her something fierce, yet his self-preservation instincts wondered how he could walk away from this weekend with everybody's expectations met, his body sated and his conscience intact.

The only decision he could make right now was to pull into the parking lot of the dimly lit convenience store and gas station and park the Porsche in the shadowed space farthest from the door. It was a defensive habit long ingrained after his years with the Bureau, prying into the lives of people who rarely welcomed a federal investigation.

Though he didn't think he had any reason to be on guard, he nonetheless scoped out the lone attendant and two visible customers inside the store before parking his car beyond their direct line of sight. He could grab five minutes of sleep while Caitlin napped, then gas up the car and buy some drinks and snacks for a midnight meal. Feeling more relaxed after making that plan, Sean killed the lights and engine.

Leaning back, he stretched his legs and closed his eyes. He'd let this weekend play out as it may, and deal with whatever came up.

Caitlin stirred in the seat beside him, drawing his attention. *Dealing* with the situation that presented itself, he reached out and brushed a lock of soft, kinky hair off her cheek. He stroked his fingers along her jaw and tucked the curls behind her ear.

"Mmm." She stretched and purred like a cat, and Sean lingered to stroke the skin down her throat and find the vibration of that sexy moan. He marveled at the electric sizzle he felt whenever he touched her. Was this incendiary reaction to the creamy perfection of her skin just a lonely testament to his sorry love life?

Caitlin's eyes blinked open.

"I'll go with you," she murmured.

"Don't worry about it. We can rest for a few minutes."

She smiled gratefully and blinked again. "Yes, sir."

"We don't need to be so formal. Call me Sean."

"Yes, my lord."

Her comment made no sense to him, but he was entranced.

Without any further comment or protest to ward him off, Sean left his fingers resting against her throat. He could imagine this was how she awakened every morning. With dark, drowsy eyes. A come-hither smile. A sleepy tumble of curly hair framing her face. Would she awaken with that same doe-eyed satisfaction in her expression after a night of making love? It was an expression that would make any man feel lucky. Feel potent.

His body lurched in a needy response to her lambent sensuality. He'd like to be that man. He wanted the whole night *and* the morning after with Caitlin.

Unbuckling his seat belt, he leaned in closer. Fatigue and desire had lowered the protective shield of common sense that normally kept him from making such a tactical error.

But it wasn't quite midnight yet. He deserved something special for his birthday. And right now, this was the only gift he wanted.

"May I?"

As Caitlin's eyes drifted shut, Sean pressed his lips to hers. It was a sweet, tender kiss. A taste, really. Her lips were firm and full, with the tempting give of a ripe peach, yet twice as delicious. And when they responded with the same supple energy that made the rest of her body so fascinating to study, he traced his tongue along the seam of her lips and pushed his way inside.

Her lips parted with a breathy sigh, welcoming him. He ran his tongue along the strong arc of her teeth and circled the yielding warmth of the sensitive skin inside. She nipped at his lips with delicate kisses of her own. And as he licked and sucked and tasted, her throat hummed with pleasure. The low-pitched coos entered his brain and traveled like a soft, steady caress down to his groin. Something about those moans—whispers of erotic sound—danced along his nerve endings and triggered an answering sigh deep in the rumbling recesses of his own throat.

They were sex sounds. Mating sounds. More evocative than a cry of rapture. More personal than words. Intimate. Wholly untrained and natural.

As Sean plunged his tongue inside to twirl and dance with hers, the sounds deepened. He shifted position in his seat, giving himself room to expand. Drawn to the seduction of touch and taste and sound, he stroked his thumb along the column of her neck, tracing the vibrations and absorbing them into his skin.

"Mmm, yes," she whispered against his mouth. "Right there." Caitlin tipped her head back and arched her neck, stretching like a cat.

Answering the invitation, Sean palmed the side of her neck and savored the sensation of her softly beating pulse, teasing his fingertips and warming his hand. He followed the path with a sweep of his fingers, the way an electrical charge follows a current, marveling at the responsive length of skin and muscle. He let his left hand fall to the inside of her thigh and slide upward. Callused fingertips gently abraded velvety skin and coarser denim at the same time.

The contrast of textures and the coos in Caitlin's throat acted like a control switch inside him. The voltage careened through his body, sparking light and life and energy in places that had lain dormant for way too long.

"You wanna try the back seat?" he whispered heatedly, running his tongue along her neck. The fevered request stirred her hair and filled his nose with the tangy-fresh scent of her. "We can use the practice."

She didn't answer. Instead, she lifted his mouth back to hers and opened for a long, drugging kiss.

He hadn't expected this kind of surrender from her. Not this soon. Not this perfect. They were virtual strangers, thrown together by chance and necessity. And yet she already had the power to spark impulses in him, to trigger desire.

And there wasn't anything *pretend* about the way he wanted her right now.

He cupped himself, enjoying the healthy strain of physical needs too long denied, as he kissed his way down the graceful contours of her throat. He drew his fingers along the line of her shoulder, then pressed his palm flat atop her chest. He pulled back just enough to look down and admire the way his big hand spanned the width of all that bare skin. Her skin was a peachy-gold velvet beneath his long, tanned fingers, as eloquent a contrast as the dueling tones of husky desire in their throats.

"Is this okay?" he asked, wishing she'd open her eyes so he could read her expression. But she communicated with a slight nod of her head, the rapid beat of her heart and the shallow swell of her lungs beneath his hand.

"Please," she whispered, a drowsy articulation of breath.

She felt the electricity, too.

With a wolfish grin of conquest he watched the rhythm of her breathing stutter as he slid his index finger along the edge of her bra just beyond the scoop neckline of her dress. Her cheeks flushed when he dipped beneath the ribboned trim to touch the soft, responsive swell of female flesh. Then he moved lower still to catch the rigid bead of her nipple in the crook of his finger.

"Mmm." Caitlin shifted position, opening her body to

his seeking hand. The pink triangle of cotton and elastic stretched to accommodate his sensitized palm, and she pressed her breast into his squeezing grasp. "Yes."

"Come here," he stated suggestively, wanting more than those little bursts of electricity that crackled between them. He wanted much more than playing touchy-feely like a couple of curious teenagers in the front seat of his car. He needed something more than his own hand to ease all those months of sexual frustration boiling inside him.

He was a swollen, aching powder keg and she was the lightning that could ignite a fiery conflagration.

He unbuckled her safety belt and reached for her. He was too big to scoot between the seats the way she had. But he'd find a way to stretch out on top or beneath or beside her— if she was willing. And thus far, she'd been very willing.

He knocked his knee on the gearshift and swore with pain and impatience. If he couldn't get to her, then he'd bring her to him. He released his seat and slid it back as far as it would go. Then he scooped his hands beneath her and lifted her right onto his lap.

The curve of her hip twisted against his groin and he nearly came undone beneath the press of her healthy, womanly weight. "Wait," he warned as she rolled onto his chest. He wanted to do this right.

He gathered her into his arms and sank back in his seat with Caitlin sprawled on top of him. "Better," he growled in a husky whisper. He grasped her bottom and spread her legs so that his thigh could ease between hers. Much, much better.

His moan collided with hers as he tunneled his fingers into her wanton curls and covered her seeking mouth with his own. She was falling down all around him—her hair around his hands and face, her breasts to his chest, her legs around his thigh, her heat to everywhere.

With the erotic push-pull of a man and woman more intimately joined, she pushed away, then covered him again. She pushed away, then fell to his chest, all the while teasing him with the questing curiosity of her probing mouth.

She braced her hands atop his chest and curled her fingertips in his shirt, digging into skin, adding fuel to the burning flame. "Take me. Make me yours." She opened her hot, wet mouth over the stubble of beard that marked his jaw. Her tongue delved into the cleft of his chin. He took one of her hands and pressed it to the heated juncture where his hips cradled hers.

Falling into the same madness that consumed him, she lightly squeezed the bulge in his jeans, sending him bucking up against her.

"God, Caitie." He could barely breathe, much less talk. "Are you sure about this? I didn't think—" When she squeezed him again, he went completely speechless.

He interpreted that as a yes.

He reclaimed her mouth and swept his hands down the length of her back and grabbed two handfuls of that sexy ass. He could tell her with his body what he couldn't say in words.

He wanted her. Badly. Now.

He didn't get this hard this fast with any woman. Maybe the forced celibacy had made him impatient. Maybe the woman herself was doing this to him. Maybe it was some combination of both.

All he needed to make this birthday complete was to move her so that she straddled his lap. Or pull her beneath him in the back seat. Or stand her up against the hood of the car. Just so he could slide those pink panties aside and give her room to wrap those legs around him as he buried himself inside her.

His shaft throbbed with the possibilities. He had to slow

this down before he embarrassed himself with all their clothes on. He had to think. He had to maneuver them into a logistically workable position.

"Caitie." His hands were up under her dress, his thumbs hooked beneath her panties, his fingertips right *there,* reaching from behind, pulling her open. They were damp with her sweet-scented honey, on fire with her heat. "Caitie, we can't do this here. There isn't room. I can't angle—"

"Don' talk, sir." Her bottom gyrated and squeezed, pushing his fingers against the nub hidden in her slick feminine crevice. She was pleasuring herself. Pleasuring him with her eager invitation. "Just touch."

"Yeah, babe." He slipped her panties aside and worked two fingers inside her, swallowing her moan with a deep, slaking kiss. "We can do it like this." This woman was thinking. She was hot and she was coming for him. "Then you can do it for me."

He moved one hand to the front and curled a finger inside her, rubbing her tender lips from both angles. She twisted and he pushed with the palm of his hand. Completely open like this as she was, the raw sex scent of her filled the car and seeped into Sean's overloaded brain.

She twisted. He rubbed. She moaned. He kissed.

She came.

"Mmm! *Oh yes!*" He felt her release in the rapid flutter of muscles around his fingers, the warm gush of success that spilled onto his hand, the long curve of body that stretched along the length of his, prolonging the taut sensations that rocked them both.

"Yeah, baby, just like that." She was still pulsing around him when he pulled his fingers from her swollen clit. "My turn." He let his hand slide up between them to unhook the snap atop the zipper of his jeans. "Touch me, Caitie," he begged her, trying to guide her grasping hand to the zipper itself. "Do me."

"Yes." The fingers of her free hand raked through his hair and clutched at his scalp, angling his head back. Her lips scudded along his jaw and opened wet and hot against his Adam's apple. "You're mine now, Beast. All mine."

Beast?

And then she bit him—a tender little nip near the base of his throat. It didn't hurt, but the unexpected show of erotic force surprised him enough for her words to register.

Oh God.

"Did I hurt you?" He twisted free from the clutch of her hand and nuzzled the crease where her chin met her throat, offering her a silent apology. "I may be out of practice, but I wanted you so bad—"

"No, my lord."

She was still kissing him. Maybe he'd misjudged. "Are we playing a game? Was I too rough?" She was too much of an innocent. Oh, God. What if she never... He framed her face with his hands and demanded an explanation. "Caitie."

Boom. With the sudden clarity of a transformer overloading and shorting out, Caitlin froze. Hands, mouth, body—everything about her luscious figure stilled like a statue. Her eyes popped open. They were round and dark. And alert.

"Sean?" He saw her lips move more than he heard the word.

"Damn." Sean's breath rushed out with an angry sigh. He pushed her hair off her face, zeroed in on her eyes and called himself every foul name in the book.

She'd been dreaming. Half-awake. Fantasizing.

She was lying on top of him, her legs tangled with his, her dress hiked up past her hips, her hand clutching his erection through his jeans. Her hair was a glorious tumble, her lips swollen with his kisses.

This untrained Amazon had been a natural in his arms. Willing and wild. A perfect mistress. And she'd been asleep.

She hadn't been with *him*. She'd been getting off with some dream lover.

"Oh, my God." Her words came out in a crystal-clear tone, unlike the sexy whispers she'd used before.

Sean held himself still as self-conscious color crept up her neck and cheeks. And then she was suddenly a jerky scramble of arms and legs and prudish inhibitions.

She snatched her hand from his zipper as if the short-circuiting electricity arcing between them had given her a stinging jolt. Sean protected himself from a slipping knee, but could do little else to help her crawl off him and shrink into her corner of the front seat.

Moving much more slowly, fighting for control of his emotions as well as his primed body, he turned in his seat and gingerly positioned himself behind the steering wheel. He should apologize. Hell. *She* should apologize for leading him on like that. "Something you want to share with me, Caitie?"

She stopped tugging at her clothes long enough to apologize. "I am so sorry."

But then she hadn't known she was driving him crazy.

He swiped his hand across the abrasive stubble of his jaw. The tiny little pinpricks on his palm matched the random thoughts pricking at his conscience. For a few minutes there, he'd lost sight of the mission. Lost sight of who he was. Lost sight of his vow to protect her.

She was the innocent dreamer out to find adventure.

He was the dedicated agent out to find the truth.

And he'd practically raped her.

"Did you know what was going on?" he demanded.

She hesitated long enough to throw his conscience into overdrive. "Yes. I was dreaming. But then I wasn't. I was living out my— It was a hell of a way to wake up." She tried to smile reassuringly, but succeeded only in making herself look young and vulnerable.

The truth was, dreaming or not, he still wanted her. But he was still four states away from his destination, the clock was ticking, and now his substitute mistress was cowering in the corner, repulsed by the big, bad beast-man she had to pretend to like this weekend.

His impulsive birthday present to himself had backfired. Big time.

"I didn't mean to take advantage." He had fences to mend, ruffled feathers to smooth, ass to kiss. "Are you all right?"

"I'm fine." She jerked her fingers through her hair. "I'm just embarrassed. I hardly know you. You must think I'm whacko to get all turned on like that."

"I'm more concerned with why you got turned off so fast. I take it you weren't consenting."

"But I was. I wanted you. I wanted that. It." Her cheeks bloomed with fresh color and her thighs suddenly clenched together. "You said whatever happened between us would be top secret."

"I meant that. But I promised our relationship would just be pretend. That got real pretty fast." He concentrated on his breathing. In and out, slowly. Anything to distract him from the dissatisfied ache in his lap and the guilt that sat like a rock on his chest. He adjusted his shirt where it had bunched beneath the shoulder strap of his holster, and opted for honesty. "When you said yes, I thought you were talking to *me*. I thought you knew what was going on. I didn't mean to scare you or hurt you."

"I *was* talking to you. You didn't scare me. And it sure

didn't hurt. It's just… I've never actually done anything like that before. Not for real." She sat with her bare legs curled beneath her, her arms hugging herself around the waist. "Have you?"

He almost laughed at her naiveté. "Never quite like that. I usually try to make it to a bed before I get carried away."

"I've never—" her heavy swallow and gasp for air tickled every nerve ending in his body "—come like that before."

Damn. She had to use *that* word? Pressure throbbed against his zipper, demanding release. He breathed delicately and stared up into the stars through the open sunroof. "I'm glad it was good for you. I'd hate to take advantage of a woman and not do it right."

Guilt filled his voice with bitterness. He deserved the pain he was in.

"You didn't take advantage. You played into a fantasy that I was dreaming about. Beauty and the Beast. I've had it a couple of times before. The villain in my fantasy—a vampire, a mobster, someone like that takes me and, because he can't resist me—pleasures me. But then I turn the tables on him and…" She shoved her fingers through her hair and shook her head. "I can't believe I'm talking about this. But sometimes in my apartment, I touch myself and imagine—"

"Caitie."

Her innocent enthusiasm was unaffected by his gruff warning. "I've never had a man play the game with me before. It was so much more intense. I wanted to—"

"Caitie!" His jaw ached with the pressure of gritting his teeth.

She allowed him a few seconds of breathy reprieve. "I'm sorry. Usually, in my fantasy, I return the favor. I didn't plan to stop so soon. But I thought *I* was the one taking advantage.''

''It was my pleasure, believe me.''

''Does it hurt?''

''Yeah.'' He looked over at her and considered turning in his badge when he saw the stricken look on her face. She was staring at the bulge in his pants. ''Don't worry.'' He found the strength to reach over and pat her on the knee. ''It's not your concern. I won't hold you to whatever goes on in that imagination of yours. I'm just glad you don't think I'm a real monster. I'll get a cold can of soda and ride with it between my legs when we're done here.''

She uncurled her legs and straightened in her seat. ''But it *is* my concern. I'm your partner this weekend. We're supposed to take care of each other.'' Her cheeks flooded with color as soon as the words were out of her mouth and she picked up on the double entendre. But then she swept her hair behind her ears and energized herself. Was she angry? At him, finally? ''I'm supposed to be your mistress, aren't I? I want to be somebody more worldly, more exciting this weekend. I want to play out *your* fantasies, too.''

He didn't want her angry at herself. ''Yes, I need you to play a part, but I went too far. I don't want you to do anything that makes you uncomfortable.''

There was a long pause as she considered the sense and self-respect of his words. ''But if I want to, I can?''

The earnest look in her eyes baffled him. ''Want to what?''

''Do you.''

Sean bolted upright to protest, but immediately regretted the swiftness of his actions. ''Damn.'' He grabbed the steering wheel in a white-knuckled grip and waited for the pain to pass. ''Do you even know what you're talking about?''

''I think so.'' She was shaking that hair about her face

and shrugging. "Like I said, I haven't done this before. But you said you'd do me first and then I'd take care of you."

"You remember that?"

"That's what the villain always says to me. That's how I know I'm safe. He takes care of my needs first."

"Then I wasn't taking advantage?" His entire future as a cop and a man and a lover depended on her answer.

"No." Her skin flushed with a soft glow like she'd had when she'd spilled herself into his hand. Was she remembering what it felt like? "I was just shocked to discover that my fantasy had come to life. That's why it was so good." An apologetic frown creased her face. "Do I sound like a complete idiot?"

So good? He'd made it *so good* for her?

Maybe he wasn't as rusty as Thomas seemed to think. The heavy weight of guilt eased from Sean's chest. He reached for her hand and held it as gently as he could in his big, clumsy grip. "You sound a helluva lot sweeter than what I deserve."

"Sweeter? That's all?"

Sheesh. Hadn't even that simple compliment come out right? He tried again. "You're doing me a huge favor this weekend. And for that I'm grateful. I just didn't want to spoil it for you before we even got to the island."

She was staring at his crotch again. "So you don't want me to help you—" the nervous gesturing of her hand mimicked exactly what he wanted her to do to him "—finish?"

His traitorous body lurched in response and her pupils dilated with a wicked light. "I'm just fine with reality, thanks. You don't have to do that for me."

But she was climbing up on her knees and pushing him back into his seat even as she spoke. "I'm a different woman this weekend. I'm a better, badder, more adventurous me. And this me wants to do it."

She hovered over him, her fingers gently tugging on his jeans. He grabbed her wrists to pull her away, but the damn witch was fighting him. "What I want isn't necessarily what's going to happen."

"You do want me to touch it."

"Yes." Shit. "No. I won't force you to—"

"It's *my* fantasy."

"Caitie—" He heard the hiss of a zipper and felt himself springing free into her determined hands. "The villain, huh?"

"The big, bad-ass, misunderstood villain." She squeezed, and he couldn't stop himself from thrusting up into her hand. "Now show me how."

Sean had a feeling he wouldn't have to teach her a thing.

6

"HAND JOB."

Caitlin giggled as she whispered the words out loud.

She'd actually given a man a hand job!

She'd never had cause to use the words before. She could barely think them.

But now she'd done it. And judging by Sean's breathless "wow!" when they were finished, she wasn't half-bad at it.

Oh man, she was getting to be such a woman of the world these days!

Well, for one weekend, at least.

Her heart fluttered with smug satisfaction as she surveyed the selection of candy inside the convenience store. She could do this. Just like in her secret fantasies, she could play the bad-boy's mistress. Granting sex and taking pleasure. Just because it felt good. Because it was fun.

And Dad and Ethan and Travis never had to know.

Secret Agent Caitlin McCormick, mistress to Special Agent Sean Maddox, was a title she was enjoying a hell of a lot more than Miss Caitlin McCormick, sheltered school-marm and all-around good girl.

She picked up a bar of milk chocolate and one of dark chocolate, absently wondering which was the better aphrodisiac.

As if she even needed one!

Sean had done something to her, working his way into her dreams like that. He'd turned her from a woman who only dreamed about wild, spontaneous sex into one who actually had wild, spontaneous sex. Sort of.

All those times alone in her apartment, when she'd clutched a pillow between her legs or rubbed a towel against herself, and imagined succumbing to the insatiable desire of her kidnapper, she'd been able to give herself mini-orgasms. She'd been able to mimic the pressure of a man in her tenderest places and give herself a healthy release that she hadn't experienced in either of her previous sexual encounters.

But Sean Maddox was no pillow, no towel. He was the real deal. With him playing the part of her beastly fantasy lover, she'd come unglued. There'd been nothing *mini* about the way her body had convulsed around the probing pressure of his hands. She'd been on full-blown maximum overdrive. It had been liberating. Wonderful.

Totally unlike her.

And she wanted to do it again.

She'd spent several minutes in the bathroom, washing up and reapplying her lipstick and mascara. But she still couldn't shake the little aftershocks that left her body feeling flushed and edgy.

What the man lacked in charm, he made up for in sheer power and honest desire. He'd picked her up and played with her as if she was one of those dainty little women who looked so feminine and men were so helpless to resist. He was her equal and more—in will, in strength, in lusty impulses. He'd made her feel wild, delicate, desirable. And so unlike the good girl her father and brothers expected her to be.

And just think, Sean and her impulsive experiment with life on the wild side would remain her own little secret. She had a whole weekend ahead of her to play that exciting, naughty role. And, she hoped, to experience a few more of Agent Maddox's intense training sessions.

She felt herself grinning from ear to ear in anticipation.

"Can I help you find something, Legs?"

Even the lame come-on line from the crusty biker with the tattoos and potbelly couldn't dampen her enthusiasm. She dropped both candy bars into her basket and turned to face the rows of chips and salty snacks without making eye contact. "I think I can handle this myself, thanks."

"I'd be happy to carry that heavy basket for you," he offered, licking away the stream of tobacco juice that trickled from the corner of his mouth into his scraggly brown beard. Charming.

Caitlin glanced down at the two candy bars, packaged sandwiches and bottle of water she carried. Heavy? Hardly. Did she rebuff this unwanted suitor like the innocent adolescent students who developed a crush on her from time to time? Or would Mistress McCormick use a sterner approach to put off his unwanted attentions?

She opted for the comfort of her own sarcasm. "It's a gallant offer, but I'm strong enough to carry this big ol' basket all by my lonesome." She added a bag of honey-roasted peanuts to the snacks she and Sean would munch on for a midnight dinner, and turned toward the soft-drink counter at the back of the store. Her biker friend barred the way.

"I insist," he said.

She jerked the basket to her side when he reached forward and touched the handle. Nailing him with an irritated glare, she didn't drop her gaze until he lowered his hand to his side.

Though she bested him in height by a good two inches, she nonetheless felt the unspoken challenge in his actions.

It wasn't quite a threat, yet his slitty-eyed attentions were definitely unwelcome.

Her father would order this potbellied pickup artist to move. Travis would have tossed him aside by now. Ethan would simply intimidate the hell out of him until he chose to leave on his own. But Caitlin had to handle this one all by herself.

"Excuse me."

Ignoring the firm hint, he stretched out his arm and leaned against the rack of chips, halting her in her tracks and preventing her from walking around him. "You're one of those high-class chicks, aren't you?"

Caitlin wasn't amused by the backhanded compliment. "I need to get a cup of coffee."

"Norm, you'll scare her off." An overwhelming odor of cigarette smoke and mechanic's grease stung her sinuses and made her eyes tear up as a second biker walked up behind her. "Let her get her coffee."

The man named Norm made a face before dropping his arm and backing off. Caitlin glanced over her shoulder to Norm's aromatic cohort. As tall and gaunt as Norm was short and stocky, this one wore dark glasses that hid most of his face except for his gap-toothed grin. Attractive or not, he'd helped her out and she was grateful. "Thank you."

But when she went to the concession area to pour the cup of coffee Sean had requested, she noticed that she'd gathered an entourage. She tried to catch the attendant's attention in the curved mirror that hung above her, but he was sitting behind the cash register, immersed in one of those tabloid newspapers, completely oblivious to her predicament.

Irritation became a frisson of panic as the two men not only positioned themselves behind her, but also made themselves at home watching her butt. Either the dress was too

short or she was too tall. Feeling a sudden, distinct breeze
where she hadn't before, she reached behind her and tugged
on the hem. Big mistake. Her hand on the back of her thigh
seemed to be an invitation to stare at the spot, judging by
the way Norm and his buddy shifted their stance. Where
were her brothers now when she needed to get rid of these
jerks?

She drooped her shoulders while she waited for the coffee
cup to fill, and wished the short hemline went down past
her knees. If she hadn't been mooning over her sexual rush
with Sean, she'd have seen these two bozos coming, and
avoided them entirely.

This was the kind of trouble Cassie would get into, not
Caitlin. Cassie could handle men hitting on her. She could
have fun with these persistent suitors, then turn them down
and make them feel glad for having tried and lost. After the
encounter had ended, she'd call Caitlin and beg a ride home,
and Caitlin would oblige.

But Caitlin wasn't used to having men hit on her, and
while one successful sexual encounter might have tripped
her joy buzzer for the first time, she wasn't any more savvy
now about how to deal with a man who wanted to put the
moves on her than she'd been twenty-four hours ago, much
less deal with two of them. What should she do?

Her nervous fingers jiggled the plastic lid she was pressing onto the tall foam coffee cup, and hot liquid sloshed
over her hand. "Ow!" She snatched her fingers back and
blew on the tender skin the way her father had blown on
her scraped knees and elbows when she was a little girl.

It was the wake-up reminder she needed.

The old Caitlin might step back and let her family take
care of her. But the all-new and improved Caitlin would
handle the situation herself. Just like her more worldly-wise

roommate. Just like her father. Just like Agent Caitlin Mc-Cormick, notorious femme fatale.

She took a deep breath, shook her hair back from her face and stood up straight to transform herself from cautious Caitlin into a confident Mata Hari.

There was even a bit of a clipped European accent in her voice when she spoke to the leather-clad lotharios. "Excuse me, gentlemen, but my date is waiting for me."

"So that's what it's called these days, huh?" said the tall one.

Was he speaking in some sort of man code? With an elegant sweep of her arm, she placed the basket's handle at the crook of her elbow and pretended she understood. "That's what *I* call it."

"We have money." In the mirror above her she saw Norm reach into the front pocket of his jeans.

Not good. "So do I." She picked up the coffee and spun around before he could pull anything she didn't want to see from that pocket. "I'll buy my own groceries, thank you. Now I really must be going."

Norm veered into her path when she tried to leave. "He's hired you for the whole night, has he?"

The tall one was right there when she tried to escape in the other direction. "What's a hottie like you go for these days?"

Hired? Go for? Hottie? Suddenly the lecherous grins and unwanted overtures made sense. Caitlin's cheeks flooded with enough heat to make her light-headed. Mata Hari she wasn't. "You think I'm a—?"

Oh God, she couldn't even say the word. These dim bulbs thought she was a hooker?

"I saw you when I went out for a smoke." The tall one leaned in close enough to give her a good whiff of his acrid odor. "That's all we want. A quickie like that. We'll pay you double if you do us both at once."

"Both?" Eeew! "You saw—?" Her and Sean? Her hands…there…on him. Caitlin's lungs seized up in shock. That had been a private lesson, part of her fantasy. She'd been so proud of herself. How humiliating. "You watched—?" The accusation wheezed through her throat.

"You were done when I went out to have a smoke." He trailed one grease-stained finger up her bare arm to her shoulder. "But why else would you be hiding around the corner? I recognized the positions. Your date was smiling."

Caitlin backed her hips into the counter and shivered with an overwhelming rush of anger and revulsion. If she'd had a hand free, she'd have slapped his face. As it was, she set the coffee down in the corner of the basket and concentrated on the healthier of the two emotions.

"That was private." She coughed to try to clear her congesting lungs. "I am not what you think I am." But her sharp words came out in a breathless denial that sounded more like an intimate whisper.

Now Norm was touching her other arm. "I'll bet you are for the right price."

Enough! Some of that McCormick backbone kicked in, overriding embarrassment and shock and the preliminary indicators of a full-blown asthma attack.

She planted her hand in the middle of Norm's chest and shoved him back a step. They were too thickheaded to believe the truth, and she was too angry to hide it. "That *date* is a federal agent. And he is so gonna kick your ass for even thinking—"

"She thinks she's too good for us, Deke." His hand closed over hers.

Oh my God, she was touching him! Caitlin snatched her

fingers away and tried to rub them clean. "I'm booked this weekend."

"We're free next weekend."

No doubt these two charmers had every weekend free. "I'm from out of town."

"I can get there on my Harley."

The front door jingled open. Though the attendant apparently had no qualms about Deke and Norm accosting an innocent woman in his store, the potential customer was enough to finally make him look up from his paper.

When Caitlin rose up on tiptoe to try and capture the clerk's attention, Stinky Deke stepped in front of her to block her from view.

"Would you move?" she demanded.

He put his hand on her wrist, as if to silence her. "This is just between us—"

"Like hell—" She jerked against a grip that was suddenly tight. "My father is a United States Marine Corps—"

"Caitlin."

Deke froze. Caitlin froze. Norm whirled around toward the dark, perfectly articulated voice behind him and froze.

The Terminator was in the building.

Caitlin looked to the end of the long aisle where Sean stood. She took note of the loose fists that hung at his sides, the tense set of his massive shoulders, the narrow, pinpoint focus of his eyes.

He definitely wasn't smiling now.

His cold, unblinking gaze fell to Deke's hand where it clutched her wrist. Deke snatched his hand away as if he'd been zapped by an indivisible heat ray.

Caitlin's wheezing sigh of relief was the first sound to break the silence. "Sean. I'm glad to see—"

"Get over here."

Sean cut her off before she could say another word. Her cheeks blanched a deadly shade of pale at his harsh command, and the wide-eyed trepidation she radiated twisted in his gut. Yeah, he was coming on like territorial gangbusters, frightening her as much as Lenny and Squiggy of the motorcycle set. But he didn't have time for lovey-dovey diplomacy and making nice with the locals.

She'd nearly blurted out her father's identity.

So much for top secret.

He wondered what other little tidbits of pertinent information she'd uttered in self-defense. Her name? His? Their destination? Trust a woman to screw up this mission before it ever got off the mainland.

"*Now,* Caitie," he ordered when no one in the store showed any signs of movement.

Fifteen minutes. He'd left her alone for all of fifteen minutes while he filled the gas tank, called in his location to Chief Dillon and tried to clear his mind of the sensations of her eager-to-please hands on him.

He'd been doing his damnedest to get his focus back on business, and she'd been flirting with the locals. Maybe this was part of her fantasy life. Get herself into a little bit of trouble and then wait for the hero to come to her rescue.

Oh wait. She'd labeled him the bad guy in her crazy little scenario. Sean almost laughed out loud at the irony of *him* being the villain with these two bozos on the scene, but he couldn't afford to compromise his tough-guy facade. For the moment, the greasy twins had been intimidated easily enough with some commanding talk and a mean look. But since he didn't know them, he wouldn't put anything past them. He wouldn't drop his guard until Caitlin was out of arms' reach and safely back in the car with him.

Besides, she didn't want him to play nice. Thank God her fantasy hadn't been about a sweet-talking poet type. He could do this big, bad boss routine in his sleep. He fisted his left hand and held it up to expose the watch on his wrist. "The clock's ticking. We need to hit the road."

"'Get over here?'" she mimicked, moving from shock to sarcasm. Uh-oh. Had he missed something? Color flooded back into her cheeks, and he had a feeling he'd never understand how her crazy mind worked. "I told you not to call me Caitie. These men were just—"

"I'm done talking. Get in the car."

He didn't give a damn what those men were doing. Or maybe he just gave a damn about the fact they were doing it to Caitie— Damn. Caitlin.

The skinny guy had had his hand on her. She'd clearly been trapped. They'd been arguing.

She'd been afraid.

Sean wanted her away from them. Now rather than soon. He wanted her safe in his car. Even if close quarters with Caitlin wasn't the safest place for *him* to be, he wanted her out of harm's way—far away from the grubby hands and leering looks of these two goons.

He'd given her plenty to deal with this weekend. A blind date to Pleasure Cove Island. The pressure of undercover work and confidentiality. Him.

She didn't need to be afraid for her safety on top of all that.

"Let's go." He extended his left hand in invitation. The two men dutifully stepped aside, giving her a clear path down the aisle to him. But she didn't budge. Of all the times to get defiant. He needed to say something to convince her. "Darling."

Her eyebrows shot up at that one. "I haven't paid for the snacks yet."

Move your kiester, McCormick. Somehow he managed to keep the words to himself. "I'll take care of it."

"I'll bet you will. Darling."

Damn. Had the word sounded as unnatural when he'd said it?

At least she was walking toward him now. Actually, it was more of a stroll, a saunter, a deliberate sashay that garnered the attention of every man in the room. A perfect role-play for Pleasure Cove Island.

But not here.

Not with the fabulous biker boys ogling her butt.

"The time?" He urged her to quicken her pace.

"I'm well aware of the time." There was hell to pay glaring from her eyes, and he could see the only way he'd get her to move faster was to pick her up and carry her out of here himself.

She studiously acknowledged, then walked past, his outstretched hand. She didn't smile until she'd set her basket on the counter and made eye contact with the clerk. Sean brought his hand to his face to stifle an impatient curse, and rubbed at the tense muscles lining his jaw and mouth. This just got better and better. Now the clerk was eating up her belle-of-the-ball act, too.

Sean braced his hand on the counter and leaned in beside Caitlin. He wasn't taking this drama queen attitude of hers lying down. He purposely brushed his chest against her shoulder and felt her flinch. This close, he could hear the rattle in her chest as she sucked in a shallow breath. She *had* been in distress when he'd walked in.

Something infinitesimal shifted inside him. He felt a little less frustration and a little more concern—and a lot more anxious to get her out of here. "If you could hurry things along…" he advised the clerk.

While the man finally put down his paper and rang up their gas and food, Sean turned around and noticed Thing

One and Thing Two had sidled halfway down the aisle, their wishful expressions still focused on Caitlin.

Sean narrowed his gaze to its coldest squint and dared them to take him on. "What?"

The men puffed up like twin toy poodles banding together to take on a Doberman. There was a lot of bark and posturing, but the threat was almost comical.

"How much did you—?"

"Is she—?"

"Deke. Norm." The clerk shushed them. "Mind your manners." He turned his detached gaze to Sean. "They're harmless by this time of night. The lady said she was with you."

Maybe she hadn't said it strongly enough. When he turned his back on the bikers, Sean draped his arm possessively around Caitlin's stiff shoulders. "The lady's mine." Whatever they hoped to get from her wasn't going to happen. "All mine."

Her skin was cold to the touch, though he suspected her sudden chill had more to do with his familiarity than with the store's air-conditioning.

"I'm ready." Without another word or a friendly smile, Caitlin picked up her bottle of water and handed Sean a steaming foam cup. "Bitter and black. Just the way you like it…" she paused "…darling."

"Give it a rest, Caitie," he warned beneath his breath.

The clerk took Sean's money and counted out his change. Caitlin picked up their bag of sandwiches and snacks. When she shrugged off his touch and headed for the door, Sean let her go. When she was several steps ahead of him, he nodded to the clerk and followed her.

He noted Deke's and Norm's fascination with her departure and traced the path of their bleary gazes to the hemline of Caitlin's dress. The dress itself was plain. But he hadn't shopped in the Talls department, hadn't considered how a regular above-the-knee dress would look so small and hug so tightly a woman of her stature.

He hadn't considered how a short dress would become a miniskirt. A ninety-miles-of-leg-baring micro-mini.

He hadn't considered how it would cup her butt and stop just short of baring anything indecent.

But he noticed every hormone-stirring detail now.

Deke and Norm had noticed, too.

Possessed by demons he might never understand, Sean stepped into their line of sight, blocking Caitlin from their ogling view. "She's taken."

With that, he knew this was about more than establishing a convincing cover, more than protecting Caitlin from their drooling appreciation for her finer attributes, more than making amends for being such a hard-ass earlier.

In three long strides he caught up with her. For this weekend at least, she *was* his. Wicked body and guileless looks and outrageous fantasies and all, she was his alone. Everyone in this store needed to understand that fact.

Including her.

He caught her at the door, slipped his palm beneath her chin and tipped her mouth up to kiss her.

It was all for show, he told himself. He opened his mouth over hers, boldly staking his claim. It was quick and hot, more territorial than seductive.

When he pulled away, her cheeks were flushed, her eyes were dark and her mouth was poised to put him in his place.

He kissed her again.

The instant he felt her posture relax and her fingers brace against his chest to balance herself, the moment her lips softened with curiosity and began to respond, he pulled away fast. Before he lost himself in this crazy craving to touch her. To possess her in every way he could.

Her eyes looked a little less fierce this time. Her tongue darted out to lick the rim of her lips, as if testing for damage—or tasting him again. Sean traced the same path with the pad of his thumb, unsure whether it was a stroke of apology or one more chance to sample the moist heat and gentle ripeness that was unique to her kiss.

"What was that for?" Her husky whisper danced along his skin.

He swatted her rump and urged her on out the door. "Let's just call it one of *my* fantasies."

Before she could gather steam again, he took her by the elbow and ushered her around the corner of the building. That adorable blush of innocent passion got lost in a series of blustery gasps as she started and then dismissed several protests. "How could—? You have no— I'm not a katydid. I said to call me— Don't think I'm going to put up with your high-handed tactics."

"*My* tactics?" When he got her to the car, he spared a look for the men inside. With the show finally over, their attention had moved on to their beer. "I don't know what those two brain cells wanted in there, but I could tell it wasn't anything good."

"It wasn't." She dug in her heels and forced Sean to release her. "They wanted to buy me for the weekend. They think I'm a prostitute."

"You're kidding."

"No." She raked her fingers through her hair. "*They* actually think I'm sexy."

Like he didn't? Her hair cascaded down around her face. And he curled his fingers into a fist to keep from touching those silken curls.

His instincts about messy entanglements with Caitlin had been right on the money. Sean was torn between going back inside and setting those two goons straight, and dumping her in the car and driving her back to her apartment in Alexandria where scum like that never entered her world.

But if he put the job first, as he knew he had to, he didn't have time for either option. One way or another he had to make this work. He appeased his guilt by giving in to the urge to touch her. He brushed a tendril of hair off her cheek. "They didn't hurt you, did they? I'm sorry. And I didn't call you 'katydid.' Was that a childhood nickname?"

She didn't answer that one. "I'm fine." She pulled away and stepped off the sidewalk. "But you should be sorry. I was handling things just fine until you came in. Your Neanderthal impersonation just reaffirmed the notion that I was your property, not your girlfriend."

Sean reached around her and unlocked the door. "You weren't handling anything. Your eyes were full of panic and you could barely catch your breath."

She opened the door and pushed him aside. "How am I going to learn to play my part this weekend if your response to my mistakes is to bulldoze your way in and take care of them for me?"

"I thought you liked a good villain."

"I want to tame him, not be bullied by his lack of manners. Your whole control freak thing is a real turnoff."

Control freak? "I'm not the one who almost blew our cover. *I* was thinking on my feet. *I* was doing my job." She climbed in. When she would have shut him out, he grabbed the handle and knelt beside her in the triangle of space between the car and the open door, forcing her to listen. "Why don't you explain how you can be a man-hungry siren when we're all alone and you're playing at that fantasy in your head? But when we're actually in front of an audience where it counts, you can't even pretend you like me?"

She defiantly met his probing gaze, but had no answer. He shook his head. "If you can't convince two drunks and a bored night clerk that we're lovers, you'll never convince Douglas Fairchild.''

"I can learn how.'' She chanted the words like a pledge. "I want to do this for my country. I want to be treated like a capable woman. Give me another chance. I promise I'll do better next time.''

"You'll have to,'' Sean warned her. "Because if Fairchild doesn't buy our ruse, then there's no point in even going to Pleasure Cove Island.''

7

CAITLIN HAD TO FIND a way to make this work. Sean seemed to think his mission to Pleasure Cove Island was in jeopardy because of her.

If only he hadn't jumped in and started controlling that fiasco at the convenience store. Her brothers had called her "katydid" when she was a little girl and had tried to tag along on their adventures. Even then, she'd understood the teasing, belittling name. She couldn't keep up. She was too much responsibility. Did she have her inhaler with her? Did Mom know where she was?

She'd gotten around their efforts to escape her by sneaking after them and pedaling her bike harder to catch up. It hadn't taken them too many run-ins with her showing up, wheezing and pale-faced, to finally understand that she wouldn't be left behind or ordered about. Her older brother, Ethan, probably owed his current diplomatic skills to the trade-offs and negotiations they'd learned to use with her. Instead of commanding her to stay put, they'd invite her to play for a while. Then they'd ask for time to themselves in exchange for loaning her their G.I. Joes to play with her dolls.

Diplomacy worked.

"Come here, Caitie" did not.

Sean's stern orders in the store had raised her hackles, but those two kisses had been pure, raw passion and she'd nearly melted in her tennies.

Crashing out on her own was all so confusing. Caitlin's sigh fogged up the side window.

She wiped the window clean, noting the Rhode Island state line rolling by.

"Do you want me to drive?" she asked, hearing Sean yawning for the third time in as many minutes. She turned to face him. "I make a better driver than I do an undercover agent."

Her effort to lighten the mood earned her nothing more than a squinty-eyed scowl from across the car.

She stiffened her spine and tried using reason to make her point. "If we're in an accident, I'll hardly be able to keep that secret from my father. You'd have a hard time explaining how a simple date landed me so far from home. And even if we do reach Maine safely, you'll be too exhausted to do any investigating. That *is* the point of your mission, isn't it?"

"This car is my baby. You're unpredictable, so you're not driving, McCormick."

Screw reason. She hugged her arms in front of her and glared out the window at the shadowy, tree-lined fields zipping past. "You're just as pigheaded as my father. You know, if you men would back off and give me some credit, you'd see I actually can do a few things on my own. I've taken care of all kinds of problems for other people—my students, my roommate, Dad's health, Travis's love life—"

"I thought you said you didn't have a love life."

"Thanks for reminding me." She watched three more telephone poles go by. "Travis is my brother. I've smoothed over a lot of broken hearts that he's left in his wake." She turned and poked her index finger into Sean's shoulder. "The point is, I'm a responsible, adult woman."

"You were about to blurt out your father's name. You're the one who said secrecy was so important." He glanced down at her finger, then over at her. "If they wanted, those bums could do a little research in a military database and figure out who you really are. Boom. Daddy comes to get you. End of mission."

End of adventure.

She tucked her hand back into her defensive hug, but gamely held Sean's gaze until his attention reverted to the long road ahead of them. Then she looked out her own window into the night, watching the black silhouettes of trees and barns and fence posts go past as they headed north away from the coast toward the heart of the New England countryside.

It was probably a beautiful drive by daylight, with fresh spring plantings of whatever Rhode Island farmers raised. But at two-thirty in the morning, it was just an endless stretch of dismal twilight.

Caitlin sighed.

Some adventure.

Sean yawned again, and she knew she had to make this right. "I expect to be disappointed," he'd told her when he first invited her to fill in as his undercover mistress. Something from his past had cost him his faith in people—in relationships, at least. He was willing to share his body, but not his trust.

And she needed his trust. Desperately.

She needed someone to believe in her unconditionally. Not write her off as an invalid. Caitlin knew she acted as a reminder to her family of a woman who had been dearly loved and lost. Her father and brothers didn't want to lose her, too, and she understood that fear, that need to protect the youngest member of their family. The one who'd been sick as a child.

The one who had been at their mother's side when the cancer finally took her.

Ethan had been stationed at the embassy in Kuwait. Travis had been on his first ROTC training cruise in the Pacific. Her father had been caught at a meeting in Washington, overseeing engineering deployments to Bosnia.

They hadn't been there to take care of her mother.

Now they wouldn't miss an opportunity to take care of Caitlin.

"You're right. My father would blow a gasket if he found out that two strangers offered to pay me for sex. And he doesn't need to find out that I let you…" She pressed her legs tighter together and tried to ignore her body's vivid response to the memory of his fingers inside her. She gestured with her hand. "That we…" Now her palms were burning. She rubbed them together and tried not to remember how smooth and hot and hard he'd been when he'd jumped into her hands and let her play. "He'd worry that I wasn't being careful. He doesn't know the kind of fantasies I have about men. He doesn't understand my need to—"

Sean's breath whooshed out in an audible sigh. "I get the idea."

"And Dad wouldn't have given me a chance to get away from Deke and Norm on my own. Just like you didn't."

Sean punched the wheel with the palm of his hand. "You were failing your chance. You don't get a second try when you're working undercover."

Caitlin adjusted her seatbelt and faced him. "Well, then tell me what I could have done differently. I tried a polite no, a firm no. I told them my boyfriend was a secret agent—"

"You told them I work for the FBI?"

She absorbed his colorful string of curses with an apologetic shrug. "I didn't give your name or any details. I merely hinted that you might beat them up."

"I doubt that they're a security risk, but I'll have my

partner try to run down their names, anyway.'' Sean slid her a look that was pure bafflement. "And I might be a little macho, but I don't generally beat up anyone on the first date.''

"I panicked, okay? I'll admit that. They wouldn't leave me alone. They needed some serious personal hygiene and they creeped me out.'' His incredulous expression softened with protective concern. And she soaked up the welcome absolution, grateful he was letting her ramble on without placing blame. Sean had listened to her secrets and wishes and fears in a way no other man ever had. Maybe he didn't want to, but he listened all the same. "Teach me how to do better. Don't do it *for* me.'' Still turned to the side, she sank back into her seat, not wanting to take her gaze from the strong angles of his noble profile or the hint of a smile that turned up the corner of his mouth. "That's what Dad and my brothers try to do.''

"You don't rebel against their authority the way you do mine?''

"*You* don't have a bum heart.''

That hint of a smile vanished. His lips pressed together, matching the narrow focus of his eyes. "There are some who say I don't have a heart, period.''

"I don't say that.''

He turned and gave her a look so charged, so deep, that she found herself rubbing goose bumps along her bare arms. Was that disbelief she read in his eyes? Longing? Pain?

"You don't even know me.''

He'd exposed her to something hot and tortured from deep within. But the chill she felt was real. What were Sean's secrets? And did she really think she could handle the emotions burning inside his soul when she could scarcely manage to handle her own?

Feeling more ill-equipped than ever to fulfill her woman-of-the-world act this weekend, she scooted around in her seat, breaking his mesmerizing hold on her. She needed to laugh. Now. Before she did something foolish like break into tears.

"I'll give you macho and pigheaded," she teased, "but not heartless. If you were truly heartless, you would have left me holding the vacuum cleaner back at my apartment. Instead, you gave me a chance to pursue a dream—to be more than what my world allows me to be." She kept on talking, anxious to fill the tense silence between them. "Maybe if we knew more about each other, we'd be able to communicate better. You know, we could read each other's signals—like a code. You'd know when I was in trouble. I'd know when to shut up and play along. You'd know when to back off and let me fly solo. I could..." Caitlin stopped talking when she realized they were slowing down. "Is something wrong with the car?"

Sean didn't answer. He tapped on the brake and pulled over onto the shoulder of the empty country road. The light of the closest farmhouse was nearly a mile away, but the glow from the dashboard lights gave her plenty of illumination to watch Sean's stony face before he killed the engine, unhooked his seat belt and turned to face her.

A nervous beat of anticipation tripped through her veins. Should she be worried? Sean hadn't hurt her. But she knew he wasn't exactly pleased with her help thus far. And she was babbling. She combed her hair back from her temple and tried to remain calm. "What's going on?"

He turned even more in his seat. In the confines of the low-slung car, he suddenly seemed awfully close. The clear light of the moon came in through the sunroof, lighting the jut of his cheekbones and shadowing his eyes to a dark, midnight green. An intense color. An intense man.

''Why did we stop?'' she asked, leaning a little closer to the passenger-side door.

''I've decided you're right,'' he finally answered, his grim expression never changing. ''We're going to get to know each other.''

''THE MUSCONGUS BAY FERRY leaves in just over twelve hours. We need to get a few things straight before then.''

Sean's tone was all-business, impersonal. ''What are you comfortable with? What nicknames can we use to give the appearance of intimacy? *Caitie* felt natural to me—I didn't intend it as a put-down. But if you don't like it, give me something else. I don't know about you, but I about gagged on that 'darling' shit.'' He rubbed his palm along the rugged contours of his jaw and his shoulders heaved in a weary sigh. ''We'll need a signal so I know when it's okay to touch you and when I need to let you have your freedom.''

So Caitlin's fantasy weekend had been reduced to this cold discussion of procedure. It wasn't exactly the kind of hands-on training she'd been hoping for.

''I don't know.'' She looked away from the twin strands of hair that had fallen over his brow, and ignored the urge to brush them back into place. ''I guess I thought you'd take the lead, and I'd just follow along with whatever you started.''

He shook his head. ''That didn't work in Connecticut. I need to know that I can kiss you or hold you and that you won't tense up. If we're not convincing lovers, then Fairchild will wonder what I'm doing on his island. I won't be able to ask questions or poke around if he suspects we're not legitimate guests.''

''Are you asking what I like a man to do when he's with me?''

"Physically," Sean amended. "What sort of public displays of affection did you enjoy with your previous lovers?"

She felt a flame of embarrassment scorch her cheeks.

Then she laughed self-consciously, clearly perplexing him, if that frown was any indication. "I wish I could tell you."

"Explain."

She tucked her hair behind her ear and started in, praying she wouldn't sound like a complete idiot. "To be honest, I don't have that much experience with men. So I'm not sure exactly what I like or what I can handle. When you have an overprotective family like mine—and you're taller than most of the boys in your class…" her voice started to fade "…and you teach grammar and you have no figure—"

Sean swore harshly. "Are you a virgin?"

He'd asked the question with all the dramatic aplomb of one of those reality cop show investigators.

"No!" Her gaze locked on to his. She'd answered too quickly for him to believe her. Great. Just great. Now she'd have to tell him everything. "Does one time count? I mean, one guy, a couple of times?" She sped through the rest of the explanation before she lost her nerve. "It was back in college. In a back seat." She glanced behind the seat and stuttered, remembering Sean's invitation to join her back there earlier. Michael Patterson's beat-up Impala had nothing on Sean's sleek, black Porsche.

Michael Patterson's fumbling hands had nothing on Sean.

"We were on a road-trip kind of a thing. Like this one. But not. We were going to a rock concert. It didn't work out." Her cheeks were on fire, but it was too late to cover up her embarrassment. "Don't get me wrong. I date. I date lots of men. I just…I haven't…a lot."

Sean's face was still too unreadable for her to gauge his reaction. When he spoke, his crisp, British tone sounded stilted and unemotional. "So, inexperience is the only reason you aren't comfortable with me touching you. It has nothing to do with regrets—" He finally turned to her, and the doubt in his eyes was easy to read. She had the same doubts herself. "—about what happened between us in the car?"

"No." She reached out and touched his forearm, trying to apologize and reassure him in one consoling gesture. His gaze dropped to the point where her fingertips rested on the nubby tweed of his jacket. Caitlin sensed that her reaction was important. But was the burning intensity of his eyes caressing her? Or warning her away?

She rallied her courage the way her father would. It was an innocent enough gesture, but she tightened her grip and refused to let go. "What you did to me at that gas station was the first time I ever—with a man... I mean, on my own I've...oh hell." She raked her fingers through her hair, wishing she was anywhere but here. "I'm sorry. I guess you can see why I was available to go with you this weekend."

And then she realized she was still holding on to him. But when she pulled away, he reconnected them. He put his hand on her knee. It was an equally gentle gesture. He had very nice hands, really. Big enough to conquer. Big enough to control. Big enough to comfort.

She didn't flinch. In fact, she rather liked the warmth of his hand there. She felt safe with that touch.

She was still watching his hand when he spoke. "You're telling me that men aren't beating down your bedroom door to get at those legs of yours?"

"My legs?"

His voice rumbled at a deeply musical pitch, with all the best intonations of his British-American ancestry. "They were the first thing I noticed about you. Surely someone's told you what a gorgeous pair of stilts you walk on?"

"No." Just Deke and Norm. And their form of flattery hardly counted.

Now she watched Sean's eyes. They were fixed on his hand. Or rather, the movement of his hand as it slid a few inches higher toward her thigh. She liked this touch, too. A whisper of sensation skittered along the surface of her skin, raising goose bumps.

"Consider yourself told." The weight of his hand settled against her leg, and his fingers curled around the inside of her thigh in a lightly possessive grip.

Caitlin didn't mind. "Thank you."

A nervous anticipation caught in her lungs. His hand stayed in place until her breathing evened out. And then it slipped higher. He stopped when the heel of his palm met the hem of her dress. A flood of heat rushed to the spot. His eyes sparkled and danced as they watched the trembling contraction of muscles in her leg. "I can't believe men don't have their hands all over that soft, creamy skin of yours."

"My brothers might have something to say about that." Caitlin swallowed hard. She wanted this touch. She wanted more.

"Does my hand make you uncomfortable?"

"No, it's…" She looked from his eyes to his hand and back to his eyes. "It makes me think of…before."

His fingers tightened for a moment. Then he released her and rolled back into his seat. She nearly snatched for his hand, wanting him to touch her again.

"So that's a way I can touch you you're okay with? A hand on the knee?" He stared straight ahead into the darkness.

"Of course. But touching my knee is hardly enough to convince Douglas Fairchild we're lovers. Sean, I want to do more."

Sean raked her with a look that bespoke something weary

and wounded inside him. "Not right now." He opened the car door. "I need some fresh air." He was out and striding down the shoulder of the road before Caitlin could even react.

Confused, anxious to prove her willingness to cooperate, she threw open her door and hurried after him. "Where are you going?"

His thick, angry voice cut through the still night air as he marched away from her. "I used my best friend's birthday present to find a woman who was ready, willing and able to act as my mistress, and I end up with a frickin' virgin. This will never work."

"I'm not a virgin." She defended herself, hurrying after him, drawing on pride to keep shame at bay. "I told you I did it twice."

"You just told me I gave you your first orgasm."

"So I'm learning on the job. We can work this out."

Suddenly, Sean stopped and whirled around. Caitlin back-pedaled a step to keep from plowing into him. "*We* don't have to do anything. *I* have to get the job done. The fate of a kidnapped little girl is on the line. I have an entire country demanding to know answers about one man's death. Ultimately, this mission comes down to *me*."

With his hands propped on his hips, his chest thrust out and his shoulders stretching the seams of his jacket, he seemed very big, very imposing. It took every bit of backbone she had to stand her ground.

And underneath his formidable demeanor she saw the desperate determination gleaming in his eyes.

And this man thought he had no heart?

Something soft and feminine blossomed inside Caitlin, something warm and compassionate that had her reaching out and grasping a tentative handful of his jacket lapel. She needed to connect to Sean somehow, to break through that wall of strength and stubbornness that hid from the rest of the world whatever hurts and feelings and guilt he had.

"It comes down to you. And your mistress."

The tweedy material radiated the warmth of his body, the soft rasp of fabric reminding her of the brush of his fingers on her skin. Caitlin smiled at the analogy. They might come from different backgrounds, they might have different goals and personalities that made them continually butt heads and confound each other. But there was one way that she and Sean communicated very clearly.

Fisting her hand in his coat, she leaned forward and pressed her lips to his.

It was a gentle kiss, but he was as startled by her actions as she'd been startled by his kiss in Connecticut. She felt an instant rush of pressurized heat from her mouth down to that heavy juncture between her thighs with just that simplest of contacts. His hands came to her elbows. At first he was pushing her away, but then he was simply holding her.

He held his mouth in a stiff line, giving her but a sample of his unique masculine textures, allowing her only a taste of the salt on his skin. Without his cooperation, the spiky abrasion of his golden beard stubble stung her lips and she pulled away, disappointed that she hadn't been able to entice or even comfort him.

As she pulled back, breathless with arousal, weak with embarrassment, she studied those unmoving lips and the rigid jaw that framed them.

"What did I do wrong this time?" she whispered. "How do I do it better?"

"Who am I this time?" The sneer in his voice warred with the tightening clutch of his fingers on her arms. "Count Dracula? Hannibal Lecter? Bluebeard the pirate?"

She raised her gaze to meet the taunt in his. She was beginning to think that all his high-handed, tough-guy bluster was just a cover for something much more vulnerable hidden inside.

That inner man was the one she wanted to reach. The McCormick in her tried again. ''You're Sean Maddox, New England Administrative Chief of the Federal Bureau of Investigation. You can call me Caitie or sweetheart or anything but darling.'' Her body was already drifting closer to his. ''And I'm all yours.''

This time Sean met her halfway. She tugged him closer by the lapels and he tunneled his fingers into her hair, palming her cheek and temple to guide her mouth to the perfect angle for receiving his kiss. His mouth was open and hot and eager to claim hers.

Sean's day-old beard scratched against her chin like the rough caress of a cat. There was a right way and a wrong way to stroke a feline. And once she learned the prickly delights of rubbing her cheek in a downward rasp against his, Caitlin developed an insatiable catlike curiosity to run her lips along his jaw, to open her mouth against his neck and even draw her teeth together to catch the sandpapery cleft of his chin in a tender nibble.

There was something intrinsically male about the ruggedness of his beard against her softer skin. Each flex of muscle, each brush of his mouth on hers teased her lips and face with a dozen little extra caresses.

With Sean's tawny crown of hair it was like being embraced by a lion. A big, rangy king of beasts.

And Caitlin had no desire to tame him. She wanted the beast to run wild.

She'd long since abandoned her grip on his jacket and had wound her arms around his neck, pulling herself up onto tiptoe as he buried both hands in her hair to turn her face one way, then the other, while he plundered her willing mouth.

She wasn't aware of the pulse pounding in her ears, or the quick, shallow gasps of air that pushed her chest in and out, until she realized his chest was expanding with the same throbbing rhythm. Engorged by the stoking friction of his body, her nipples grew hard, puckering and poking against their cotton sheaths like twin pressure valves trying to hold back a sudden swell of heat.

"Mmm...Sean?" she gasped with her next two breaths. She didn't know how to make this better. She couldn't think of how to move past the crazy notion that she wanted him to devour her, that she was damn near ready to jump out of her skin and devour him. "Please."

She didn't know how to ask to take this kiss to the next level, but Sean knew how to answer.

8

CAITLIN REVELED in the needy press of Sean's hands as he slid them down her back and lifted her by her buttocks— clear off the ground. She tightened her grip around his neck, partly for balance, partly to ease the overwhelming friction of her body sliding along his.

"Put your legs around me," he ordered in a fevered command against her throat. "I've got you."

But she was too tall, too big, too much woman to trust his strength. Her lips scudded across his mouth. "Your back. You'll hurt— You shouldn't—"

"Caitie." He growled that one word to silence her before he reclaimed her mouth.

She couldn't protest. She didn't want to. She heard nothing belittling in the shortened version of her name when Sean said it like that. Articulated in his growly voice, it sounded almost desperate. Needy. Intimate.

And then he was lifting her higher, cradling the backs of her thighs in his palms, splitting her legs apart and wrapping them around himself. She clasped the back of his head and moaned, savoring the stretch of muscles in her thighs that opened her taut, female heat in an erotic caress against the double layer of denim at the front of his jeans.

Oh God, he was so strong. So strong.

"Hold on." Her breasts flattened against the wall of his chest as he shifted his hold yet again, jostling her against the growing bulge in his jeans.

She cried out with the agony of unleashed pleasure that throbbed in the very heart of her. She linked her ankles behind his hips and rubbed herself against him. But it wasn't enough. She wanted more. She needed more. She needed Sean.

As she climbed up his chest, searching for the best fit of her arms around his shoulders, she realized they were moving. He was carrying her, high in his arms, breathing hard from the passion they shared, but striding with the speed and grace of a man whose load was easy to bear.

In Sean's arms she wasn't a five-foot-eleven freak. She wasn't an asthmatic, motherless little sister. She wasn't a dutiful daughter who sacrificed her fantasies to keep her father's heart beating at an even pace.

She was woman.

A feminine, potent she-cat, primed and ready to surrender to her mate.

She arched her back, preened and stretched along his chest and torso as he carried her through the dark. With his hands firmly planted, his lips danced along the base of her throat. And still she stretched, urging him to go lower.

She was dizzy with desire. The pressure was gathering in her body, seeking an outlet through every pore, building with a power that was driving her mad.

She caught her breath in a moment of temporary sanity when her bottom hit something hard, something warm— something as smooth and sleek and solid as the man holding her—the Porsche.

He was setting her down!

"No," she cried, throwing herself shamelessly forward and clinging to his neck. "Don't stop now."

"This is crazy. Caitie. Sweetheart." His breathing came in deep, swift gasps between each word. Each kiss.

And then she understood that he had set her on the hood

of the car beside the passenger door to free his hands. First they were beneath her, cupping her butt, sliding beneath the hem of her skirt and shoving the material up around her hips. The fading heat from the hood of the car radiated through the moist crotch of her panties, and the pressure that had been building inside her rushed with an almost painful madness to that most tender spot.

Caitlin felt like roaring with frustration. She was so close. So close.

She channeled that frustration into her hands, pushing the jacket off Sean's shoulders, battling with him to see whose hands would be freed first as she tugged first one, then the other, sleeve free. Then her hands were at his shoulders again, skimming across the erotic strip of black leather that bound his holster across his back.

"Tell me..." she begged, dragging her palms over the curve of his powerful biceps. "Tell me..." She skimmed his flanks and sank her fingertips into the waistband of his jeans, tugging loose the hem of his T-shirt and then scorching her hands on his hot, bare skin. "What should I do?"

"You're doing it." They were lusty words of praise and a breathless plea for mercy. "Damn. Caitie. Is that okay?" His hands were on her back, sweeping her up to his mouth for a kiss, sweeping down and taking the zipper of her dress with them. "I can't—" The zipper stuck at her waist and he swore. "—get—" She heard a rip of material, felt a cool breeze against her skin. And then he was pulling at the neckline of her dress, pulling the straps off her shoulders and down her arms, taking her bra down along with them and freeing her breasts. "—enough."

He pushed her back against the windshield and closed his mouth over one taut, aching breast. He curled his tongue around the distended nipple and she whimpered. He touched his teeth to the sensitive rim and she gasped for breath. He squeezed the breast in his hand and sucked hard on the tip, and Caitlin cried out.

"Sean!"

It was too much. Too much.

Hard car behind her. Hard man between her legs.

Caitlin squirmed and bucked and reached for that heady release. He slipped his hand inside her panties. Wet and slick and primed for sex, her opening easily stretched to accommodate his fingers as he slipped them inside her. With his thumb pressed against her clit, he glided in and out and rubbed his fingers back and forth along her feminine crevice. She felt the slick lubrication of her sex against her thigh, felt it in the hair that surrounded her core, felt it deep, deep inside herself.

She had never been this hot, this full before. She wanted this to be right. She wanted this to be perfect.

"No. I want *you*."

She snatched at his jeans and unhooked the snap. But he kept her pinned to the car, stroking his tongue to the other breast, suckling the tip, distracting her from her purpose. "You've got me."

She shook her head. "Not like…" With an awkward, desperate twist she unzipped him. She could barely think, barely breathe. But when the straining ridge of his desire sprang up into her hand, she shouted, "Yes!" She squeezed him through his shorts and spread her legs wider, making her invitation as plain as possible.

Sean groaned as she worked him free and drew her hand along the deliciously hard proof of his desire for her. She flicked her thumb across the tip, bringing away a bead of his moisture. "Caitie—"

"Yes." She was ready. Now. But it still wasn't perfect.

On a half-formed impulse, she pushed his hand aside and touched herself, lubricating her fingers with her own desire.

Then she touched him again, sliding her hand back and forth the way he had taught her. He moaned aloud when she found that sensitive strip of skin on the underside of his penis, and she felt the sounds of his imminent release vibrate through her.

He'd made those sounds once before. Caitlin closed her eyes and smiled a wicked little grin of ecstasy about to be realized.

She scooted to the edge of the car as the spasms began, and urged Sean closer.

"I want to feel it with a man inside me."

"What?"

Sean's hips rocked against hers as he pulled his mouth away and tried to shift his balance to his feet. The spasms exploded into pain-filled pleasure as wave upon wave of orgasm finally seized her. Not yet. Not yet.

"I've never come with a man—"

The tip of his shaft brushed against her thigh. Caitlin gripped him with a desperate need and guided him through the slick trail of her desire until the hard probe nudged the slit where she wanted him so badly. He was throbbing. He was coming.

"Caitie, stop." Sean jerked his hips to the side and spurted his seed onto the side of the road. "Shit."

Not exactly the endearment, or the finish, she'd been hoping for.

Caitlin clenched her thighs together and let the disappointing remnants of her climax pass. Sean had backed away from the car. With his hands at his waist and his face turned to the sky, he was sucking in huge gulps of the crisp night air.

He was an amazing sight, really, profiled against the moonlight. Straight nose, rugged chin. His chest formed a massive silhouette of sculpted strength as his diaphragm sank in and flexed out below it with each gut-wrenching breath. His jeans had pooled around his hips, and that jutting erection she'd wanted to possess inside her was slowly receding back beneath the body-hugging contours of his black briefs.

But nothing felt amazing right now.

She was drained physically and numb with emotional shock. She moved much more slowly, sitting up, pulling her bra back into place and hugging her arms across her naked torso. She wasn't aware that her own breathing was fractured with the telltale rattle of overexertion until she noticed that Sean's chest was rising and falling at a more even pace.

Caitlin shoved her fingers into her hair and pushed it back off her forehead. "What did I do wrong?"

He didn't even look at her. "Not a damn thing."

"But we didn't—"

"And we're not going to." Sean carefully adjusted himself, then pulled his jeans up and zipped them shut. He lectured on while he tucked in his shirt and adjusted the position of his gun and holster. "We're in the middle of nowhere. There's no shower." He swiped the back of his hand across his mouth as if his grim expression was the last thing he needed to put back into place, and finally turned to face her. "No condom."

A mixture of shock and shame left Caitlin feeling lightheaded.

There wasn't a single possible outcome of unprotected sex that wouldn't send her father over the edge or turn her brothers into a lynch mob.

"I didn't think—"

"Neither one of us was thinking."

Sean was gallant enough to share the blame, even though he'd been the one to see the potential problems and stop their crazy lovemaking before it went too far. Maybe her father was right to worry about his sheltered daughter.

As the spring night air cooled her body, Caitlin pulled the straps of her dress up over her shoulders and lowered her feet to the ground so she could stand on shaky legs and straighten her skirt. "I just wanted to prove to you that we could be a believable couple. That I wasn't afraid to touch you, and you shouldn't be afraid to touch me. I don't know how it got out of hand."

She reached behind her to zip her dress, but found the rip in the seam instead. She'd forgotten how desperate he'd been to get his hands on her skin, to get as close as he possibly could to her. If she didn't feel so empty inside, she might actually laugh at the irony of just how much distance he seemed determined to put between them now. "At least you don't have to worry about us portraying believable lovers. I didn't do too badly for a 'frickin virgin,' did I?"

The man had no funny bone left for her sarcasm. "Dammit, Caitie. This isn't real. *We're* not real."

"But that came a little too close, huh?"

His eyes filled with that same desolate pain that had spoken to her heart earlier. Maybe if she was more a woman of the world, she'd understand how a man could seemingly want her so badly, and yet not be happy when he was given the chance to have what he wanted. Whether it was her body, her allegiance or her heart.

She dropped her gaze when she felt tears of pity welling up in her own eyes. "Well, the clock's ticking." She pointed to her own watch, even though her vision had blurred too much to focus on the dial. "We'd better get back on the road. If we're still on for Pleasure Cove Island, that is."

"We're on."

Though his eyes had never left her, his posture relaxed.

He seemed relieved that she'd turned the conversation back to business. He picked up his jacket, brushed it off and turned the sleeves right side out. Clearly, completing this assignment successfully was the number one priority for Sean. Maybe she should remember that she'd volunteered for adventure, not a chance to probe the mystery behind this enigmatic man or advance her own sexual education.

Caitlin hovered beside the car, looking through the windshield at the dark, compact interior. How was she going to survive five or six more hours in such cramped quarters with Sean without embarrassing herself further? "I'm still willing to drive if you want a break."

"No, I need the distraction."

So much for that option. "What's it going to take to get you to trust me, Maddox? A signed permission slip?"

"This Porsche is my baby."

That wasn't what she was talking about and he knew it. Clutching her arms across her stomach, Caitlin looked him straight in the eye and challenged him. "You don't want to give up control. Of anything. You won't let me help you at all."

"You're my cover. That's how you can help me. End of discussion."

Dismissed. Out of her element. In over her head.

Her energy spent from the long drive and even longer battle of wills, Caitlin turned toward the car door. She shivered as a whisper of night air chilled her skin.

"Here. You're cold."

Sean slipped his jacket over her shoulders from behind, draping the soft silk lining across her bare arms like a tender hug. The familiar scents of wool and leather and musky man clung to the material. An instant warmth surrounded her, so that she felt as if he was actually wrapping her up in his own sheltering embrace. A vague impression from her fantasy life faded slowly into her imagination. Beauty taming the Beast. She went all soft inside at the notion of tender feelings from this sexy savage.

But as soon as she gave in to the urge to lean into the hands that lingered at her shoulders, he pulled away. "I'm sorry," he said, reaching around her to open the door. "I'm sorry about the dress. I'm sorry about..." he held the door until she'd climbed inside and sat down "...everything."

Caitlin had kicked off her shoes and buckled in by the time he circled the hood, checked the road for nonexistent traffic and climbed in behind the wheel.

Sean started the engine, then let it idle while he rested his hands on the wheel. "I can't let my sex drive run this mission. I have to stay focused."

"I know. The kidnapped girl and the dead guy need answers from that island."

"And I don't want you to get hurt. I'm not relationship material, Caitie."

"Who says I'm looking for a relationship?" In all honesty, she hadn't volunteered to come along because she was in search of a husband or boyfriend. But as the hours ticked by, she found herself more intrigued by the man who was her partner for the weekend than by the weekend itself. "I'm your mistress. I know that Monday morning you'll go back to work for the Bureau and I'll call my dad to tell him his little girl is A-okay. We'll never see each other again. I understand my role. I can act the part without thinking it's real."

"Are you really sophisticated enough to pull off all that?"

"I'm not going to let you down, Sean. I promise."

She hunkered down in her seat and closed her eyes, avoiding the probing doubts in his moss-green gaze.

SOMEWHERE AROUND THE HUB of Boston, Massachusetts, Sean had relented and handed over the keys to his Porsche to Caitlin. She'd accepted the offer with a teasing, "I'll try not to get too many scratches on your fancy car," and a promise to wake him once they passed through New Hampshire and crossed over the Maine state line.

Not that he completely trusted her. But she assured him she wouldn't get lost on the interstate or waste time with unnecessary stops. Her smile had been confident, her gray eyes round and sincere. And, dammit all, her offer made too much sense to ignore. He was beat. He'd need some sleep if he was going to get anything accomplished at Pleasure Cove.

She'd given her word. And he had no choice but to let her try.

But women had made promises before. His mother had promised to love, honor and cherish his father. Her string of affairs had devastated his father's pride and destroyed the foundation of their family. Roland Maddox had never remarried after their divorce. He eased his pain the way his mother had—by taking on lovers, one after another.

Sean should have learned his father's lesson better. He'd risked his heart on Elise and gotten it trashed by her betrayal. Maybe she'd just wanted him for sex, like one of his mother's lovers. He'd made the mistake of thinking there was something more between them.

He intended to be a relationship survivor. Don't love one woman too much. Don't surrender your trust completely. And put your faith in things you can control. Like your job. Like yourself.

He'd come way too close to losing his control with Caitie. *Caitie.* Hell. The name she once hated was flowing off his tongue like some kind of damned endearment now. He was slipping big time, mistaking lust for trust. Confusing her commitment to the mission with commitment to him.

He needed to back off and play it cool. Those two close encounters with her should stave off his body's sex drive for a while. And since she seemed to be getting off on the whole Mata Hari fantasy about secretly serving her country, she should be willing to cooperate with his desire to keep things strictly business between them, so they could get the job done without distractions.

Now if he could just get his hormones to listen to what his brain was trying to tell them.

Exhaustion finally won out over both hormones and intellectual debate. With one final glance through the slit of his eyelids to assure himself that Caitlin was on the right road, he settled into the passenger seat and drifted off to sleep.

By noon they finally reached Bar Harbor, Maine, on the rocky shores of Muscongus Bay. Sean checked them into a hotel for the afternoon and ordered a pizza. With the first decent meal in their stomachs in almost twenty-four hours, Caitlin lay down for a nap, and Sean stepped into the shower.

He adjusted the temperature of the water downward by several degrees until cold water was sluicing over his chest and groin. He'd been at half-mast ever since that interlude on the side of the highway, just thinking about how much he wanted to bury himself inside Caitlin's hot, slick folds— and how close he'd come to actually doing it. What he hadn't allowed his body to do, his mind had done more than once in his dreams.

But he was awake now. He was rested. He had no excuse for concentrating on anything besides his mission to Pleasure Cove Island.

With his body and goals firmly in check, Sean turned off the water and stepped out of the shower stall. He bumped his elbow on the door as he reached for his towel. The place was pretty cramped, with barely enough room for him to maneuver. But the room was functional. It possessed all the amenities they needed for their brief stay.

But it sure would be nice to have some space big enough for him to move without constantly bumping into things. His mind immediately leaped back to its previous obsession. It'd be nice to have enough space for him and Caitlin both to do some maneuvering.

"Damn." That familiar heat began to simmer in his groin. This was ridiculous. "The job." He glanced down at his still-swollen member and gave it a stern reminder of their priorities. "The job comes first."

Leaving his cock to deal with its own frustrations, Sean wrapped a white towel around his waist and opened the bathroom door. It was all a case of mind over matter. He could control this. He had to.

Fortunately, Caitlin was still asleep on the far side of the double bed. This would be easier if she kept her distance for a while. He'd have time to get his brain together and review the particulars of his investigation.

She looked so innocent lying there, curled up in a ball with her back to him. So trusting. He marveled at her ability to drop her guard in a room she shared with a stranger in a strange town.

She'd put a hell of a lot of faith in him, he realized. She trusted him to give her this secret weekend of adventure and then deliver her home safely when all was said and done. It was a powerful responsibility.

And it settled on Sean's shoulders with a profound sense of rightness. Caitlin was a strong woman, but a gentle soul. The protective urges that squeezed his heart weren't completely foreign to a man who'd carried a badge for ten years, a man who'd sheltered his little sister from the harshest repercussions of their parents' disintegrating marriage.

But this need to protect had never scared him quite so much.

The broken zipper of Caitlin's dress gaped open, revealing a delectable stretch of soft skin. Sean squeezed his eyes shut to avoid that stimulus that was sure to disrupt his thought processes again. But thoughts of sex mingled with guilt. He'd wrecked that dress for her.

He'd done a lousy job of protecting her so far.

He hadn't protected her from himself.

It was just one more reason to turn his mind back to the job.

Sean knew what he had to do. Padding on silent feet across the room, he retrieved his phone and dialed Thomas. By the time his partner had picked up, Sean had opened his travel bag and pulled out a manila envelope.

"Hey, buddy. I hear working late paid off in a plum assignment," Thomas said amiably.

The normalcy of shooting the bull with Thomas distracted Sean from his guilt. "Yeah. When we had two investigations with contacts to Pleasure Cove Island, the chief got mighty suspicious. If there's something funny going on there, I'll find it."

"So you get to spend the weekend getting laid and call it work."

How about *almost* laid? How about mind-blowing handwork with a virginal temptress who blurred the lines between fantasy and reality? "Yeah, life's a bitch sometimes. But I'm a dedicated agent."

Thomas laughed. "So who's the lucky girl? I guess you didn't need that little black book I gave you, after all."

Sean's gaze slid over to Caitlin's sleeping figure. It was hard to fathom that he'd known her for fewer than twenty-four hours. With the way their bodies communicated so clearly, it felt as if he'd known her forever. He wouldn't let Thomas know how they'd met, or that connecting with her at all had been a fluke.

"She's a patriot," he answered, keeping her identity a secret as they'd agreed. "She's more than willing to serve her country."

"So that's what they're calling it nowadays." After a few more double entendres about being served and called to duty, Thomas got down to business. "There's no change on Rossini's status. He still claims a family problem as the reason for dumping his career. The Vargas case is a little more interesting, though."

Sean pulled two photographs from the manila envelope. The first was a graphic crime-lab shot of Ramon Vargas's bruised, bloated body slumped over in the bathtub of his ritzy hotel room. "How so?"

"The M.E.'s report confirms homicide. Blunt trauma to the head. The guy had been knocked silly before someone held him under the water."

"So he'd be too disoriented to put up much of a fight?"

"That's my take. Either the drowning was a spur-of-the-moment thing, or the perp wasn't strong enough to subdue him."

"You mean like a woman?"

"Or someone older or handicapped." He heard the rustle of papers before Thomas spoke again. "We got a financial statement on Vargas, too. The guy's drained two bank accounts in the past year—his personal savings and an embassy expense register."

"Blackmail?"

"Either that or he had a pretty expensive hobby. Each withdrawal was for twenty-five grand."

Caitlin stirred at Sean's long whistle. "Then I'm guessing drugs, gambling or one very high-class mistress."

"You can rule out drugs. His toxicology came back clean."

"Do we have any personal history on the ambassador? Know any business associates or women he hung out with?"

"I'm working on that now. So far all I can tell you is that Vargas came from old money. He inherited the ambassadorship from his father. I don't know if the San Isidrans are trying to protect the family name or recoup the money he cost them. He lived the kind of high life you and I only see in the movies, buddy."

"Which would explain the trip to Pleasure Cove Island." Ramon Vargas's money and elitism would definitely attract Douglas Fairchild's attention. Sean turned his back on Caitlin and finished the conversation. "There's something dirty on that island—I can feel it in my bones. I'll find out what it is and report in as soon as I can."

"Right. I'll tell the chief. Hey, buddy—stay safe. And keep your patriot friend safe, too." Thomas's low-pitched chuckle warned Sean of the upcoming dig. "Don't work too *hard*. Unless you're wearing a condom, that is."

Sean shook his head and groaned. So much for getting his mind off Caitlin. He'd have to walk a fine line between maintaining his cover and giving in to his desire if he wanted to solve the connection to Pleasure Cove Island. And he definitely wanted to solve it.

After signing off, Sean picked up the second picture from the envelope. It was a school photograph of a pretty girl with dark hair and amber eyes. A girl who wasn't afraid to smile and show the braces on her teeth. In the last interview Sean had had with Alicia Reyes, the girl hadn't been smiling. If her kidnapper walked free because of Justice Rossini's untimely resignation, he wondered if she'd ever smile again.

The picture was a sobering reminder of why he was here.

Setting the pictures on the table beside his bag, Sean pulled out his clothes and started to dress.

Fifteen minutes later, he was standing at the sink, working up the will to knot his tie around his neck, when Caitlin's reflection joined him in the mirror. Still soft and rumpled from sleep, she sifted her fingers through her honey-blond hair and combed that riot of long, bouncy curls into a sensuous semblance of order.

"Wow. That's a new look for you." Gray eyes met green in the bathroom mirror. "You clean up pretty good."

Sean rubbed his hand along his clean-shaven jaw and tucked two fingers into the snug collar of his white broadcloth shirt. His gaze shot straight down to the wrinkled hem of that plain black dress. "I'll buy you some clothes when we get over to the island." It was the first step in his plan to do a better job of taking care of her. "The dossier says Fairchild's sister runs a hotel-style boutique there. You can wear my jacket until then."

"Great. It'll be nice to put on something fresh." Her wide mouth tipped at the corners in an indulgent smile. "Let me."

He was her willing pupil as she angled him a half turn to the right. With capable, confident hands she buttoned the collar of his shirt, slipped the knot of his tie up to his neck and smoothed the lapels of his gray worsted jacket.

He felt the stroke of her palms across his chest. The brush of her fingers beside his neck. Each sweep of her hands was an unintended caress. He balled his own hands into fists at his sides to keep from reaching for her. There was nothing personal in her touches. She was making the effort to respect his wish to keep their relationship simple. They were nothing more than friendly business associates.

He was the one whose skin was tingling, whose fingertips were itchy with the need to sweep her into his arms and get *very* friendly.

"When was the last time you wore a suit?" she teased, apparently oblivious to his body's rise in temperature.

"On purpose?"

Caitlin laughed, and Sean paused to consider why he found that sound so reassuring. Maybe it was because it sounded natural. Normal. Real.

His body's traitorous urges eased in intensity.

In another lifetime, on another day, with a different job, he could spend a hundred hours like this with Caitlin. Getting to know her, finding out what else made her laugh. Meeting her family and comparing notes on growing up in a military household.

Showing her the proper way to get laid in the back seat of a car.

But this was here. This was now. The badge and gun he'd hidden in the secret compartment of his suitcase already held his trust. His commitment was to the mission—and to keeping Caitlin safe.

Nothing more.

"You ready for this?" he asked.

Caitlin wandered back into the bedroom and sat in the chair beside the table to slip on her white tennis shoes. "Is this the girl who was kidnapped?"

Damn. He'd forgotten to pack up the pictures. He hurried to the table, but could tell by the frown that gathered between her brows that she'd already seen more than any innocent bystander should. "Her name's Alicia Reyes. She was kidnapped by a reputed sex offender in her neighbor-

hood. Fortunately, we found her quickly. But we suspec
she's not the neighbor's first victim.''

"She's younger than my students. Her kidnapper coul
go free unless we find some kind of proof at Pleasur
Cove?''

Sean plucked the two pictures from her hands and slippe
them back into their envelope. "If we can prove the judge
was somehow coerced into early retirement, we could ex
tend the statute of limitations on the case and get a favorable
ruling on the evidence.''

Now the frown reached her mouth. "And the other one'
Is he the dignitary who was also on the island before hi:
death?''

"Ambassador Vargas." Sean shoved the envelope intc
his pocket and knelt down beside Caitlin. Forgetting better
judgment, he reached out and traced the taut lines of concern
that bracketed her mouth. "I'm sorry. You shouldn't have
had to see them.''

Her frown transformed into a rueful smile beneath hi:
fingertips. "I've dealt with death before. My mother...'
Caitlin took a cleansing breath and pulled his hand from her
face. But she folded it between both her hands and absently
played with his knuckles and fingers in her lap. "Her body
was ravaged by cancer before she finally found peace. And
my father and brothers occasionally tell stories about combat duty—but I know they leave out the worst of the details
to spare me.''

"They don't want to relive it themselves, probably.''

Her hands stilled and she lifted her gaze to his. "Is tha
what drives you, Sean? The need to help those people? The
need to find justice for those innocent victims?''

"That's part of it." His gaze dropped to her mouth and
he knew an almost overwhelming urge to kiss her. To comfort her. To seek comfort from those very demons that did

consume him. But he didn't kiss her. That would be too personal. Too real. That would put him right back into the mess of guilt and distraction he'd just managed to climb out of. He stood and pulled her to her feet, then quickly released her. "I don't want anyone else to get hurt, either."

She picked up his discarded tweed jacket and slipped it on over her dress. Her smile was determined, her eyes hopeful, her beauty and energy inspiring as she rolled up the sleeves. "Then I'm ready to do my job, Agent Maddox. Let's go get some bad guys."

9

THE FERRY DOCK at New Haven harbor was bustling with cars and bikes and pedestrians. But there was no mistaking tourists and locals from the members of the Pleasure Cove Island guest list Sean had memorized from Chief Dillon's dossier.

Keeping Caitlin's hand securely tucked within his own, Sean surveyed and catalogued mental images of each guest who would be joining them on the cruise across the bay to Douglas Fairchild's estate. One of them might be a murderer. Or they might all be potential victims of a dangerous blackmail scheme.

The short, wiry Texan with the silver-trimmed hat was oil man Les Truitt. He was accompanied by Candy Truitt, wife number five, a busty platinum blonde in a white fur coat that was too warm even for the cool evening breeze blowing in off the Atlantic. Half her husband's age, she stood a head taller than her seventy-year-old escort, carried a white cat in a plastic carrier and looked bored.

Then there was the tall redhead, Ali Turner. Still stunning at the age of fifty, the retired fashion model was signing autographs for a small circle of fans who had gathered at the foot of the walkway that zigzagged from the parking lot above them down to the dock. Her current boyfriend, Richard Powers, was the chef and owner of a trendy restaurant he'd just opened in New York City. A year younger than Sean himself, Powers followed Ali about like a devoted puppy dog.

The ramrod-straight bearing of the salt-and-pepper-haired man in the navy-blue polo shirt and pressed khaki slacks indicated he was military personnel. That would be General Pod Whitmore, USMC. He was a career man with a distinguished record of service through two wars. He had no problem ordering about the two men loading freight and luggage into the cargo hold. Though he'd arrived with a trim brunette—his secretary, Denise Fenton—the man's gaze strayed time and again to Caitlin.

Sean pretended not to notice. Pleasure Cove guests prized their anonymity. He needed to get a feel for these people before he'd risk alienating a possible source of information, or putting a potential suspect on guard. But if Whitmore's wondering eyes ogled Caitlin's butt one more time…

"Ow." Sean looked down at Caitlin's startled expression and quickly realized how tightly he'd squeezed her hand.

He eased his grip. "Sorry."

"Did you see something interesting?" He lifted her hand and massaged it between his. Her fingers were long and supple like her legs, he noticed. Soft-skinned on the surface, and fit, without being too bony or too muscled underneath. Utterly fascinating to the eye, utterly arousing to the touch. "Sean? Or should I be calling you honey or pookie or something else?"

He squeezed his eyes shut and groaned at the thought of *pookie*. "Sean will do just fine."

A cacophony of honking horns and squealing tires diverted their attention to an old tan sedan that screeched to a stop in the parking lot above the dock. The slamming of car doors and shouts and giggles preceded the appearance of a young blond woman at the whitewashed fence that lined the gangplank. "Are we too late?" she shouted.

A blond man carrying two suitcases ran up behind her and planted a kiss on her cheek. "C'mon, darling, we've only five minutes to go."

"Pleasure Cove Island, here we come!" The twentyish lovebirds kissed each other again and ran down to the ferry.

Caitlin's wry tone matched Sean's thoughts. "You said Pleasure Cove was for movers and shakers. How do those teenyboppers rate an invitation?"

"They're listed as John and Priscilla Doe from San Francisco. Apparently, one of them bought a winning lottery ticket."

"Doe? That's not their real name, is it?"

Sean shook his head. "Chief Dillon couldn't get me any more details on such short notice. That's something I'll need to find out."

"Do you want me to ask Priscilla?" Caitlin's voice had dropped to a whisper, but her excitement radiated in the air between them. "We could have a little girl talk."

"Not yet, Mata Hari." The eagerness that darkened her big gray eyes was hard to resist. But until he knew more about the cast of characters they had to hang out with this weekend, he intended to keep Caitlin and her fanciful imagination on a very short leash. He didn't want her out of his sight until he was very sure there was no danger.

He turned her around to face him, settling his hands with casual possession on either side of her waist. "I promise I'll give you an assignment of your own later. But let's get our cover established first." He felt a stiffness tighten up her body and watched her inhale a deep breath as if she was about to jump off a bridge with a bungee cord attached to her legs. "Work with me here," he coached her, leaning close to her ear. "You promised me we'd be believable lovers."

"I'm just a little nerv—"

Someone bumped into Caitlin from behind and she stumbled into Sean. "Sorry, ma'am. Sir."

Before she could respond to the apologetic dock worker with the heavy crate on his shoulders, Sean had her wrapped up in his arms. "Not a problem."

The porter shook his long ponytail behind his back before moving on. "This is the last of the supplies. The guests may start boarding at any time."

Sean winked over her shoulder, taking advantage of the opportunity for public intimacy. "When we're ready."

"Sean—" Their sudden shoulder-to-toe contact silenced her. The impression of small, proud breasts branded his chest, and an instantaneous memory of her volatile reactions to his touch made his body contract. Taking full advantage of the impromptu embrace, he slid his hands around her hips to steady her, letting the tips of his fingers branch out over the swell of her bottom.

"I'm not ready for this." Her panicked whisper was a fevered caress against his cheek. She wedged her hands between them and tried to push away. "What if I screw up?"

"You won't," he murmured encouragingly, his mouth teasing her ear. "We're here to catch some bad guys, remember?" Lifting her onto her toes and then right off her feet so that she had nothing to hold on to but him, he rubbed his hips against hers, reminding her of her role as mistress and not skittish ingenue.

Damn, he was a sorry sucker for anything that put him in contact with her body. For an instant in time they were all alone in the middle of the night again. She was spread-eagled on the hood of his car and he was about to drive himself home in the closest thing he'd ever come to a fantasy in his whole life.

His groin reveled in the sudden rush of heat, and his fingers itched to pull her even closer. *The job. The job,* he chanted to himself, bringing his wayward thoughts back to 4:55 p.m. on the dock of the ferry. He rested his forehead against hers, sucking in a deep breath and trying to coach his body on the difference between acting like he wanted to bed Caitlin and actually doing it.

"Oh my." Her breathing was as uneven as his. "P-put me down." Her fingers dug into the collar of his coat. "Not like that."

He let her slide along his body until her feet were flat on the ground. It was a torturous caress because it only made him want her more, when he needed to be thinking about wanting her less.

When she had her balance, she tried to put some distance between them. But Sean kept a possessive hand on one hip. He lifted the other hand and brushed the back of his knuckles against the flame that bloomed in her cheeks. "You're blushing."

"Can't help it." She relaxed her grip on his coat and splayed her fingers across his chest, attempting to look a willing partner in their embrace. "When you picked me up like that—" she fiddled with his tie "—it just made me think of…" Damn the distraction. He was thinking of it, too. "You're so strong. You make me feel…"

Those wide, guileless eyes scared him. When they were round and dark like this, he could lose himself there. She was clearly in the moment with him, clearly aroused, clearly worried about something. He should be running from the innocent trust shining in those eyes, and the way it sneaked around his business-only resolve. But he ignored the warning bells dinging inside his head and dived in anyway. He stroked her cheek again. "You feel what?"

"Feminine. Soft. And sexy." She gave a nervous laugh and picked at his lapel. "I don't feel like such a giant tomboy when you pick me up."

"Giant tomboy?"

Now her hands were sliding beneath his lapels, leisurely caressing the planes of his chest. "You know, in most of those fantasies I have I'm a little daintier. I'm about six inches shorter and I have big breasts."

He didn't buy her sarcasm. He loved her body in all its healthy, Amazon glory. "Have I left you with any doubts about how much I like your body just the way it is?"

Sean dipped his fingers beneath Caitlin's chin and tipped her mouth up for his kiss. He didn't bother with slow and lazy. When her lips parted, he plunged his tongue inside, laving the delicate softness with his hard, hungry attentions.

He stroked her tongue, inviting her to join the kiss. And then they played a game of tag as she wiggled her tongue and he gave chase. Finally, he caught her and sucked, pulling her tongue all the way into his mouth. He closed his teeth around her in a pretend bite. He skimmed his fingers along the answering purr in her throat, celebrating the lengthy proportion of that beautiful stretch of skin.

Her fingers fisted in the front of his shirt, aligning herself to play the same game with him. It was a shyer, slower, achingly wonderful challenge that he met kiss for kiss. And when she caught his tongue between her teeth to claim her victory, he laughed into her mouth and started the game all over again.

He tunneled his fingers into her hair, catching up a handful of those rich, wonderful curls. The twisting silk stretched and bounced and sprang around his greedy grasp, triggering a cascade of tiny shock waves that quaked along his fingertips and the back of his wrist.

He centered his left hand on her butt and pulled her up flush against the straining response in his pants. She liked when he did that, she'd said. *Him.* Not some fairy-tale beast or James Bond or any other fantasy lover. She liked his strength. And, God help him, he was getting off on hers.

The ocean breeze caught and blended with her tangy, fresh scent, filling his nose with the essence of Caitlin, filling his brain with the need to consume her. The need to claim her entire body the way his mouth had already claimed hers.

The sounds of New Harbor clanged inside his head. The beat of the tidal current slapping against the boats and the docks. The wind swishing through the moaning branches of trees along the shore. The chime from a distant church bell tolling five o'clock.

Damn. Reality. The job.

"Caitie." He rasped her name against her mouth and fought the urge to grind his hips into hers. "Caitie, you're a beautiful woman. I don't want this to stop." He let her feet slide to the ground one more time. "But we have a boat to catch."

"Right." Her head moved in a jerky nod. "The bad guys."

He felt her heart thudding beneath her breast, her hard, uneven breaths making her chest butt against his. Though he'd wisely abandoned the game before its inevitable finish, he moved his hands to a neutral position at the small of her back and held her close and still, not yet trusting his control when she was in his arms and willing like this.

"Do you think I was convincing?"

The question was barely audible. But Sean heard it. Way down in the depths of his randy body and tired old soul, he heard the niggling doubt. He felt it in the trembling sweep of her fingers across his chest, trying to smooth the wrinkled front of his outfit. They were soft, repetitive strokes, as if she was petting him, soothing him. Quieting the beast she expected her question to unleash?

He knew that kiss hadn't been all acting on her part. But did she really think it had all been work on his own? Didn't she know just how carried away he'd been a moment ago?

Maybe it was for the best if she thought that kissing game was all for show. It'd be a hell of a lot easier for her to go back to her life on Monday if she didn't develop any emotional attachments to him. It'd be a hell of a lot easier for him come Monday, too.

"Yeah. We did great." It felt wrong, breaking down that torrid kiss into a clinical discussion like this. But it was for the best to depersonalize it. "I'd say we got some people's attention. That porter's stamping his foot, waiting for us to come up for air and get in line to board."

"Is he watching us now?"

"Yeah."

She reached up and brushed a fallen lock of hair off Sean's brow. It wasn't an overtly sexual gesture, but it was a proprietary one. And its casual claim calmed his doubts about her allegiance to him and his mission more than he cared to admit.

"I'm ready to take our act to Pleasure Cove Island." She smiled.

Sean was relieved when she turned her back to him and led him by the hand up the gangplank and onto the boat.

Who was acting, after all?

CAITLIN STOOD on the observation deck at the bow of the ship and watched as the gray, rolling waves seemed to dive beneath the sparkling white hull of the Pleasure Cove ferry.

Everything about this vessel was polished or freshly painted. Even the garage area was clean. That wasn't much of a challenge, though, since the only vehicle parked below deck was a van loaded with supplies for the island. She'd learned there was no need for cars at Pleasure Cove because there was no place to go except for the estate itself, and bicycles and golf carts were provided for anyone who didn't feel like walking around the premises.

Most of the other guests had taken refuge from the wind and sea foam inside the elegantly appointed bar on the main deck. The bar's picture windows provided a warm, dry view of the endless gray ocean and the darker gray speck of land that was growing on the eastern horizon.

But Caitlin loved being out on the water. Loved the salt spray on her skin. The damp, pungent air in her nose. Even this water, cooler than that of her native Virginia, gave her a sense of rejuvenating freedom. She wasn't headed home to the lonely prospect of her books and imagination. She was headed toward adventure.

And she wasn't going alone.

She tipped her face up to the rolling clouds that shaded the last rays of the sun, and huddled inside Sean's tweed jacket. In an instant, a long, strong arm wrapped around her waist from behind and she settled back against the shielding warmth of Sean's chest.

"Are they watching us again?" she asked. The bar also gave their fellow passengers a clear view of the bow decks, and she and Sean had made a point of walking together, arm in arm or hand in hand, as they explored the ferry.

"You looked cold." His deep, accented voice articulated the words in her ear. She closed her eyes and sank into the vision of a dangerous pirate captain claiming her as his prize from his latest raid against the enemy.

But then she thought of Sean's insistence that she stay firmly grounded in the real world with him.

Her mouth curved in a secret smile. The reality of standing in the circle of this man's arms was better than any fantasy. Maybe if she'd had this kind of stimulus in her life, she wouldn't feel the need to steal away inside herself so often.

"It's a little chilly." She tucked her arms beneath his and snuggled closer. "But I'll take the fresh air over the cigarette smoke in that bar any day."

As the mainland became reduced to a ribbon of dark grays and greens on the skyline behind them, she and Sean spent most of their time away from the other couples. Partly because there were three smokers in the group, and Candy Truitt's cat had made her lungs feel congested. And partly to get some time to themselves to discuss and decide other ways they could pretend to be a convincing couple.

This was one of her favorites, she decided. Sean standing behind her, nearly surrounding her with his warmth and strength. There was a security and a confidence to be gained by having him at her back. And there was also the unaccustomed vulnerability he made her feel. Being close in height, he could rest his chin on her shoulder and whisper into her ear. But he was so much broader, stronger. There was just so much more to Sean. His physicality. His strength. His power.

His heart.

That was one part of him the man refused to acknowledge. But she'd seen glimpses of it time and again. In the guilt he felt when he thought he'd taken advantage of her. In the don't-mess-with-me tone of his voice when he thought she'd been in danger.

In those sad, sad eyes that refused to reflect hope.

She knew he was concerned about his cover, about whether she was woman enough and worldly enough to make everyone believe that he was a high-ranking FBI official who'd run off with his mistress for the weekend.

But she worried there was something more at stake here,

something Sean himself might not even realize. More than truth. More than justice.

Sean needed something for himself. Something that would ease that wounded look he worked so hard to hide. But what? And just because *she* wanted to help him find the healing remedy that would make him smile more and worry less didn't mean he *wanted* her help.

If the most Sean Maddox would accept from her was a stellar performance as his weekend mistress, then she'd deliver. She refused to disappoint him, as he was expecting her to.

"You're awfully deep in thought." His voice vibrated like a caress in her ear.

Caitlin smiled to herself. She wasn't about to let him know where her thoughts had been. He'd made it clear he wanted this weekend to be an act. It wasn't hard to act as if she lusted after the big brute. But she would do her very best to hide the fact that she was beginning to care.

Come Monday, caring for Sean Maddox wouldn't be an option. She was beginning to think that walking away from him was going to hurt. A lot. But it didn't have to be humiliating as well.

She'd wanted to be a sophisticated lady for a change— have one of those impulsive, guilt-free adventures that her roommate, Cassie, was famous for. Getting sappy about Sean's devotion to a kidnapped little girl, or promising to listen if he ever just wanted to talk about what or who had hurt him so, wouldn't fit the image he wanted her to project.

She made an excuse for her ongoing silence. "Just tired, I guess. I don't imagine we'll get much chance to sleep this weekend, either."

"No, we'll have to keep up our energy in other ways." And then he was turning her in his arms. Whether his devilish smile was real or part of the act, it warmed her all the way down to her toes. "How does something hot to drink sound?"

"Fabulous. Hot chocolate or a cup of coffee. Don't bring me a hot toddy. The liquor would put me to sleep."

"Hot chocolate it is, then." His eyes made an infinitesimal shift toward the observation window. Caitlin understood his intent. Showtime.

Dutifully, she wrapped her arms around his neck and angled her head for his kiss. It was hard and swift and way too tame to justify her body's instant, weak-kneed response. In all his styles and moods, Sean Maddox was one heck of a kisser.

She wondered if spending a week, or a month—or a lifetime—with him would allow her enough time to sample each of the wonders of his magical mouth.

But she would never find out. The kiss ended quickly, but not before it had done a little damage to her heart. Still, she managed a smile when he lifted his head. And it was more awe than acting when she raised a finger to trace the curve of his bottom lip, which tormented her so. "Don't be long," she warned him in a surprisingly husky voice.

"Nice touch." He kissed the tip of her finger before stepping back. "Don't go anywhere."

"I'll be right here."

As he turned and strode away, Caitlin looked beyond his path to the observation window above them. They *did* have an audience.

Les Truitt doffed his cowboy hat to her, then turned away to Bert, the porter with the ponytail who'd bumped into her on the dock—and who now doubled as bartender—and launched into an animated story. Les's long-winded account of each of his marriages had monopolized Caitlin's attention until the dander from his wife's cat had finally made sitting close to him a sinus-plugging, eye-weeping nightmare. Sean had promptly appeared at her side to invite her out onto the deck. She'd been grateful for the escape.

But Les and Bert weren't the only ones at the window. Farther down, the tall, pepper-haired man and his petite date from the docks sat at a table. Sean had said he was a military man. Was he still on duty? He seemed to be talking—dictating, perhaps—while the woman busily typed on a laptop computer. And he never looked at the woman; he just stared out the window, watching her.

As his eyes made contact with hers, Caitlin shivered. There was no friendly acknowledgment like Les Truitt's hat-tipping, just a lazy, unblinking perusal. She shoved her hands into the pockets of Sean's jacket and turned away. Was his fascination just idle curiosity? Jet lag? Voyeurism?

Deke, the biker with the nasty smell and sick idea of chivalry, had said he'd seen her and Sean in the car, and that had made him hot to trot. Maybe that's how this guy got off, too, by watching other couples. Maybe the brunette had been jotting the details of her and Sean's kiss into her computer for them to use later. Maybe they'd already been scanned into some kind of digital camera.

Caitlin turned her face to the refreshing spray of water that splashed up over the deck, letting it cool her rampant suspicions. "Too weird." At least *her* sexual fantasies had never lived anywhere but inside her own imagination.

Well, except for with one strong-armed federal agent. Thoughts of Sean eased her anxiety. He wouldn't let her be hurt by anyone on the island, she was sure of that.

But she supposed she'd better throw her good-girl ideas about sex out the door. Voyeurism might be the least kinky thing she ran across this weekend.

She was enjoying the ocean and her own thoughts again when she heard footsteps behind her. Donning a pouty grin that she thought gave her an appropriately mistress-like air, she turned to greet Sean.

But it wasn't Sean.

The military man from the window was striding toward her, shoulders tossed back in the face of the wind, his canvas jacket playing up the vivid blue hue of his eyes. He was tall and handsome and moving with too sure a purpose for this to be a chance meeting.

"Pod Whitmore." He extended his hand in the classic friendly greeting. "And you're..."

She took a step back, but her hips butted against the railing. Nowhere to retreat. No Sean to bail her out. She had to handle this meeting all on her own. This was the sort of challenge she'd wanted, right? The wind whipped her hair about her face, giving her a moment to calm her jittery pulse and assume her role as undercover mistress.

She pushed her hair back with her left hand and held it at her temple. Then she offered a coy grin and took his hand. "Caitlin."

"Ah, pretty name." He held her hand between both of his for a moment, then released it and turned to match her previous stance, looking out over the bow of the ship. "I get cooped up in my office for too long sometimes. I miss the sea air."

When he leaned forward and gripped the railing, Caitlin relaxed her stance. Maybe he was just a fellow sailor.

"I love the smell of it," she agreed. "Especially on the open water like this. You can forget all about smog out here."

He concurred by closing his eyes and tipping his well-chiseled nose into the breeze. But Caitlin had dropped her guard too soon. When he turned to her, his perceptive eyes were drilling into her.

"I don't mean to be forward, but you look familiar to me. I know we've met somewhere."

Caitlin swallowed hard to keep from groaning out loud. This guy's come-on line was as weak as Norm's had been. A man with the looks and polish this man possessed should be able to come up with something classier.

Feeling the upper hand in the cleverness department, she decided to divert his attention by playing to his ego. "I don't think so. You're quite distinguished. I'd have remembered meeting a man like you."

"Nope." He was persistent, if not creative. "I've seen you before. If not the face, at least the picture. What's your last name?"

A bulky figure moved into her peripheral vision an instant before she felt a hand at the small of her back. "Sean Maddox."

His voice was cordial enough as he joined the conversation, but she felt the tension in the possessive arm that slipped round her waist. Was this man a suspect?

"General Pod Whitmore."

Caitlin nearly dropped the insulated mug that Sean gave her before shaking hands. *General?*

"Retired or active duty?" Sean asked, making manly small talk while she faded from the discussion.

"You're not a marine, by any chance, are you?" she asked, interrupting Whitmore's explanation about his current position at the Pentagon.

"Yes, ma'am."

The Corps employed hundreds of thousands of soldiers all around the world. What were the chances that he'd run across her father or brothers?

She didn't want to ask this, but she had to know. She wouldn't be able to concentrate on another thing until she did. "I'm Caitlin McCormick. You wouldn't happen o—?"

He snapped his fingers and grinned in victory. "McCormick. That's it. You're Hal's little girl. I've seen your picture on his desk. We shared an office during Desert Storm."

Caitlin's sea legs suddenly went out from under her. If it wasn't for Sean's unmoving strength to lean into, she would have fallen to the deck.

It wasn't a pickup line.

This man knew her father.

10

EVEN THOUGH CAITLIN couldn't seem to breathe in, Pod Whitmore apparently didn't notice. "Where's the old codger stationed now?"

At fifty-five, her father didn't seem old. And there was nothing in his strict habits and cautious nature that she would consider codgerlike. But she couldn't comment. A tight fist was squeezing her lungs.

Whitmore plowed on, apparently used to hearing the sound of his own voice. "Well, I feel like I've met an old friend. Or the next best thing." He jabbed Sean's arm with a playful poke. "You a military man, Maddox?"

"My father was."

Caitlin tried to intervene and stop the conversation. Pod Whitmore already knew too much about them. He knew about *her*. He would talk to her father. He'd talk to someone else who knew her father. Even though Hal McCormick had retired from the Corps, he kept in touch with his buddies. If they started teasing him about his daughter and her mystery man and her ripped dress and Pleasure Cove Island, he'd go ballistic. Even if his heart survived the shock, career-long friendships might be destroyed.

But all Caitlin could manage was a shallow cough. She sipped her hot chocolate and hoped the warmth trickling down her throat would somehow ease the constricting muscles in her chest.

"I've been told that group activities are sometimes en-

couraged on the island.'' Whitmore's authoritative voice
had dropped to a hushed whisper. "I didn't think it would
hurt for us to get acquainted.''

Group activities? Oh no. He'd tell her father he'd met
her at the orgy capital of the East Coast.

"Please—''

"I'm an only child.'' Sean squeezed her around the waist,
bringing her ear to his mouth for a possessive kiss. "I never
did learn to share my toys.''

Too tight. She couldn't breathe.

Pod smiled. "Of course. I didn't mean to intrude. I understand that there will be plenty for us to do once we get
there.''

She needed to cough, but she couldn't. She needed to
protect her father from news about this sophisticated Dis-
neyland, but she didn't know how. She clutched a handful
of Sean's coat in her fist. "I need my inhaler.''

"Caitie?''

His sharp voice startled her, enough that she could suck
in a gasp of air. But her lungs wouldn't expand. A congested
wheeze rattled in her chest. She clutched Sean's arm. "It's
my asthma.''

Whitmore and Sean spoke at once.

"I'm sorry. Is there something I can do?''

"Breathe, sweetheart.''

She had to laugh at Sean's stern order. "I'm trying to.''

But she couldn't laugh. The sound came out in little
coughs—her body's instinctive attempt to loosen up bron-
chial airways that were rapidly closing.

A man of action in the face of danger, Sean took her hot
chocolate and pushed it into General Whitmore's hands. He
pushed Whitmore aside entirely, led Caitlin to a bench in
front of the observation window and sat her down. He
started to pick up her feet and lay her down, but she shook

her head and swatted away his hands. "It's better if I sit up."

"What do you need me to do?" he demanded.

Whitmore had followed them over, his face looking even paler than Sean's taut visage. "I didn't mean to shock her."

She coughed again. She'd taken a few essentials from her purse and locked them inside Sean's suitcase. But she always had her inhaler with her. "My inhaler."

She patted her pockets, looking for the tiny canister, but Sean's hands were already there. He pressed the device into her palm. "Here."

Caitlin shook the inhaler, then squeezed it in the air, spitting out a cloud of vapor.

"What good does that do?" Sean's voice was angry, as if she'd wasted a chance to save her life.

Without the breath to spare for an explanation, she squeezed her fingers around his thigh, hoping to calm his concerns. She'd been dealing with asthma for years, and knew to clear the valve first. She squirted the next dose into her mouth and breathed in as deeply as she could. She sat still, holding the mixture in her lungs and counting to five.

"Caitie? Talk to me."

He pulled out his cellphone, then cursed when it refused to work. Dropping the useless gadget back into his pocket, he circled his arms around her in a loose, protective hug. As she exhaled, she closed her eyes and savored the instant release she began to feel. Like a steel trap slowly opening its jaw, the airways in her chest began to expand.

She felt the heat of those intense, all-seeing eyes and turned to look at Sean. He was scared. For her. How about that? Muscled, macho Agent Maddox was afraid.

"I'm okay."

Moved by such a human emotion coming from this man who claimed to be so unfamiliar with the tender side of things, Caitlin laid her hand against his cheek in reassurance. He turned his head and pressed his lips against her palm. Helplessness wasn't something he dealt with easily. But he was dealing with it.

And she'd have to deal with her unexpected panic at meeting an old friend of her father's.

"I'm okay," she repeated, feeling something else, much more profound and enduring than the panic, taking root and expanding its warmth inside her. There was no fantasy at work here. This feeling was real. And it was something she didn't think she could handle right now.

Something she knew Sean wouldn't want to deal with at all.

Removing her hand from his warm skin, she shook the inhaler again and puffed the second dose between her lips. This time she could inhale deeply enough to feel the expansion down to her diaphragm.

At last she sagged back against the bench. She closed the inhaler and put it in her pocket. Then she reached inside the jacket she wore and massaged her chest above the neckline of her dress.

Sean's fearsome expression eased into one of puzzled concern. "What does that do?"

"I don't know that it does a darn thing for the asthma. It's just soothing."

The next thing she knew, his hand was there, rubbing slow circles across her chest. Less sure than his other touches had been, his hand trembled as he gentled his strength to tend to her. But the warmth he generated was the same. The cherishing caress of each stroke still woke sensations in her that made her strong in spirit yet weak with desire. Her pulmonologist had never elicited this warm, drizzly contentment inside her with his massages.

It was the sweetest bedside treatment she'd ever received.

"Is she all right?" Somehow she'd forgotten General Whitmore's presence. He sat down on the other side of her, still carrying her drink. His high forehead was still furrowed with concern.

He knew her father.

Her anonymity for her wild weekend had been shot to hell.

He knew her father!

As if she'd transmitted the sudden tension that had triggered her attack in the first place, Sean's hand stilled on her chest. "I think she'll be fine now." It was not an invitation to stay and chat.

Caitlin could breathe, but she lacked the energy to speak. Covering for her silence, Sean stood. With true military decorum, the general stood up, too.

"I'll get out of your way. I hope this doesn't put a damper on your vacation plans." Whitmore nodded with the crisp precision of a salute. "Maddox. Miss McCormick. Good to meet you."

Sean laid a hand on her shoulder, urging her to keep her seat, and answered for her. "We'll tell Caitlin's father you asked about him."

"No—"

"No. Don't." The general's refusal overshadowed hers. He smiled apologetically at his overly quick response. "I'm a married man." He thumbed over his shoulder at the observation window above them. "Denise isn't my wife."

Sean nodded in a man-to-man show of understanding. "Then we never met. Enjoy the island."

"You, too."

"I intend to."

As soon as Whitmore had gone back inside, Caitlin tugged on Sean's sleeve. He quickly sat beside her, resting one arm lightly around her shoulders, the other possessively across her lap. "Are you sure you're all right?" he asked.

Other than the fatigue that would hit her soon, after the stress and oxygen deprivation of an attack, she was fine. Physically. "What if General Whitmore goes home Sunday night and calls my father to say how pleased he was to finally meet me? What if he tells Dad's friends he saw me making out on a boat up in Maine? So much for keeping my top-secret adventure a secret. Dad'll freak."

The analytical wheels were turning in Sean's head. She could only imagine all the different motivations and scenarios he was evaluating over this potential security leak. "He and your father can't be very close. He didn't know your dad was retired. And a Pentagon general isn't going to want anyone to find out he's been to Pleasure Cove Island. I doubt he'll talk. Maybe that trip down memory lane was nothing more than a feeler to see if we'd be interested in multicouple sex."

"Ho, boy." A roomful of naked, sweaty strangers. Not a picture she wanted to contemplate.

Sean moved his hand to capture hers in a gentle grasp. He nudged two fingers beneath her chin and tipped her face up to his. The wind blew those twin locks of hair down onto his forehead, but his eyes were too serious for her to indulge the tenderhearted urge to lift them back into place. "We can claim a medical emergency and turn this ship around."

She hadn't expected that response. "Why?"

"Because I'm sending you home. Your days as a secret agent are over."

FOR SOME REASON, Sean hadn't expected a woman who'd just suffered an asthma attack to be able to move that fast.

"If I leave, you'll have to come with me. No mistress, no mission. We can't abandon Alicia Reyes's case now."

With a few pithy words about keeping her promise, and a pithier remark about him being a control freak, Caitlin had shoved his hands away and dashed up the starboard stairs before he had any chance to figure out how he'd become the bad guy.

Whitmore was the slime who'd used family ties to try to charm his way into Caitie's pants. Maybe the guy did have a legitimate connection to her father. But the old man had been eyeing her dockside, too. And he hadn't been checking her *face* to see if she looked familiar.

The way Sean saw it, there was no crime in signing off on a case if you'd been wounded in action. Caitie wasn't fit for duty. He'd felt the weight of her body, clinging to his for support. He'd seen the pallor on her cheeks and the faint blue tinge to her lips. He'd heard the air whistle through her lungs, like the scratch of sandpaper on wood, each time she'd breathed in or out.

And he hadn't known how to help her.

That had been the worst part of it all. When Sabrina had bawled over their father moving out of their lives permanently, Sean knew to take her in his arms and hold her. When Alicia Reyes had disappeared, he'd known how to piece together the clues and find her.

Kidnappers, murderers, horny sleazeballs who put the moves on his woman—those things he could handle with some tough talk, some kick-ass perseverance and some top-notch training. But Caitie hadn't been able to breathe. She could have passed out. What if she got really sick? How could he keep her safe from that?

Despite the strength of her glorious body, she was a fragile creature. Tenderhearted. Idealistic. Innocent. Too fragile to risk in the stress of an undercover investigation. Too easily hurt for him to even contemplate screwing her brains out the way his body wanted to.

He wouldn't hold it against her if she asked to quit. But she hadn't asked to quit. She'd shoved the idea of quitting right in his face and told him in no uncertain terms that this was a risk she was willing to take.

It was a risk he had to take, too.

He'd have to change his whole way of thinking about work and women. She wanted him to give her a chance to do this her way. She wanted him to trust her. He'd learned enough about Caitlin to believe she wouldn't let him down on purpose.

But what about those things she couldn't control? Like her asthma? Like a blackmailer or lover who was willing to kill a man to hide his or her identity? Like sophisticated sex games that went far beyond her limited experience? Sean could put all his faith in Caitlin's promises and she still might fail.

Didn't she see how badly she could be hurt?

He just wanted her to be okay. He needed her to be safe. Why was that such a terrible thing?

Caitlin had dived right into her Mata Hari fantasy, finding a seat in the snack bar and getting chummy with Priscilla Doe and her husband. Sean had spent the last twenty minutes of the boat ride nursing a lager and watching her live out her adventure and studiously avoid him.

He knew she was right. It was too late to back out of the game. Every person on this ship had identified them as a couple. If he pulled rank and had her taken back to shore, then his own invitation would be null and void.

An FBI agent alone on Pleasure Cove Island would be a threat to whoever or whatever had caused Ramon Vargas's death. An FBI agent with a woman to keep him busy would be a welcome guest.

The woman was set for action.

But the agent was having second thoughts.

"Having a lovers' tiff already?"

Sean tore his gaze from the aft gangplank where Caitlin and the other passengers were gathering to disembark, and turned toward the husky female drawl. Ali Turner linked her arm through his. She pressed the point of her flawless chin against his shoulder and whispered in his ear. "I recommend the dungeon room. It provides the best way to work out the tensions that pull at a relationship."

"Thanks. I'll keep that in mind."

Dungeon? Pull? Sean had an instantaneous vision of being helplessly tied to the rack while Caitlin collapsed to the floor just beyond his reach, unable to breathe. He squeezed his eyes shut and shook his head to dispel the troubling image.

Change wasn't going to come easy for him.

"The cage is my favorite," Ali continued. "Don't forget to bring extra pillows, though. The bars are made of real iron."

He tried to picture the supermodel at his side chained up inside a cage while her lover du jour looked on. Or maybe she imprisoned the lover. Or they were both in the cage. Sean dismissed the images before they could take shape and form in his mind. Too weird. This place was more seriously messed up than he'd thought.

It was a lot easier to see the opportunity at hand to ferret out some inside information. "You've been here before, then?"

"Um-hmm." She pulled out a long, brown, ultraslim cigarette and held it to her lips between two red-lacquered nails.

Sean shrugged at the silent invitation in her pout. "Sorry. I don't smoke."

"Richard. My cigarette." Still clinging to Sean's arm, she turned her head and gave the terse command. Richard Powers dropped the leather overnight case he was carrying and hurried over. He pulled an engraved silver lighter from his pocket and lit her cigarette. Her long auburn hair draped over Sean's arm as she tipped her head back and savored the first draw. "Umm. Lovely, darling."

The artificially sweet aroma of the smoke matched the woman herself, thought Sean. Her nails were perfect. Her makeup perfect. Even after a windy boat ride, her hair fell in perfect precision down her back. She was a textbook example of classic beauty.

But his gaze kept straying back to Caitlin's headful of unkempt curls on the deck below them. Jeffrey—a bulky man with a shaved head who had piloted their ferry—was holding her hand. An unexpected tension stretched Sean to his full height and expanded his chest. Jeffrey laughed at something Caitlin said as he helped her climb from the gangplank down onto the fixed wooden dock.

She looked safe enough. Healthy enough. Dammit, she actually looked like she was enjoying herself.

So why was Sean so miserable?

"This is my fifth visit. Richard's first." Ali Turner's smoky voice demanded his attention again. "Douglas offers us something new each time we come to the island. There's something absolutely thrilling about the unknown, isn't there?"

No. He'd take solid predictability any day. Clear-cut perpetrators. Reliable clues. A woman whose choices and motivations he could understand.

In little more than twenty-four hours, Justice Rossini's unexpected resignation had jeopardized Sean's case against Diego Marquez. Caitlin's unanticipated blend of red-hot passion and teach-me innocence had turned him into a sex-charged, distracted agent. And her chronic health condition had intensified the guilt about his growing feelings for her a hundredfold.

But if Caitlin was still determined to play the game, he could do no less. Ali Turner seemed willing to talk, and he needed information. "I haven't had a real vacation from work in several months and I want this weekend to go smoothly. Have you ever encountered any problems here on the island? Met any dissatisfied customers?"

"None that I've run across. Some guests are more adventurous than others. At Pleasure Cove you can have just as much fun—or relaxation—as you want."

"And privacy is guaranteed?"

She gave him a smile that had once graced the cover of one of *Sports Illustrated*'s seductive swimsuit issues. "Unless you want an audience. I'm sure it could be arranged." Her red nails squeezed the gray-suited curve of his biceps. "I can show you around the place myself, if you'd like. I've been here with five different men. The first time as Douglas's own personal guest. I know all the ins and outs of his estate."

Ali Turner was a legendary beauty. She was flirting with Sean, offering just the kind of no-strings fling that could ease the frustrated tension from his body.

He wasn't interested.

"I'd better catch up with Caitlin. I'll keep your offer in mind, though."

"Please do. Richard?" The tall, dark and doting chef had been standing patiently off to the side. He crooked his arm and Ali switched escorts. Didn't the guy get jealous of his girlfriend's extracurricular flirtations? Was he really okay with her coming back to the home of a former lover? Or was he of the persuasion that two's company, but three's more fun?

Powers's dark eyes slid over to Sean and demanded acknowledgment. The men traded curt nods before Richard lifted Ali's hand for a kiss and took her down the stairs to disembark.

A chill rippled across Sean's shoulders. Had the pretty boy just marked his territory? Or seconded the supermodel's invitation?

Hearing Caitlin's laughter above the chatter of the crowd gave Sean the impetus to set aside his distaste and hurry down the gangplank to join her. She'd convinced him she could provide his cover for the weekend. But he didn't intend to let her out of his sight while she was doing it.

As soon as he jumped the last step from the ferry to the dock, the ship's pilot stepped forward and stopped Sean with a restraining hand against his chest. Interesting. Apparently Jeffrey's duties on the island included security. Sean slowly raised his arms in surrender, tamping down his instinctive reaction to repel the unexpected constraint and throw the man to the ground.

"Relax, Chief Maddox." A man who matched the Bureau's picture of Douglas Fairchild—from his tall, portly stature to his uniform of a long-sleeved Hawaiian shirt and white pants—stepped forward from the crowd of passengers and crew. The welcoming smile of shiny capped teeth confirmed his identity as their host. "I assure you this is standard procedure. You had a phone on board ship?"

"It doesn't work."

"Perhaps the battery's dead. But functional or not, we don't allow them on the island. I'm afraid I must insist."

"It's on my belt." Sean left his hands in the air until Jeffrey reached inside his jacket and retrieved his cellphone. Over Fairchild's shoulder, he saw Caitlin's concerned glance. But she made no move to come closer. He wouldn't let her keep her distance for long. Sean adjusted his cuffs and jacket while Jeffrey scanned him from top to bottom with a hand-held metal detector. When a telltale beep stopped the inspection, Sean let the man reach inside his suitcoat and pull out his wallet with his badge and fake ID. "Is it standard procedure to frisk all your guests?"

Jeffrey returned the wallet and stepped back. "He's clean, sir."

Sean noted the plastic bin into which Jeffrey packed his phone. Through the clear plastic sides, he could make out several phones, a laptop computer, cameras and other various electronic devices that had been confiscated from the other guests. That meant his bag had been searched, too. His first objective, once he and Caitlin were in their private room, would be to check the secret compartment to see if his Bureau-issue Sig Sauer pistol was still hidden inside.

Douglas Fairchild moved forward to shake Sean's hand. "To ensure absolute seclusion, we can't allow any contact with the outside world. No phones, faxes or e-mails are allowed on or off the island. We can't afford a leak to the press and paparazzi, even an unintentional one."

No communication to the outside world, Chief Dillon had said.

If someone was writing news briefs or filming incriminating tapes or photos about Pleasure Cove guests, they had to be using equipment that was already in place. Or Fairchild's men were conveniently forgetting to search someone's belongings.

"What if there's an emergency?" Sean asked.

Fairchild had an answer for that one, too. "My sister, Ramona, is a registered nurse." He gestured across the dock to the middle-aged brunette who was helping load supplies onto a waiting golf cart. "If something comes up she can't handle, we have a ship-to-shore radio we can use to contact the mainland. But it's kept under lock and key and only used for medical or weather emergencies. Anything we take from you now will be secured, and then returned at the end of your stay.''

Sean's questions had garnered the interest of the other guests, and they'd gathered in a semicircle around Douglas Fairchild. Their host, with an Orson Welles–like boom to his voice, seemed to be eating up the attention. He swept his arms in a wide circle to include everyone. ''Think of your stay here as forty-eight hours of uninterrupted time with the one you love. Or the one you want to love.''

Sean sought out Caitlin again as Fairchild acknowledged a smattering of applause and laughter. She was staring right back at him, her flushed cheeks and pale eyes betraying a mixture of defiance and desire that was heating him up to a slow boil.

''Since I have everyone's attention, I want to welcome you to Pleasure Cove Island. Allow me to explain a few party rules before we drive up to the house.''

While Fairchild went through his well-rehearsed spiel, Sean edged closer to Caitlin. Everyone else had paired up with a mate. It looked odd that the two of them were standing so far apart. It felt wrong to have so much distance between them.

''Each couple will be shown to your own suite of rooms in the main house.'' Fairchild beamed a showman's grin. ''But if you're looking for something more *creative*, I invite you to check out the east wing of the estate. There is one key for each room—again to insure privacy. Read the brochures in your suites, then feel free to ask me or anyone on the staff for the key of your choice.''

Those must be the notorious theme rooms. Did they offer complete privacy? Or were they traps for unsuspecting guests? Sean kept playing devil's advocate. ''What if we get locked out and the key's inside?''

''I have a master key for any emergency.''

One man with free access to any room. The setup for a con just got better and better.

Caitlin played the game well, too. "What's in the west wing?"

"Staff quarters. Back-up generator. Storage facilities. All the boring necessities we try to hide from our guests."

John Doe, clinging to his new wife, asked a question. "Does this place have a honeymoon suite?"

"Every room is a honeymoon suite, young man."

Priscilla giggled and John gave Fairchild a thumbs-up.

"Let's go see if we can find one you like." Their host invited the newlyweds to climb onto the first golf cart waiting to drive them up to the house. Pod Whitmore and his secretary joined them.

As everyone moved toward their transportation, Sean caught up to Caitlin. When he was by her side, she leaned over and whispered, "The west wing sounds like a perfect place to hide a secret communications room. We'll have to check it out."

Sean touched his hand to the small of her back. "*I'll* check it out. If there is such a place. You need to lie low and keep your nose out of trouble until the ferry returns on Sunday."

She sighed with a huff that stirred the bangs on her forehead. "I'm your partner in this whether you like it or not. You can't lock me in my room and go play without me."

"This isn't a James Bond movie." He growled the reminder beside her ear. "It's the real thing. I'm trying to protect you."

"Dammit, Sean, if there are going to be repercussions to my coming here, I at least want to do something to deserve them."

"I won't let there be any repercussions."

"Problem, Chief?" Douglas Fairchild interrupted before

Sean could explain to Caitlin how worried he'd been about her health. How scared he'd been that he might lose her.

First the woman battered at emotional barriers he'd erected in stone, and now she didn't want him to care.

A celibate life on the job was looking more appealing by the minute.

Letting his frustration ease out in a silent sigh, Sean put his hand on Caitie's back. She held herself stiff beneath his touch. But he'd be damned if he'd give in to her attitude and let anyone in the crowd watching them think she was available in any way, shape or form. He was going to control who got close to her, and keep her safe.

"Caitie and I were just having a little discussion. We didn't realize there were going to be so many rules here. You sure we'll have fun?"

Fairchild took the teasing tone as Sean had intended. "I'm sure. Our intent at Pleasure Cove Island is to spoil you. You have the run of the grounds and the house." He turned to include the other guests. "Though we do ask that everyone be inside by 10:00 p.m."

"Curfew?" Les Truitt laughed. "That doesn't sound like the free-wheeling sex party you promised."

Fairchild patted the air in a conciliatory gesture. "It's for your own safety, Mr. Truitt."

Candy Truitt's face scrunched in the first sign of life Sean had seen since they'd met at Bar Harbor. She cuddled close to her husband and wrapped her arms protectively around her cat. "Are there wild animals on the island?"

Fairchild shook his head. "High tide. Our rocky shoreline has some very steep drops that aren't well illuminated at night. I wouldn't want anyone washed out to sea."

"Les?" Candy was still worried.

"We'll stay inside, sugar," he promised.

Caitlin, fine-tuning her role as a sophisticated woman and

ignoring Sean's warning, complimented their host. "Sounds like you plan to take very good care of us."

Fairchild beamed. "The very best." With a chivalrous flourish, he extended his arm to her. "We'll take the carts up to the house. You'll have an hour to settle in and change for dinner. I know some of you want to be alone, but it is a tradition at Pleasure Cove to take our first meal together in the dining room. Shall we?"

Sean fumed silently. Caitlin was enjoying this way too much. She gave Fairchild a cocky grin and draped herself on his arm. "I can hardly wait."

11

"CLOTHES! At last."

Snugging the belt of the fuzzy white courtesy robe around her waist, Caitlin fluffed her damp hair and hurried from the bathroom toward the packages stacked at the edge of the king-size bed.

"Room service delivered them while you were in the shower."

Sean's tie and jacket were tossed across the double-wide chaise longue at the foot of the bed, but she didn't see the man himself. "Sean?"

"Try them on for me."

She spun toward the closet and pinpointed the source of his voice. He was standing inside the open door, running his hands along the top shelf.

"What are you doing?" she asked, enjoying the view of his tush as he stooped down and checked something on the floor of the closet.

He turned around on his haunches and pointed to the parcels of tissue and plastic. "I want to see you in them. Now."

Huh? "Is this how it's going to be? You giving me orders all the time? If you remember back in Connecticut, that whole he-man act—"

Sean surged to his feet and crossed the room in two powerful strides that had Caitlin backing up to escape his unexpected attack. He snaked his left arm behind her waist and covered her mouth with the palm of his right hand, stopping her retreat and shutting her up at the same time.

"Please." He bent his mouth to her ear and whispered. "I need you to make some noise. Maintain a normal conversation, but in the role of my mistress, while I finish searching the room."

"Hmm-umb?" she asked from behind his hand. He trapped her like that for several breathless moments, until she opened her eyes wide and silently told him she understood the need to be quiet.

He removed the hand that covered her mouth, though not the one that pulled her hips flush against his. It felt wonderfully reassuring to be held in his firm embrace again, but she ignored the girlish impulses inside her that were delighting in the contact. Sean had made it clear he wasn't happy about having her here. She wouldn't interpret his hold on her now as anything but a necessity of the job.

"For what?" she repeated, her muffled words angling her lips close to his ear.

He reached into his shirt pocket and pulled out a tiny square of plastic and metal that looked like a computer chip. He dropped it to the carpet and ground it beneath his shoe. "Another one of those."

She'd seen something like it in a movie. "They're listening to us?"

"I'd like to know who's on the other end listening. Maybe it's how Fairchild gets his jollies, or maybe somebody else is taking advantage of a prime setup." His green eyes narrowed and scoped the perimeter of the room before settling back on her. "My gun is missing from my bag."

"What?" She clutched the front of his shirt in a frisson of panic. "Do you think they're onto us already?"

He brushed his fingers across her cheek and tucked a strand of hair behind her ear, calming her with the gentle caress. "They know I'm with the FBI, and I have a license to carry it. That in itself shouldn't make anyone suspicious."

"But you're worried." Now she was, too.

"They had to search pretty thoroughly to find it. That makes me think they're keeping an extra close watch on me. On us." The hand on her cheek slipped into her hair and palmed the side of her neck. "That device was easy to find. A dog bone to lull us into a false sense of security. But I suspect there are others, better hidden than that one."

"So we have to be *on* all the time?"

He nodded. "I'm trying to create one secure room for us, but until I'm convinced it's clean, we'll have to play our parts even in here. Be natural, but…remember you're my mistress. We have to look and sound like lovers."

The heat from his thighs seeped into hers as she unconsciously snuggled closer, seeking reassurance and support. "So you accept that I can handle that now? You'll treat me as an equal partner instead of ordering me about and controlling my every move?"

His pensive sigh stirred the hair at her temple. "Caitie, it's not that I don't—"

A simple yes would have sufficed. "I withdraw the question." Caitlin pushed against his arm and shooed him away. "I'll make some noise."

The threat of being overheard probably kept him from calling after her and making a pretty apology as she scooted around the side of the bed and left him standing in the middle of the room.

She'd become well aware of his attitude toward her. He was more than happy to comfort her. To ease her fears and take care of her safety. He was willing to do all those things for her. Sean was gallant, heroic and kind.

But it also meant he didn't believe she could take care of

herself or help with his mission. He thought she might break. Or cave with the pressure or blow her lines or get hurt. In other words...he still didn't trust her.

What was it about the men in her life that they wouldn't let her make her own mistakes? Or celebrate her own successes?

Sean resumed his search and she noisily ripped open the first package. Several small bits of cloth fell into her hands. It was underwear. The size she'd ordered, according to the tags, but skimpier and filmier than any panties she'd ever worn. A string bikini in red silk. A thong of black lace. Knit-cotton tap pants trimmed with crystal beads around the hip-hugging waist.

He wanted natural? She let the sarcasm fly. "These would be useful if I'd brought my doll collection with me."

"McCormick."

"Oh, look. They coordinate with the outfits." She continued unwrapping, taking great care to crinkle and wad each piece of tissue and plastic to hide the noise of Sean opening and closing drawers.

A red silk dress, trimmed with sequins at the high neck and keyhole back, came next. Then a black tube top with a tigerprint, wraparound skirt.

"I suppose that one's for the jungle room," Sean said.

She pulled out a chiffon scarf with matching black-and-gold stripes. "The jungle room?"

"I read the brochure. There are vines to swing on and a tree house." He tossed her the glossy pamphlet enroute to the nightstand beside the bed. "The room has its own climate control unit and sunlamps, so the heat and humidity help maintain a steamy environment."

Caitlin was almost afraid to open the brochure and see what other playlands were available. "I'm not much of a fun-in-the-sun kind of person myself."

"Read on, sweetheart." The endearment startled her. But when she glanced at Sean, he was busy looking behind the framed painting over the bed. He was just playing his part. "There's a North Pole room, too, with a brisk thirty-two-degree setting. You strip in the igloo and cover yourself with pseudo whale oil, or you can snuggle in the layers of furs that cover the floor."

She'd promised to play her part, too. Setting aside wishful thinking, she opened the next package and discovered a casual outfit consisting of a cropped T-shirt and a pair of denim shorts that wouldn't cover any more than a swimsuit bottom would.

"None of these will work for the North Pole room." Apparently, Ramona Fairchild's boutique catered to her customers' more seductive needs. "I guess *you'll* have to keep me warm."

It was Sean's turn to be startled. She felt the laserlike intensity of his eyes on her even before she turned to face him. He wasn't looking for anything but an explanation right now.

Everything about his stance told her he wanted her—the flare of his nostrils and deep swell of his chest as he breathed in deeply; the clench of his fingers, fisting and releasing at his sides as he fought the urge to move and touch; the unblinking scan of those eyes, stripping her naked and caressing her flesh. He was looking at her the way he had *before* the asthma attack. The way he had when he'd carried her to the hood of his car.

But he wasn't doing a damn thing about it.

"I won't break, you know. In body or in spirit." Caitlin looked away, knowing that same intense desire was heating her face and betraying her shameless need for the man.

So she'd convinced him to let her stay for the weekend. She hadn't proved a thing. Mistress by default. If he couldn't trust her to *pretend* to be his sex partner, then he certainly couldn't let her be the real thing.

"Dinner's in twenty minutes." She gathered her new wardrobe and carried it to the closet. "I'd better change."

"Caitie—"

She couldn't find the nerve to look him in the eye for fear she'd blurt out something way too personal for this business-only undercover game.

But she watched his reflection in the mirrored door as he shook his head and forced himself to move on from the supercharged moment. "I'm gonna shave. Don't worry about making conversation."

She didn't understand his cryptic exit until she heard the hum of an electric shaver from behind the closed bathroom door. It was loud enough to drown out any conversation a listening device might pick up.

If only they had something left to say.

"ADMINISTRATIVE CHIEF Sean Maddox and Ms. Caitlin McCormick."

Since Caitlin had no fake ID, and Pod Whitmore had already recognized her from her picture, Sean had decided there was no point in trying to assume names. Though she'd probably prefer something from one of her fantasies like "Beauty" or "Princess" or even "Mata Hari," he liked "Caitie." Not for the first time, Sean questioned the wisdom of continuing the charade with her.

Maybe if he'd had time to get to know her before issuing his spur-of-the-moment weekend invitation, he wouldn't be worrying so much about her health and dangerous impulses now. Who was he kidding? If he'd known about Caitie's asthma and her determination to pack a lifetime's worth of adventure into one weekend, he'd have left her in Virginia.

His desperation to find a woman to create his cover, and

the inexplicable fascination he had for her sexy body and sheltered soul, had prevented him from sending her home when he'd had the opportunity. Ultimately, he'd kept her with him because he liked having her around. Because she swore she was committed to seeing this through with him.

He wasn't very good at trusting a woman's word, but he'd do his damnedest to believe in her loyalty to him. Even if it was only about the job. Even if it was for only one weekend.

With all the pomp of a costumed ball, Douglas Fairchild announced them as the last couple to arrive, and ushered them into a formal dining room that could have come straight from the pages of an Agatha Christie novel. Heavy brocade drapes filtered out the warmth of the sunset while an ornate crystal chandelier and silver candelabras illuminated the nooks and niches of the room with a muted light.

As Sean set foot onto the dark Oriental rug, all eyes at the long mahogany table turned toward them. Caitlin's fingers clenched the crook of his elbow, and he felt her shoulder brush his.

She was nervous, more about the sensual details of the outfit she wore than by the command performance that was about to begin, he guessed. Just like during their first meeting in her apartment, she was self-consciously tucking in her chin and hunching her shoulders to make herself appear smaller.

Sean paused and reached over to caress her cheek. In front of God and Fairchild and nine other guests, he slipped two fingers beneath her chin and tilted her face toward his.

"You wanted this adventure," he reminded her beneath his breath before he lifted his lips and kissed the sculpted line of her jaw. He feasted on her creamy skin while her hair tickled his nose and filled him with the tangy scent of her shampoo. "You're gorgeous."

So what if she topped him by a couple of inches in those killer spiked heels that had come with the packages from the boutique? She was a glorious thing in that traffic-stopping minidress and those strappy red sandals—which showcased every inch of bare, beautiful leg in between.

She looked the part of a woman he wanted to take to bed. Now if she could just convince the others she was everything she appeared to be.

And he could just keep reminding himself she really wasn't his for the taking.

Just as he felt the heat of her responsive blush against his lips, Fairchild politely cleared his throat and pried her from his arms. Sean managed to disguise a territorial growl behind a pensive sigh as their host guided her around the table and pulled out her chair.

"I'll seat you to my left and right." Fairchild's pale, fleshy hand made itself at home in the center of Caitlin's bare back while he spoke to all his party guests and his sister, Ramona, who sat at the foot of the table. "I hope everyone's hungry. Jeffrey's prepared a sumptuous meal for all of us."

Ship's pilot. Security guard. Chef. What other talents did Jeffrey possess? Spy? Con artist? Blackmailer?

And just how long did it take a man to pull out a chair and seat a woman, anyway?

"Should I ask why the two of you were detained?" Now Fairchild was giving her shoulders a friendly massage. "If there's anything you don't like about your accommodations, or the staff has neglected you somehow, please let me know and I'll take care of it right away."

Caitlin seemed to be counting the number of forks and spoons beside her plate. "The room is fine, thanks."

Confidence, sweetheart, Sean silently urged.

"We were having a discussion and got sidetracked," he said, offering a plausible version of the truth.

Actually, she'd been dressed and ready to go by the time he finished in the bathroom. He was the one who'd stalled for time. He'd misjudged Caitie more than once. Thought she was a flake. Thought she was a sexually experienced woman. Thought she was going to give up the charade when it got too intense.

But she'd stayed with him every step of the way. Beyond his crude impulses, beyond her asthma, beyond her naiveté, beyond his distrust. She hadn't given up on his mission. She hadn't gone back on her word. She hadn't given up on him.

He'd been the one who was ready to give up.

A curious epiphany tried to work its way into Sean's mind. His parents had taught him all about neglecting commitments, allowing them to fail. When he'd gotten involved with Elise, he could see the pattern repeating itself. He'd expected their relationship to fail. He'd never given her the chance to work through the rough times with him. He'd just called it quits and determined that no woman would ever go the distance.

But then, he'd never met a woman quite like Caitlin Mc-Cormick.

For the first time in his adult life, he wanted to set the security of the job aside and see where a relationship with a woman might take him. Straight to bed? Straight to a justice of the peace? Straight past his disbelief in the enduring promise of a one man–one woman commitment?

But he couldn't set the job aside. Someone was watching them. Setting them up for blackmail or something worse.

He couldn't cheat the job right now. Caitlin wouldn't let him.

Once she was settled and Fairchild moved on, Sean took his seat across from her and tried to assess whether she had her head in the game yet or not. Would her lusty natural intelligence kick in? Or would she refuse to play the loving mistress out of spite because of his insistence that she was better off safe at home?

"I think the two of them had a spat and haven't made up yet." Ali Turner's ruby-tinted lips smiled in wicked amusement, and the others laughed at her teasing tone. Sean failed to see the humor of being out of sync with Caitlin when it was so vital that they come across as a real couple.

When he wanted them to be a real couple, period.

Les Truitt, bald as a bowling ball without his cowboy hat, laughed the loudest. "You'd better say you're sorry, Chief, or you'll miss out on all the fun." He winked across the table at his wife, Candy. "The little lady is always right."

While Sean pondered that pearl of folksy wisdom, Fairchild snapped his fingers. "Bert. You may serve us now."

The ponytailed porter cum bartender now played waiter. Dressed in a black tuxedo, he stepped out from the corner and bowed to his employer. After handing Fairchild a long, flat basket, he set bowls of a creamy white soup at each place setting. Fairchild made a toast and continued the show.

"I always like to start the party with a get-acquainted dinner. I know some of you will become quite close before the weekend has ended. As I said earlier, each of the east wing rooms has only one key." He lifted the basket and rattled the contents. "Here they are."

"When can we check them out?" Les asked. "I'm not getting any younger, you know."

"Lester." Candy rolled her eyes at her husband's unabashed eagerness.

Douglas Fairchild seemed pleased by Les's enthusiasm. "Right after dinner, if you like." He set the basket on the corner of the table next to Sean. "There are a few rules of etiquette I'd like us to cover before you split up, though."

"More rules?" Sean asked. He nudged Caitlin's foot under the table, urging her to join the conversation.

She looked at him with hooded eyes. "I thought you liked it when people follow rules."

Not the supportive response he was looking for. "*My* rules, sure." Was this one of her fantasies—staying mad at him long enough to jeopardize his investigation?

"I think someone needs to do some making up. Or should I say, making out?" Priscilla Doe drank her wine and giggled as she looked back and forth from him to Caitlin.

Fairchild's loud voice silenced her. "I thought we might play a game to get to know each other while we continue the conversation."

"A game?" General Whitmore didn't sound any more interested in playing than Sean did.

"To put everyone in the mood."

"I'm already in the mood," Les exclaimed, a response Sean could have predicted.

"The game is simple," Fairchild explained. "Every time you speak, you have to work in a sexual innuendo. It can be a word or something *longer,* if you know what I mean."

Priscilla laughed out loud. "That's such a goofy idea. Why, there must be *sixty-nine* different things I can think of off the top of my head."

John Doe raised his glass and toasted his wife. "That's it, baby. That's as good as winning the lottery with you."

"And the sexual overtone there is what?" Whitmore asked.

John winked. "'That's it, baby' is what I say to her when…you know."

"I know a lot more about sex than you do, *lover boy.*"

Damn. Even the general had succumbed to the game.

Priscilla's high-pitched giggle taxed Sean's patience. This wasn't much of a format to ask questions relating to past dates and visits to the island. And there'd be no opportunity to snoop around the estate as long as Fairchild insisted they party together as a group.

Soup became salad before the first round of that game had run its course. Caitlin had jumped in with a couple of lines. Sean refused to play.

"Douglas," Ali Turner said, her husky voice quieting the table, "tell them what to do if you want to use a room where another couple is conducting *private business.*"

"You must wait until they've finished *networking* and hand the key over to you. Or you may get their permission to *join* them. And please remember, there is a supply of condoms in every room. I expect each of you to have a safe party experience." Fairchild seemed to be enjoying his control over the sex lives of his influential guests. "Anything and anyone you see here must remain strictly confidential. We count on each other's discretion to protect your own reputations, as well. It spoils the fun for everyone if you *let your cat out of the bag,* so to speak."

Sean felt a toe nudge his foot beneath the table. Caitlin. Her gaze slid over to Pod Whitmore. Sean read the discomfort brewing in her eyes. Did she really think he'd allow anyone else near her? Or that he'd let her secret excursion to Pleasure Cove Island get back to her family?

He hooked his ankle around hers, hoping she'd understand it was the closest thing to a reassuring hug he could give her right now.

Sipping her wine, she looked over the rim of her glass and nodded once at him. Sean supposed it was a subtle thank-you, but he began to wonder if, beneath the table, she was trying to communicate a different message. She crossed her legs just so, tugging his ankle between both of hers. Being locked between her legs had been a heady fantasy of his from their first meeting. It didn't take much for the subtle pull to flutter all the way up his leg to his crotch.

"Caitlin."

The jerk on Sean's foot told him Douglas Fairchild had startled her. But above the table she played it cool, offering him as genuine a smile as he'd ever seen.

"Would you like to help me start the next dinner game?"

"I'm not sure. I was really..." she shrugged coyly "...*getting off* on the last game."

Fairchild's loud laugh rattled the windowpanes. Reaching over and punching Sean's arm wasn't the least bit endearing, either. Douglas Fairchild was moving higher and higher on Sean's suspect list—of annoying rich guys with way too much time on their hands.

"She's a winner, Chief Maddox. Sexy *and* smart."

As if Sean hadn't figured that out for himself already. Caitlin blushed at the compliment. Sean fumed.

"The new game, Douglas?" Ramona Fairchild suggested, encouraging her brother to move on.

With all eyes on him, Fairchild rubbed his hands together with the delightful glee of an adolescent who had gotten away with something naughty. "I like to call it Physical Contact."

This did not sound good.

"You have to touch the person to whom you are speaking." Fairchild trailed his fingers up the line of Caitlin's bare arm to demonstrate. Sean's toes clenched inside his leather oxfords.

"What if that person is sitting at the far end of the table?" she asked, thinking at the last moment to run her fingers across the back of Fairchild's hand.

"Be creative." The bastard teased his fingers through her hair. Sean's feet flattened on the floor. "You can also touch something that person is touching. But you can't get out of your chair.''

"I see.''

She'd said she didn't want Sean to interfere with her undercover work, swore she could handle whatever came up. But, dammit, Fairchild was playing with her hair! Why wasn't she *handling* that?

"You forgot to touch Douglas that time.'' A perverse need to point out her easy familiarity with the host simmered in Sean's blood. A fake endearment sounded perfect just about now. "Darling.''

Her round, soft eyes hardened to battleship-gray. "You didn't touch me just now, either. Darling.'' She covered her sneer with a dazzling smile. At the same time her toe slipped inside his pant leg, stroking the base of his calf. Definitely touching.

He picked up the bread stick from the plate beside his salad and held it out across the table. It was crude, it was phallic, but he wanted to make his message clear. "I'm the only one you need to be touching. Darling.''

She gripped the bread, her fingers wrapping around its cylindrical shape with the same firm eagerness she'd used around his dick. "It's just a game. Darling.''

He wasn't playing.

Above the table, her eyes locked on his, her voice and smile a defiant challenge to his protective jealousy. Beneath the table, she stuck her leg out, sliding her foot over his knee and straight up his thigh.

A dozen muscles clenched inside him. A few in particular started to expand.

Was she flirting? Comforting? Reassuring him she was still on his side? Did she even know what she was doing to him?

Sean surrendered the bread stick and glanced at Fairchild.

'How much longer do we have to keep making nice and playing these games?''

Fairchild raised his glass and indicated Sean should do the same. ''Aren't you forgetting something, Chief?''

He wasn't going to clink glasses with him. ''I don't think so.''

''Temper, temper, Mr. Maddox.'' Ali Turner reached over from the chair beside him and squeezed his thigh. Sean jerked. Caitlin's foot grazed a little too close to home for him to stand much more of this.

Priscilla grabbed Les Truitt's hand and giggled. ''I think he's sexually frustrated. Don't you?''

''Enough!'' Sean jumped up, snatched a key from Fairchild's basket and grabbed Caitlin. ''We'll be skipping dessert.''

Leaving chairs askew and questions unanswered, he took her by the hand and dashed out of the dining room.

'''Bout time somebody took some action! Let the party begin!'' Les Truitt's loud whoopee! echoed down the hallway behind them.

''WATERWORKS. Waterworks.''

Caitlin hurried along behind Sean as he marched swiftly from door to door in the estate's spacious east wing. It was a start-and-stop race as he checked the brass plate on each door against the key ring he gripped in one fist. With her hand firmly clasped in the other, she fought to maintain her balance and keep up with him—a precarious challenge considering his snarling mood and her four-inch heels.

Should she be thrilled? Worried? Mad that he'd lost control and had whisked her away for a private party of their own? Had she gone too far with her subtle, under-the-table defense of her fitness for the mission? She'd been nervous,

sure, but she'd done a damn good job. She had Dougla
Fairchild convinced she was a sexy siren, at any rate.

"Here's our room."

She slammed into Sean's back when he suddenly stoppe
and inserted the key into the lock. She tucked back her hai
as he pushed the door open. "I was hoping for something
more along the lines of a Victorian boudoir."

But Sean was in no mood to laugh. He stormed into th
room, dragging her behind him. He closed and locked th
door before finally releasing her.

At first glance, it looked like a giant bathroom, a long tub
the size of a wading pool sunk into the tile floor, a tall vanity
cabinet with a mirror on either side, a bidet, plenty of potte
silk plants. Sean crossed the room to the switch above a
raised hot tub and turned it on. Jets swirled to life and a
heater hummed into action.

Since he wouldn't talk, she would. "Did you get a sudde
urge to wash up?"

When he turned on the water in the sinks as well, she
finally understood that he was creating noise so that they
could talk without being overheard. "We got what I
grabbed, okay? I had to get out of there."

Caitlin's frustration eased a notch toward concern. Ha
she missed something important at dinner? Was there a
problem? "Why?"

Without touching her anywhere, he pinned her to the
door, backing her into the hard wood and bracing a hand
on either side of her. His mouth swept past her cheek and
hovered beside her ear as he leaned in. "Because Fairchild
was groping you, Whitmore was trying to show off how
clever he is, you were laughing at every damn thing Les
Truitt said—"

She pushed at his chest, urging him back enough so she

could read the heated message in his narrowed green eyes. "Aren't we supposed to fit in as guests?"

"You're *my* mistress, not theirs."

Feeling suddenly shaky with a rush of relief and emotion, she curled her fingers into the front of his jacket. He'd just said something wonderfully possessive. Something fiercely male. About her.

"Sean, are you jealous?" She splayed her hands flat and skidded them up over the imposing contours of his chest and neck. She framed the stiff set of his jaw between her palms. "I thought I was making it clear which man I was attracted to. The rest of it was all part of my secret-agent act."

He didn't relax the taut rein he held over his body, nor did he answer. He pulled away, leaving her breathless in his wake, and prowled around the room like a big jungle cat. "I think we've established our cover just fine. It's time we got some investigating done."

"We?" He'd said *we?* Funny how one little word could give her such pleasure. "You're asking me to help?"

"Are you going to question every damn thing I say?" He tried to stare her down and look all tough, but the silly urge to grin wouldn't go away. With a dramatic sigh, he shook his head. Something close to a smile relaxed the corners of his mouth as he loosened his tie and unbuttoned his collar. "Don't let it go to your head. But you were right, I need you to be my partner on this. I have to trust you to do your thing so I can do mine."

Her grin erupted into a full-blown smile. "Oh, Sean." She stumbled across the room and threw her arms around his neck. She hugged him tightly, pressing her cheek against his, giving herself the right to savor the heat that emanated from his body into hers. "That's the best part of my fantasy, you know. To be your equal. Not your burden."

He closed his arms around her. "If you don't mind, I'm still going to worry about you, though."

"I don't mind. Just let me try to take care of myself first."

Okay, so maybe trusting her competency wasn't the *best* part of her fantasy weekend. He'd found the bare skin exposed by the back of her dress and spread his broad, hot palms there. Caitlin stretched like a cat against him as he swept his fingers lower and cupped her bottom in the sure fit of his hands, waking all kinds of tingly responses in the needy parts of her body that had already learned to crave his touch.

But before she had a chance to seek out his mouth and complete the embrace, his hands tightened on her hips and firmly pushed her away. "Okay, Mata Hari, we might as well start looking in here."

Oh right. The hot and tingly part was just a fringe benefit. This was where she had to prove she was worthy of his trust. "What are we looking for?"

He opened the vanity doors. "Hidden cameras, microphones—"

"Secret journals about the romantic trysts of past guests?"

"That's the idea, Sherlock. Later, if we can get into the west wing, I want to try to find a communications center, see if I can get a message out of here."

Caitlin wandered off in the opposite direction. Inside one cabinet she found stacks of fresh white towels and, as Douglas had promised, a basket holding a variety of condoms. So guests came here and did it in the hot tub? Nothing terribly creative about that. "What about Douglas's office? Maybe we could find some financial records or past guest lists."

"Good thinking."

She opened what she thought was a closet door. But inside, instead of hangers and storage, she found a plastic shelf built high into the wall above her head. The spongy floor, covered in a soft synthetic carpet that reminded her of clipped grass, sloped gently down toward the main part of the room. "Weird."

"What's that?"

She traced the joint of floor and jamb behind the door and discovered a rubber-lined trough running around the perimeter of the entire room. The main floor wasn't entirely level, either. It all tilted in a subtle slant toward the sunken bathtub. "I thought this place was just a glorified bathroom, but it has some amenities I've never seen before."

"Weirder than an igloo or a tree house?"

"I'm not sure."

She ran her fingers along a wall that had been painted with a pastoral mural of rocks and flowers and trees. The small, round black center of one flower caught her eye. But it wasn't a microphone as she had suspected.

"What do you think this button does?"

"Caitie, I wouldn't—"

She pressed it.

12

"WHAT'S THAT SOUND?"

Caitlin lifted her hands to steady herself as the floor started to vibrate. Maybe it wasn't the floor, but rather the walls that were moving. Her heart skipped a beat and then resumed at a faster pace. Maybe the entire room was shaking. Taking careful little baby steps, she backed away from the mural. Did they have earthquakes off the coast of Maine?

"Sean?"

She felt his hand at the small of her back. "Something's happening in the ceiling."

A grinding sound, louder than the noise of the hot tub and the sink combined, clamored overhead. Caitlin tipped her face up. A cool drop of water splashed her cheek. She blinked and turned away, wiping the moisture off her skin. "Is there a leak in one of the pipes?"

"The hot tub and sinks just turned themselves off." Sean was slowly pulling her back toward the door.

A second drop hit her shoulder, another the tip of her nose.

Caitlin shaded her eyes and looked up again. "It's opening up."

The slats that had formed the solid ceiling were separating. Every other one rose up, to reveal a complex sprinkler system. A series of large fans oscillated back and forth, dispersing the water in a random pattern across the room.

She and Sean both stopped as the few drops became a steady downpour.

Caitlin held out the palm of her hand. "It's raining."

"Inside? What button did you press?" Seeing less of the wonder of it all than she, he slipped off his coat and draped it around her shoulders before darting across the room. "This one?"

He flipped a switch beside a tall, painted fern.

"No." Too late. "The daisy."

The grinding sound from up above gave way to a rhythmic pulsing from behind the mural itself. Like her own steady heartbeat, the sound in the wall picked up speed, thumping faster and faster. She traced the pumping sound as it thudded along behind the wall, turned upward at the closet door, faded a moment and then— "Sean, move!"

Like her favorite theme park ride, a torrent of water gushed over the top of the closet's plastic shelf, knocking Sean to his knees on the spongy carpet. "What the hell?" His sputtering curse got lost in a mouthful of water.

"It's a waterfall." Now she understood the construction of the floor. The water cascaded to the spongy deck inside the closet, then channeled along the sloping floor toward the sunken tub and into the drain. Any excess water was caught in the trough at the edge of the room.

"It's not exactly what I was hoping to find." Sean pushed himself to his feet and climbed out of the newly formed brook that flowed into the tub. His unbuttoned sleeves hung from his arms; his gray wool slacks clung like a second skin across powerful calves and thighs.

"I get it. Waterworks!" She stuck out her arms and twirled around with her face tilted to the ceiling. The rain splashed her face, her throat, and trickled inside her dress. "I feel like I'm in a special-effects movie scene."

"Caitie, you're getting soaked." Sean peeled his jacket

from her shoulders and held it over their heads like an umbrella.

"So are you."

She smiled at his scowling countenance, blinking a prism of raindrops from her eyelashes. This was like kid's play. He shouldn't be frowning so. They had to stand close together to share the shelter of his coat. It was close enough to feel the heat from his body, but not close enough to touch.

She wanted to touch.

Water dripped into his eyes from two strands of hair that stuck to his forehead. Caitlin reached up and pushed the errant locks back into place. She lightly traced the contours of his hairline around his face. With each caress, his scowl softened. His mossy eyes narrowed and focused. She felt the intense perusal of his gaze on her face like a probing laser ray.

The steady rain pelted his jacket, but standing beneath it, she was protected. She felt protected in other ways as well. The arrogant cut of his features held no menace for her.

But she wanted more.

Did he still want that, too?

She trailed her fingers over the jut of his chin and let them settle at the open collar of his shirt. Her fingertips trembled at the startling contrast of cold, wet cotton and steamy heat from his skin.

She paused to breathe—and drop a hint. "Don't you get it? This is somebody's fantasy. To make love out in the rain."

"Is that one of your fantasies?" he asked. Echoing in the intimate tent of his jacket above them, his deep voice seemed to shimmer along her nerves.

"I hadn't thought about it before." She ran her right hand up her left arm, finding it slippery with droplets. "There is something fresh and invigorating about the rain. And, of course, all the water would make things slippery. And there's something about water running across your body that makes you think of..."

Her voice faded away into silence. The water might be cool to the touch, but her skin was suddenly hot and flushed. The contrast was too much for her to bear, and goose bumps puckered her skin. Her nipples beaded against the wet silk of her dress.

She felt Sean's gaze on her lips, her breasts. Narrowed. Piercing. She squeezed her eyes shut and shivered at the vision that began to formulate.

With just his look, her breathing stuttered, her pulse started to hammer.

She imagined herself in a secluded glade. She imagined the sounds of rain hushing the rest of the world and leaving her with the desperate agent who had kidnapped her and dragged her to this crystal waterfall and dappling brook. She imagined his kiss, hot and wet upon her open lips. She imagined his hands on her body, his mouth upon her straining breasts. She imagined the gathering of heavy heat between her thighs.

She wanted this. She wanted him.

As much as she'd wanted her adventure in the first place.

"Caitie." Sean's hoarse cry invaded her vision. She opened her eyes and saw the deep, controlled movements of his chest as he breathed in time with her.

She looked down and realized that the hands on her breasts were her own. She was touching herself through the raw, soft silk. She was hot. She was confused. She was well on her way toward fulfillment of that vision.

But even *her* fantasies were nowhere as good as the real thing.

With a wrenching cry of her own, she grabbed Sean's jacket and threw it to the floor. The sudden force of the rain

on her face and body was cooling, reviving, real. She slid
her hands into his wet, clingy hair, and invited herself over
for a kiss.

He wrapped his arms loosely around her. She felt his
hands on her back, roving islands of heat against her cool
skin. Water splashed between their mouths and teased the
tips of their noses as they breathed in and out.

But he was holding back, she could tell. His mouth was
hungry, his hands were seeking. But she missed the press
of his body, the crush of his strength taking what she so
desperately wanted to give.

"Sean?" she whimpered, sipping the moisture at the cleft
of his chin.

"We shouldn't." His mouth brushed a warm cloud of
steam against her ear, but he didn't nip or nuzzle. "Caitie,
I—"

"Shh." She pressed a finger over his lips to quiet his
argument. She leaned back against his hands and read the
torment in his eyes. "You want to. I want to."

"But sweetheart, you're so..." With the pad of his
thumb, he traced the track of a raindrop down her face until
it pooled in a dimple. "I'm so..."

She felt a burning jolt of sexual awareness as his lips
thinned into a taut line beneath her fingertip. She could feel
the frustration simmering beneath the surface, could sense
what it cost him to keep his volatile emotions in check. She
could recall with perfect clarity the way those lips had felt
against her mouth and her breast.

Something wise and worldly blossomed inside her. The
confidence of a woman who needed her man. The heart of
a woman whose man needed her.

"Please, Sean." She swept the hair from his eyes and
cupped his face, wanting him to see and hear the truth.
"Make love to me. The way you'd love your fantasy

woman. I don't want kid gloves or noble sacrifices. I want you. Sean Maddox. Please. You make me feel like I'm the sexiest damn thing you've ever seen.''

A jerky clutch of his hands drew her closer. ''You *are* the sexiest thing.''

She tilted her hips against his, feeling the unmistakable jut of his desire through their wet, body-hugging clothes. ''Everything, Sean. No excuses this time. I found a whole basket of condoms in the cabinet over there.'' She rubbed herself against him, not knowing how to make her desire any clearer. ''I want everything.''

''No excuses,'' he promised with a kiss, lifting her off her feet and carrying her across the room until her bottom butted against the wall behind her. Her toes touched the tile, but he suspended her with his strength, pinning her with his grinding hips in the warm cascade of water that ran down the wall. His mouth scudded across her cheek and nipped at the lobe of her ear. ''And no regrets.'' His words were a throaty request in her hair. ''Promise me. No regrets.''

Caitlin wound her fingers into his own hair and pulled his mouth to hers. ''No regrets.''

She melted into his kiss, hanging on to the firm anchor of his shoulders and neck as a whole slew of new sensations buffeted her from inside and out. Pellets of rain dotting her skin. The fiery brand of his mouth on her neck. Frantic gasps of moist, cool air. The molten weight of desire in her belly.

She needed this. This welcome. This reassurance. This reconciliation of two strong wills giving in to the thing they wanted most.

Sean's water-slick hands skimmed the bare slope of her back. He slipped one to the front and palmed her breast, squeezing silk and flesh in his big, bold grasp. Every moan of sensation, every pinch of delight, fed into the kiss, filling her with hot, wet, mad desire.

"Don't hold back," she begged him. "I want it all."

He slid his hand over the curve of her bottom and cupped her thigh. Without fanfare or finesse, he bent her leg, and sliding his hand to her knee, lifted her higher onto his hip and walked into her, pushing, grinding. Finding the slice of heat exposed by the spread of her legs and the thin, wet silk of her panties, he rubbed against her.

"More." Her nipples dragged across his chest as she gasped for air and tried to speak. She dangled atop his rock-hard leg, riding him like a mount, stretching to grant him greater access to her heavy, weepy center. "I want more."

Feverishly plundering with his mouth and hands, he dropped her leg and let her feet hit the floor. He unhooked the back of her dress. She tugged his shirt from the waist of his pants. He swept his fingers into her hair. She unbuttoned his shirt and pushed it from his shoulders.

He was a magnificent beast. A mat of tawny hair covered the angles and planes of his chest. Emboldened by the pulsing surge of fire in her veins, she kissed him there. She laved a flat male nipple with her tongue and teased the other with her fingers. The responding flinch of his skin made her heady with the potency of her feminine power. She nuzzled the golden curls, breathing in the crisp bite of his cologne and lapping up the bitter tang of salt from his skin.

She heard the thunder in his chest, a seductive mix of throaty moan and hammering heartbeat. It matched the feral growl in her own throat, a trembling jumble of words and sensations too overwhelming to be spoken.

"Sean— Mmm— Please—"

"Not yet."

He silenced her with a broiling kiss, distracting her with the lick of his tongue while he peeled her dress away from her skin. It came down in front, exposing her breasts to the cool rain.

"Sean..." She tried to cross her arms and cover herself, but his hands were there, kneading and rolling and plucking and squeezing until her skin was hot and waiting for his mouth.

While he kissed the tips, he peeled off her dress the rest of the way, taking her panties with it. Each new chill on her skin became a blaze of heat beneath a brush of his rough-tipped fingers, the gentle nip of his hungry mouth. He traced her legs from thigh to foot, the dent of her knee, the curve of her calf, the length of shin all subject to the attentions of his hands and mouth.

He guided her hands to his shoulders as he knelt in front of her and slipped the dress off her feet. Balancing on shaky legs, she lifted one foot and reached for the strap of her sandal. But Sean caught her ankle and batted her hand away.

Like a sea creature from the deep, he rose up in front of her, catching her mouth in a kiss on his way. "The shoes stay," he ordered, kissing her again, making her thighs clench with an instinctive response to his feverish demand. "That's *my* fantasy."

And then he left her clinging to the wall, naked and needy, unable to tear her gaze from the prominent tent at the front of his pants. He pulled a condom from the cabinet, then shed his clothes as he came back to her, crossing the room with a purposeful stride.

She held on to the wall as he sheathed himself, and knew her first moment of panic. How could she be enough for him? He was so big, so powerful, so much more experienced than she.

But he saw the flare of doubt in her eyes. He came close enough to share the heat from his body. She reached out, but he grabbed her wrists and wouldn't let her touch.

"Trust me, Caitie." His eyes narrowed to mossy slits and

looked deep into her soul. "I'll make this as good for you as you'll let me. No excuses."

Her anxious heart calmed in the truth of his vow. "No regrets."

She expected him to impale her then, but he picked her up and carried her beneath the cascading force of the waterfall. He wrapped her in his arms, chest to chest, heat to heat. The water crashed down, sliding over their twisting bodies in a cocoon of chills and sensations that made the fiery tension of skin on skin feel even hotter.

The wave of water blinded her to all but his touch and scent and taste. "Stand here," he commanded, turning her hip and pushing her back with a kiss.

"I don't understand."

He kissed her throat and nipped at her breast and supped from her navel on his way down to his knees in front of her. With the force of the water hitting her directly, she nearly fell forward. She latched on to Sean's shoulders and tried to pull him back up to her. "What are you—?"

"Trust me."

He ran his hand up her belly and between her breasts. With the guidance of his strong hands to support her, she learned that he wanted her to arch her spine. As she leaned back into the water, he grabbed her hips, squeezing her bottom with his fingers, pressing his thumbs into the seam between her hips and thighs.

She grasped at his shoulders for fear of falling, but did as he asked. She tipped her head back, beyond the veil of the waterfall, and found dry air to breathe. With a slight adjustment of his hands, she understood.

"Oh!" She cried out as the water hit the thrust of her breasts. It was more than gentle, but not too hard—a steady pulse of water on her fevered skin. But what was Sean—? "Mmm—oh!"

He put his mouth on her. A soft kiss at the lips of her opening. She held herself still in shock at the unfamiliar touch. He rubbed his nose in the wet thatch of hair and pressed his mouth to her again. He licked his tongue along her swollen crevice and she jolted in his grasp.

"Sean—"

He kissed her again, harder this time, opening his mouth against her heat. She snatched at his head, raking her fingers through his hair, clutching the back of his skull and holding him between her legs.

The gentleness of his teaching vanished at her body's unspoken invitation. He pulled her open with his hands, squeezed her bottom and thrust his tongue inside her. Caitlin twisted at the growing pressure, but there was more to learn.

With his teeth shielded by the masculine texture of his lips, he bit down, pushing his mouth against that tender bud that would unleash the firestorm kindled inside her. He drove his tongue in, again and again, squeezing her between his mouth and hands.

"Sean…"

As the waterfall sluiced over her skin, a similar current of relentless pressure was pounding in her veins, with every river of sensation flowing straight to the pressure of Sean's mouth on her.

Her knees began to shake. Her fingers trembled. Her toes clenched in the red, high-heeled shoes.

"Mmmm—" She gasped for air and tried to think. "No…I want you inside me. I want—"

"Trust me, sweetheart."

One hand left her hip and palmed her belly, arching her back into the water. He slipped the other hand square on her bottom and pulled her against his open mouth.

At his first draw on her, the dam inside her cracked. Cold water on the outside, hot, weepy passion on the inside…

"Let it come." Sean's urgent voice reached her ears. "Go for it, honey. Let it come."

Caitlin arched back. Sean pulled hard. The water beat at her breasts as he sucked and sucked.

He thrust in his tongue and everything exploded inside her. Caitlin cried out. Her knees buckled at the flash of heat that melted her core. As wave after wave of the conflagration consumed her, Sean caught her in his arms and laid her on the soft, spongy floor beneath him.

"Are you all right?" he asked, dipping his lips to the purring vibration in her throat.

She caught his face in her hands and angled his mouth for her kiss. "I've never been so all right."

She tasted her honey on his tongue and a new fire sparked low in her belly. This was life. This was the adventure she hadn't known she'd been yearning for.

And this man—this brutish beast with a macho thirst for action and a troubled, doubting heart—had been the one to give her that adventure.

Not the thrill of undercover work. Not the speedy drive in the fancy car. Not even the sex itself.

The caring. This man cared. He treated her like a normal, desirable woman. She'd never been given such a generous gift.

And in the waning innocence of her hopeful heart, she understood that he was caring for her even now. His rigid penis butted against her thigh as he sprinkled kisses across her face and breasts. But he wouldn't enter her. With all her fuss about barking orders and taking control, he was waiting for her to ask.

"We're not done yet." She pushed a clinging strand of hair off his forehead. "You promised." She put the other wayward lock of hair into place and smiled up at him. "I'm not wearing these red shoes for nothing, am I?"

He smiled back. "I hope not."

Without wasting more words, he slipped inside her. Her slick, swollen labia stretched and stretched to accommodate him. He was big and powerful, like the rest of his body. And she loved it. He was more man than she'd ever known before. All the man that she could ever need.

His hips were already rocking against hers. She spread her legs and let him drive himself in to the hilt. He sank against her pelvic bone, and that sensitive nub, hidden in her folds, flared to attention once more.

"Sean?"

He glided his hand down her left side, taunting her nipple with his thumb, cupping her butt, squeezing her thigh. He caught her knee and bent it up beside his hip, opening her more to the stroke of his shaft. He repeated the action on her right side, bending her knee and opening her wider.

He slipped in and out, letting his dancing member tease her lower lips while his tongue did wicked things to her mouth.

"Sean?"

Everything that had spilled from her before seemed to be gathering again. He stroked his hands from her knees to her thighs, dipping his thumbs inside her and dribbling the proof of all he did to her around her aching mound.

"Sean." Now she was begging him to release her from the exquisite torment.

He swept his eyes over her, the intensity of his gaze burning every secret, sensitive place inside her. "You're beautiful." Then he looked into her eyes and smiled. "You're the sexiest damn thing I've ever known."

With that, he plunged deep, pushing and grinding and driving her to the edge. She clutched at his shoulders as he rode her with a powerful, pulsing rhythm.

"Mmm…"

And as the waves of her climax took her for the second time, he dragged his hands all the way down her legs—from her clenching thighs to the tips of her toes pointing from their red, spiked shoes. He pushed them straight into the air as he gathered her in his arms and emptied himself inside her.

"Damn!"

It was the happy curse of a satisfied man.

SEAN DRIFTED BACK toward sanity once he realized the rain and waterfall had stopped.

The contraption must be on some sort of timer—for randy lovers like himself and Caitlin who got carried away and forgot about everything until their passion was spent. He must have dozed for a few minutes after the fact because the water in the pool where they were lying had nearly drained away.

Caitlin was snoring softly, her face nestled in the crook of his arm. She was definitely one of a kind. He wasn't completely sure what to make of her yet, but he knew he'd never met anyone quite like her. He doubted he ever would again.

While the soft lap of the water trickling past cooled their bodies, he propped himself up beside her and studied the drowsy contentment of her smile. He brushed the backs of his knuckles across her soft, cool cheek and tangled his fingers in the silky curls at her temple. All that water and his own greedy hands had made her hair kink up into a wild mess that framed her unlined features and gave her an even more youthful beauty.

Was this innocent the same creature who had boldly commanded that he make love to her—no kid gloves, no holding back?

She looked so soft and vulnerable, as if she really could succumb to her asthma, as if she really needed her father or another man to keep her out of trouble. As if the only place she could even think about sex was in her eccentric fantasy life.

Sean smiled at her. He knew better.

They were still lying with their legs tangled, the hard press of his thigh caught against that slice of honey-sweet heat. Those irresistible red heels were still on her feet, calling to him like a red flag to a bull.

She'd wanted it down and dirty, and he'd obliged. He'd never had it so good. He'd never wanted it so badly. And judging by the stir of interest down there from just thinking about it, he'd never wanted it again so soon.

But Caitie was just a babe when it came to sex. He was only the second she'd ever had. He steadfastly refused to acknowledge that little voice inside that said he wanted to be her last. Her only.

It was just too damn unrealistic.

Despite giving her word that she wouldn't regret giving in to their sizzling attraction to each other, he worried that she'd read something more personal into it. Great sex was just that—great sex. Nothing more, nothing less. It qualified as one of those fantasy adventures she kept talking about.

But because they'd connected at such an intense physical level, she might think they'd connected in other ways, too. She might think she could change his beliefs about the endurance of marriages and monogamous relationships. She might try to convince him that it wasn't a stupid tactical move to surrender his complete trust to a woman. She'd wind up getting hurt.

He'd be the one to hurt her. And he wasn't sure he could live with that.

He should get up right now and just walk away before he botched this mission and screwed up her life any more than he had already.

Because a connection *had* been made. He'd dropped his guard without fully considering the consequences. She'd promised to be his for the weekend. One weekend. That was all. Then she'd go back to her books and her irresponsible roommate and her overprotective family and her safe, anonymous existence, without making any claims on his time or heart or conscience.

He traced the tip of his finger across the sweet mouth that had made such a promise to him, and tried to ignore the regret already spreading its numbing tension through him.

Look how he'd botched things with Elise. He could no longer blame her for running off to the Bahamas with her old boyfriend. He'd practically pushed her into that other man's arms because he was so damn scared he'd wind up getting hurt that he'd never really given them a chance.

He'd conveniently struck a bargain with Caitlin, too, to protect himself, guaranteeing her nothing beyond Pleasure Cove Island. He'd promised her adventure in exchange for a no-strings-attached relationship.

And, dammit all, he was beginning to believe that she might be the one woman who would keep her word to him.

He stroked his hand down the long column of her throat, already wanting to soothe the pain he thought he might cause her. She purred beneath his gentle petting and snuggled closer.

"S'nice," she murmured, brushing her lips against his chest in a sweet reminder of the kisses she'd given him earlier. She opened her eyes and gave him a smile that was part gratitude, part vamp, and loaded with contentment.

"That *was* nice." It was a woeful understatement of the

truth, but he hesitated to let her think making love to her was anything more than a mutually satisfying reprieve from the work that filled his life. He pressed a kiss to her forehead, thanking her for the wild release that she'd drawn from his body, apologizing for the need to move on with their lives.

"I think my butt's pruning up with all this water." She chuckled and wiggled her hips. An instant flare of interest clutched in his groin. He braced his hand on her hip and stilled the unwitting torment. He wanted to do the right thing here. But if he made love to her again…

He gentled his hold and carefully rolled to his side.

"But I'm too tired to even move." Her cheeks turned pink as she rolled onto her side to face him. "Does great sex always make you feel this way?"

He stroked her hair and tried to think of an eloquent response to that loaded question. She was the one who was so great. So daring. So uninhibited. "I suppose."

"Is it like that for you every time?"

"Umm…" No. It had never been like that for him. But answering with the truth could give her the wrong idea. He had to look somewhere else besides those trusting gray eyes. The waterfall looked like an ordinary closet again. The paintings on the wall were just decorations once more.

But something in passing caught Sean's eye. He pushed up on his elbow to get a better look. There it was again, a shiny glint of reflection from the leaves of one painted plant. He squinted his gaze into razor-sharp focus. But suspicion was already curling up from his toes by the time he confirmed what he saw.

"Shit."

"What is it?"

Sean rolled away from Caitie, every muscle in his body clenched against the violation he felt.

He crawled across the floor toward the heap of sodden clothes in the middle of the room.

"Sean?" He pulled on his shorts and searched for her dress. "Did I say something wrong?"

There. In a puddle by the closet. "It's nothing."

"Nothing? Then why…" She sat up in the tub, crossing her arms across her naked breasts.

"Get your clothes on." He tossed them at her. "We're going back to the room. Now."

His voice was too sharp. He knew she'd argue.

"You're giving orders again." She scrambled to her feet. *Oh no. No, no.* He draped his jacket across her shoulders, but she tossed it aside and stood there naked. Beautifully, beautifully naked.

"You tell me what's going on or I'm not moving."

"Dammit, Caitie…" He moved behind her and wrapped his arms around her waist, picking her up and carrying her out of the tub.

"Put me down." She twisted and wriggled, and her wet skin slipped from his grasp.

She planted her hands on her hips and turned to lecture, but he grabbed a towel and looped it around her. She fought against that, too, but he was determined to hide all he could, from her breasts to her thighs. With something dry to hold on to, he squeezed her in his arms and shook her once. He lowered his voice and got right in her face. "Please. Let's go back to the room so we can talk privately."

At last she stilled within his grasp. Though she pushed at his chest to put space between them, she didn't run away this time. "At first I thought you were being a jerk, but now you're scaring me." She clutched the towel together herself, and Sean opted to wrap a towel around his waist rather than trying to pull on his soaked pants. "What's wrong?"

He gathered their things and put his arm around her shoulder, turning her toward the door. "There's a camera in the room."

She went slack in his arms and he pulled her against him. He shouldn't have told her. He hadn't wanted to tell her. Making love to Caitie had been perfect. He'd hoped to leave her with a dreamy afterglow and a few things to smile about when she looked back on their night together. But now he'd tainted the memory of it for her.

He half carried, half walked her to the door. He wanted it to look as if they were still lovers, hurrying eagerly on to their next trysting place.

But he hadn't let Caitlin in on the plan. She planted her feet, forcing him to stop. Her cheeks were bright red. "Was it running when...?"

He knew she meant while they were making love. He had no answer for her. "I don't know. I can't even tell if it's running right now. All I know is it's aimed at the tub. There may be others."

She hugged herself so tightly her knuckles were turning white. "My father..."

Sean caught her face between his hands and commanded her attention. "Will never see a thing. You'll still be his good little girl. I promise."

"Sean, he won't just be shocked at seeing me on film. It could damage his reputation. And what about my brothers? Ethan's in diplomacy. He can't have a sister who—"

"We'll find the tape."

The worried lines between her brows relaxed a bit. "I love it when you say that *we* stuff." Bracing her hand at the center of his chest, she leaned forward and gave him a kiss. It was wet and soft and full of feeling. The simple enthusiasm in that grateful kiss left him feeling calmer, stronger—and much less sure of his jaded conceptions about women. "Let's go."

He grabbed her by the towel before she got out the door. "Fine, Mata Hari. But let's get some clothes on first."

13

"THE CIRCUS ROOM? You've got to be kidding."

Sean unlocked the door and stepped aside for Caitlin to enter. "It was the only room available, and we have to start somewhere."

"Sounds like our fellow guests are having a busy morning."

"Everybody gets their kicks somehow." His own sexual fantasies would always involve cars or shoes, and one very long pair of legs.

But he wasn't going to think along those lines right now. It was a new day and he was a new man with a new mission.

He had to be.

Sharing a bed with Caitlin last night had given him a fitful sleep. He hadn't minded the tangle of arms and legs as she tossed about in her sleep. What worried him was the way she quieted when he hugged her in his arms and nestled against her back. It was as if she belonged there, felt safe there. And he'd lain there trying to figure out why simply holding a trusting woman in his arms made him feel safe and contented as well.

He wanted his weekend with Caitlin to be about sex and work. Great sex. Fruitful work. He didn't want it to be about tender moments or guilty pleasures like burying his nose in the sweet, soft scent of her hair as she slept. Those were long-term indulgences. Silly, secret little habits that developed over the course of a relationship.

This was *not* a relationship. He wouldn't do that to Caitie. Relationships with him tanked. He either got caught up in his work or he shoved them by the wayside as he had with Elise. Caitlin deserved to be front and center in some good man's life, for the long haul. Not a weekend fling or aberration of judgment.

But, for the sake of her family and her own reputation as well as the two cases he'd come here to investigate in the first place, he was determined to get his head back into the game. Making love in the Waterworks Room had been a mistake—a perfect one, but a mistake nonetheless.

It left him thinking about Caitlin at unexpected moments. In the shower—would she be willing to join him? Packing his clothes away—would the T-shirt he'd given her to sleep in always carry her scent? Over room service coffee—was she always such an adorable little grumpy butt in the morning?

Would he be thinking of her when a clue presented itself? Would he be thinking of her when he came face-to-face with a perp and needed to defend himself? Or her?

No. He wouldn't allow it.

And even Caitlin's pretty figure, covered in those deliciously indecent shorts and T-shirt, wasn't going to distract him from the business at hand, either.

She stopped beside him and whispered in his ear. "Couldn't we just accidentally 'get lost' in the west wing and see what we can find there?"

He shook his head. "Fairchild told me he'd be working in his office this morning. But don't worry. We'll find a time and way to get there."

"It gives me the creeps to think of him watching me. Us." Her shoulders lifted and shook as a shiver ran through her body. "I don't know which grosses me out more—the idea of him getting his jollies by watching us, or knowing he thinks he can use it to influence us.'' She fluttered her hands. ''And I feel like I've been selfish. That tape could do as much damage to your career as it could mine.''

Sean closed his hand over her shoulder and kissed her cheek, already doubting his objectivity. ''It'll never get that far. I promise we'll find the tape and destroy it.'' As they'd plotted out their strategy that morning, they'd discussed that such a tape, if it existed, could be used to hurt her father or even damage her personal reputation and cost her her teaching license. Big bucks weren't always the goal of a blackmailer.

''Then I guess it's showtime.''

''Ladies first.''

Sean locked the door behind them and slipped the key into the pocket of his khaki slacks. The room was like an amusement park. Awnings with bright red-and-white stripes hung from the ceiling. Along one wall was a series of vending machines and arcade games—hot dogs and cotton candy, a baseball toss and a shooting gallery. At the center of the room hung a trapeze and a suspended cargo net. Farther along, he saw a mechanical horse. There was clown makeup and kiddie cars. There was even a whip and a cage and a lion's costume in one corner.

''This room feels more like Les and Candy's style,'' Caitlin suggested, petting the fake white fur that covered the horse. ''I wonder if they were in here last night. Do you think they…?''

She left the question unspoken, but Sean understood. They were looking for more hidden cameras and listening devices. Peepholes. Anything that would establish a pattern of invasion of privacy on Pleasure Cove Island. Anything that could be traced back to a source and lead them to a telecommunications network room and someone with a very voyeuristic hobby.

As they'd agreed beforehand, they would first start producing some kind of noise to serve as a distraction, and then conduct the search in such a way that, visually, they'd appear to be using the room for fun and pleasure.

He crossed over to her and tucked a honey-blond curl behind her ear. "Let's start turning on the games and rides."

She patted his cheek. "Got it, Chief."

Soon the room was a cacophony of grinding gears and a garish calliope rendition of "The Circus March." Private conversations would definitely not be a problem here. The investigation was back on track.

Caitlin watched Sean make a big production out of throwing baseballs at stacks of wooden milk bottles, drawing plenty of attention to himself while she scouted out the wall behind the arcade. When he awarded himself a giant stuffed kangaroo and handed it over to her, she accepted it with a dramatic kiss and reported her findings. "Nothing."

She sniffled and rubbed at the tip of her nose. "I've got an idea so we don't waste so much time."

"I'm listening."

"The camera last night was focused on the point where a couple would be most likely to do something naughty that could be caught on tape." She slowly turned, sweeping her gaze across the crowded room. "Where would a couple do it in here? On horseback?"

"In the lion's den?"

Their gazes swept around the room in opposite directions and connected in the center ring.

"The trapeze," they echoed together.

Looking like an eager couple discovering a new sex toy, they hurried arm in arm to the center of the room. "I don't get it." Caitlin traced her fingers across the horizontal steel bar and its suspension cables. "What's the—?" An unseen force tickled her nose. She turned her head and sneezed. "Excuse me."

"Bless you."

"Thanks." She patted her pockets, hunting for the tissue she usually carried with her. Duh. These shorts barely had enough denim for seams and a zipper. There were no pockets. "I don't suppose you have a handkerchief?" She sniffed again.

"Sorry. Not old-fashioned enough." He narrowed his eyes in a curious frown. "You okay?"

Her sinuses were plugging rapidly and her eyes were beginning to sting. "I must've stirred up some dust when I was checking behind the games."

"Do we need to go back to the room?"

"No." He was reverting to caveman protector again. "I'm fine. You have my inhaler in case I need it, though?"

He touched the pocket of his jeans. "Right here. Are you sure you're okay?"

"I'm fine." She stroked her fingers across his lips in a gesture that seemed to be as soothing to him as it was arousing to her. It would look pretty intimate to any audience who might be watching them, too. "Now wipe that frown off your face. Or someone might think we're having another quarrel."

He curled his lips in a toothy smile that made her laugh out loud. "Better?"

She'd never seen a silly side to Sean before. He'd been all about control from the moment he'd walked into her apartment. Even in their lovemaking, he'd been the one in charge—partly because he was the one with the experience, and partly because...well, she didn't really understand the other part. Something inside Sean hated when his emotions got away from him. It was as if he was giving in to a weakness of some kind. Was it a law enforcement thing? Having control over any given situation did add a large degree of security.

But making love wasn't a crime and she wasn't a criminal. There had to be something else going on in that rugged, temperamental head of his. Something that refused to allow him to just let go and be himself.

Making a face meant he was lowering his guard around her. She liked seeing that little inroad toward trusting her. It brought him that much closer to believing in her abilities—as a woman, a friend, a civilian partner…and a lover. Trusting her put him one step closer toward seeing the positive in life, instead of waking up every day with the expectation that he'd be hurt or disappointed. And she intended to do all she could to keep him on that journey toward enjoying life with the rest of the human race.

She puckered up her lips for a pouty kiss and pinched his cheek, playing right along with his goofy game. "Much better, punkin."

"No punkins, no pookies. Got it?"

Caitlin sneezed. "Got it, tough guy."

"Are you sure—?"

"Enough." She pushed the kangaroo into his arms and went back to work, reaching up to wrap her fingers around the trapeze bar and trying to figure things out. "I can see how this room would be a great place to play or unwind. But where does the sex theme come in?"

Tightening her grips she picked up her feet and swung forward. The instant she put her weight on the bar, a strobe light came on, bathing the whole center ring in a bright, sparkling glow.

Sean stopped the trapeze on the return swing, his attention focused on the ceiling. "Nice touch." When Caitlin stood up, the light went off. Sean pulled on the trapeze. The light came on. He released it. The light went off. He looked down at Caitlin. "I wonder if the observation devices get activated at the same time."

If that hypothesis was true, then the same theory could be applied to the Waterworks Room. To every room in the house! Caitlin hugged herself and leaned close to Sean. "If that's the case, then everything we did last night..." Her breath rushed out in a shameful sigh. "From the moment I pushed that button. All on tape."

His arm closed around her shoulders, infusing her with his abundant strength. "We don't know that for a fact yet."

"But that's what you think, too, isn't it? That someone videotaped us without our permission?"

He pressed a kiss to her temple instead of answering. "Get up on the trapeze."

"That sounded an awful lot like an order."

His dark green eyes squinted with impatience. "Please."

She rewarded his effort with a smile. "Okay."

Utilizing rusty skills from her backyard swing days, Caitlin grasped the trapeze in her hands, then curled her legs up and swung them over the bar. She climbed her hands up the ropes until she'd shifted her balance and was sitting on top. She threw one hand up into the air and shouted, "Ta-da!"

Sean watched her sway back and forth. "Nice moves, but let's keep this all looking real in case the cameras are on."

She sniffled and coughed to loosen the hint of heaviness that was settling in her chest. "So a trapeze is sexy, huh?" She kicked out her legs and started to swing, touching Sean's hair or face each time she got close. "I just don't get how."

Two powerful fists reached out and stopped the swing. "I get it."

Eye-level with her crotch, Sean's heated gaze made everything suddenly clear. He was looking straight at the goods.

"Oh." She reached down and stroked his hair, torn between wanting to spread her legs wider and invite him to work his magic on her as he had last night, and closing her legs like a proper lady and insisting they get back to their search. But as that familiar heat Sean's intense gaze inspired began to gather at her center, he looked away.

The camera. Caitlin's cheeks grew hot. It was all the reminder she needed to focus on the task at hand. He was an agent with an investigation to conduct. And she was his cover. They weren't really here to explore each fantasy theme in Douglas Fairchild's bawdy boudoirs.

Ignoring the raw physical and emotional needs of this man that kept calling to her, she flipped around on the bar and hung by her knees. "Is this better?"

His hand on her bare knee conveyed a silent agreement. So while Sean slowly circled her in the center of the room, looking for a camera pointed their way, she hummed along with the high-volume rendition of "March of the Toreadors" blaring from a hidden speaker.

She hated the idea that had popped into her head almost as much as the wheezing sound that made her voice raspy. "You know, Sean, if there is a tape, maybe we shouldn't destroy it."

"We'll destroy it," he answered, his vow to protect her as solid as ever.

She cleared her throat. "But wouldn't it be evidence you could use against that kidnapper? Or to help solve that murder? If someone taped us, then surely other guests have been recorded, too."

"I won't use you that way."

"But if you need it to make your case—"

"No." He'd moved halfway around the circle now, his intense focus trained anywhere but on her. "We'll find something else."

"It might not be that easy." She gripped Sean's thighs to stop her swinging.

"Caitie…" His growled demand betrayed the same physical impulses she'd been trying to ignore. Hanging upside down like this, her face was just about level with *his* goods. Now that she understood the concept, all sorts of possibilities for a raunchy circus act flitted into her brain.

But the excitement of her sudden discovery helped her keep everything in focus. Looking right between his legs toward the wall, near the lighted makeup table and the rack of circus costumes, she saw it. "The camera," she whispered.

She flipped her feet over her head and dismounted. She grabbed on to Sean's arm to steady herself until the dizziness of being right side up again passed. But as soon as her head was clear, his arms were around her. "Show me."

Wrapping her own arms around his neck to ensure the believability of walking straight toward the camera, she backed toward the wall, swishing her hips as if she'd issued an invitation to join her on the makeup table. When her thighs butted against the table, she stopped. "It's right underneath us."

"Okay. Let's slowly work our way down to the floor so I can get a clear look." She nodded in understanding and surrendered her strength to Sean's hands as he went down on his knees. He slid his hands over her bottom and squeezed for the camera's benefit. "Just a little more."

As Caitlin lay down on the floor beside him, she sneezed. She sneezed again. "Sorry." Her lungs seized up and her eyes watered and she sneezed a third time.

"Caitie." Concern as much as physical frustration sharpened his voice and turned his grip around her waist from sexual to sympathetic. "Something's wrong with you."

She sat up and frowned in apology. "I'm sorry." Her

voice sounded nasal. "I have an antihistamine in my purse in the room. I'd better go get it. I usually don't have this severe a reaction unless I'm around one of my allergy triggers."

A low, moaning cry caught their attention. Caitlin sniffled and tried to hold her breath. There it was again.

A meow.

Sean hiked her up onto his lap. His mouth creased in a wry smile of amusement and frustration. "Like a cat?"

Caitlin nodded. "Where's it coming from?"

The cat meowed again.

"Sounds like it's here in the room."

"Kitty?" Caitlin crawled off his lap and looked under the table. "Here, kitty, kitty." She checked behind the costumes. "Kitty, kitty. Where are you?"

The meowing got louder in response to her calls, and Sean homed in on the sound. "Over here."

He'd traced it to the hot dog machine. Caitlin knelt down beside him. Another sinus-shaking sneeze told her he'd found the source of her allergy attack. From behind a ventilation register in the wall came the plaintive cries of an unhappy feline.

"Oh, poor baby." Sean lifted the grate from its frame and a long-haired cat, whose snow-white fur was matted with a dingy coat of dust and grease, jumped into Caitlin's waiting arms. "It's Candy Truitt's cat."

Her nose and lungs reacted immediately to a fresh assault of cat dander. Sean took the feline from her hands and handed her the inhaler instead. "Here. Can you use it before your asthma gets as bad as it was on the ship?"

Caitlin nodded and walked across the room into relatively cleaner air, where she took her medication. Sean, on the other hand, whom she never would have pegged as a cat man, held the critter in his arms and scratched its ears while he…crawled around on the floor?

"What are you doing?" she asked from across the room, giving her lungs a chance to recover before going near the cat again.

"He came here for the food, but how'd he get in?" Sean was poking at something next to the grate. "Candy wouldn't forget and leave him in here overnight."

"I think she likes Snowflake better than Les, don't you?"

Instead of an answer, Sean jumped to his feet and snagged a handful of costumes off the rack. He tossed one to her, threw another over his shoulder and dropped the third one beneath the makeup table.

Caitlin stared at the sequined acrobat's costume in her hands. Hadn't he promised this morning would be all work and absolutely no play? "Um, should I put this on?"

He shook his head. "Just making it look good." He draped a ringmaster's jacket over the front of the table. "Now they'll think we were playing dress-up and got carried away—tearing off our clothes and accidentally covering the camera lens."

"And we want them to think this because…?"

"Because I don't want them to know I found this."

He crouched in front of the grate where Snowflake had been trapped, and reached inside the opening. A few seconds later, she detected the hum of a machine beneath the din of calliope music.

A section of paneling, two feet wide from ceiling to floor, moved. It slid behind the drape of an awning and revealed a black hole in the wall.

"A hidden passageway?" It was every cloak-and-dagger fantasy of hers come true. "We get to check it out, right?"

Oh please, please, please?

He smiled a wicked grin. "After you."

"THIS PLACE IS A DAMN maze," Sean muttered into the blackness. The only certainties in this long, narrow passageway were the wall he trailed with his right hand, and Caitlin's hand clutched in his left. "I should have gone back for a flashlight."

"Wouldn't that have looked suspicious?"

"Yeah." He jammed his shoulder into another junction box and swore. "You'd think this place was built for pygmies."

"Relax, tough guy." Though he couldn't make out her face in the darkness, Caitlin's husky voice calmed his frustration. "This tunnel has to lead somewhere. Snowflake didn't just materialize behind that grate. He had to get in from another room."

Sean figured they'd covered about fifty feet, judging from the number of steps he'd taken. After the first few feet, they'd taken a sharp turn and had been moving in a straight line ever since. "I guess we just keep walking."

Though extensively remodeled, Fairchild's estate was an old mansion built when the Industrial Age had first hit American shores, creating hundreds of instant millionaires who wanted to show off their wealth. It wasn't that unusual to have these servant's hallways built in to allow swift, unseen passage from room to room to light fires or turn down a bed. In more recent years, the tunnels served as ready-made conduits to run modern pipes and electrical wires.

Or the feeds and power supply for audio-visual equipment.

Caitlin tugged against his hand and he stopped. "What's that up ahead?"

Either his eyes were playing tricks on him or there was a faint glow in the hallway ahead of them. Sean set off again toward the possible exit, but a shrieking caw sound stopped him in his tracks. Caitlin plowed into his shoulder, but he stood fast. She huddled right behind him. It had been too high-pitched to be the cat again. "Did you hear that?"

The fingers of one hand clenched more tightly round his own. Her other hand latched on to his shoulder. Her lips were a ticklish caress against his ear. "It sounded like a bird. A big parrot or macaw."

"Maybe the cat's after it," he reasoned, though he'd seen no indication of any pets on the estate other than Candy Truitt's.

Another shriek, louder and more frenzied than the first, echoed through the passageway. Sean's defensive instincts fired in his blood.

"That sounded human," Caitlin murmured.

"Let's go." With senses sharpened by the rush of adrenaline, Sean hurried toward the muffled sound. Closer to the muted light, he could make out more of their surroundings. The unfinished walls. The dusty plank floor. The layout of mechanized pulleys and hinges that indicated another hidden door like the one he'd found in the Circus Room.

"What is it?" Caitlin asked, her voice no more than a breathless whisper.

"You doing okay?"

"Sure. Why'd we stop?"

"I think I'm onto something. Don't go anywhere." Sean released her hand and traced the outline of the door with his fingers. The Circus Room had had a latch hidden at the bottom of the panel. He stooped down, feeling his way along the wall to locate another ventilation grate and switch.

Caitlin had figured out what he'd found, too. "Do you think someone's in trouble in there?" He heard the bird call again, louder this time.

Without enough space to pass around him, Caitlin was blocked by his crouching body. When Sean felt her knee dig into his arm, he realized she was trying to climb over him. He grabbed her leg and arm and pulled her back to the ground, then rose to his feet. "Where do you think you're going?"

"I want to see where the light's coming from." She pointed past his shoulder. "If it's a crack in the wall, then that means the light's from one of the theme rooms. Shouldn't we look before we barge in?" She settled her hands on his shoulders, calming him and urging him to action at the same time. "I know you're a big, macho superhero and all. But you don't have your gun. If something's happening in there, I don't want you to get hurt."

Someone screamed from the other side of the wall—a man in terrible agony.

Sean backed up to the light source—a long, thin crack that followed the grain of the wood. He closed one eye, blinked through the dust and focused. Caitlin scooted his legs aside and knelt in front of him, catching a peek herself.

"Damn."

Les Truitt, naked as the day he was born, stood on a raised platform above a forest of artificial trees, pounding his gray-haired chest and yodeling a version of the Tarzan yell that wouldn't even call pigs back to the barn. When he reached for a vine and swung down to the floor where Candy sat fluffing her hair, Sean had to look away.

Caitlin already had her back to the wall, her arms hugging her legs to her chest. "I could have lived my entire life without seeing that."

He pressed his back to the wall above her. "I never thought the old coot had it in him."

"No wonder he's already gone through four wives."

"Caitie." He touched her shoulder to turn her attention to their left. Snowflake had followed them down the passageway. But with the same indifference as his platinum-haired mistress, he strolled right past them, jumped up onto a knee-high ledge and squeezed past a loose board back into the Jungle Room.

But Sean wasn't interested in the cat. He stooped down beside Caitie to get a closer look at the recessed shelf. On it was a tiny video camera, its red light blinking. He traced the wires from the back of the camera up into a metal conduit. He followed that past the next wall stud and found a junction box.

The circuitry was simple enough to figure out. This box wasn't powering anything in the room on the other side of that wall. Grasping the rubber-coated wires in his fist, he yanked them out the box, killing the red running light on the camera.

"Sean." Caitlin's fingers closed around his forearm, transmitting her concern. "Won't that alert whoever's watching at the other end?"

"It's Lester's fantasy. The man deserves his privacy."

They all did.

"You think all those other boxes you hit—?"

"Are powering other cameras? Yes. The Jungle Room is at the end of the hall closest to the common area." Sean swiped his hand across his jaw, doing the calculations as he mentally retraced their path. "That means every room is being watched. There are enough spy holes and hidden cameras back here to make this a voyeur's paradise."

"Is that enough evidence to solve your case?"

"It's enough evidence to get a search warrant." Even if he couldn't connect it to the Reyes or Vargas cases, there was something seriously twisted and wrong going on at Pleasure Cove Island. "Come on, we'd better get back and cover our tracks in the Circus Room."

But Caitlin, of course, was already headed the opposite way. "If this is the end of the hall, where does the rest of the tunnel go?"

"With this many electronic feeds, there has to be a command room."

"Fairchild's office? Should we check it out?"

Sean snaked out his hand and caught her around the wrist, stopping her from going any farther. "I need to make a phone call first."

"There aren't any phones on the island."

He needed Caitlin, her natural curiosity and her overblown craving for adventure, tucked away safe and sound in their room before he did this. "There's a binful of cellphones stored somewhere on this estate, and there's the ship-to-shore radio."

"None of which Mr. Fairchild will give you permission to use."

Sean pulled her to his side and started back toward the Circus Room. "I don't intend to ask."

14

"SEX SOUNDS?"

Caitlin sat on a pile of bright silk pillows on the floor of the Harem Room and watched Sean pull off his turban and stuff a flashlight and some sort of manicure set into his jeans. The sweeping background music of *Scheherazade* didn't fit his villainous tough-guy image at all.

She jammed her fingers into her hair and swept if off her forehead. "I thought we were working together."

Their morning had been productive, discovering the secret passageway and hidden cameras. They'd nibbled on fruit and cheese and each other in their private room over lunch, planning how they'd make contact with the outside world and alert Sean's partner to their suspicions about Douglas Fairchild.

They'd been a team. Equals. But Sean's latest plan sounded like a dubious setup to get her out of the way.

And a surefire setup to get him into trouble.

"I can't do this without you," he insisted, double-checking that the tent flap he'd secured in front of the camera lens would stay in place. "I'm counting on you to make it sound like we're still in here together so no one questions my disappearance. Don't worry. I'll be back in time to change for dinner."

"How long will that be?" She stood up and adjusted the ridiculously low waistline of her sheer silk harem pants. "I mean, you might be the greatest lover I've ever had, but even you can't keep me oohing and aahing for an hour.''

"It's mmms and ohs."

His uncharacteristic smile made her suspicious. "What is?"

"The sounds you make." He gathered her into his arms and stroked his fingers across her throat. "It starts off as a little purr right here."

"Mmm."

He dipped his head and kissed that spot, tracing his tongue along the hot pulse beneath her skin. "Then, as you really get into it, you start adding vowels."

Caitlin smoothed her palms over his hair and then gripped his head, savoring the tantalizing friction of his tongue and tawny beard stubble along her sensitive throat. She felt powerful. Beautiful. Sexy. When he held her this way, the strength of his body made her proud of her own, the gentleness of his hands made her feel cherished, the neediness of his mouth made her feel...loved.

"Ohh."

It was an almost painful realization. She snagged her hands into his hair and brought his mouth up to her own to claim him. To demand answers. How much of Sean's tenderness and teaching and gruff honesty and shielding protectiveness was the job? And how much was the man himself? How much about this kiss and all the others was about catching the bad guys? And how much was about her? About them?

His hands slipped down the bare skin of her back and settled possessively on her derriere. He kissed her lips, her cheek, her neck. He kissed her lower, down in the low-cut cleavage of her blue silk harem bra.

"Sean..." She gasped for a breath. "Umm..."

She knew he cared about her. It was evident in his concern about her health, in his efforts to ask instead of order, in the careful, thorough way he made love to her.

But did caring necessarily lead to love?

He'd given her everything she'd ever wished for in her fantasy world and more. He'd given her the chance to be herself without holding back, without apology. But after only forty-eight hours could she dare call that inexplicable longing she felt in her soul love?

Did she really know what she was feeling?

She didn't even know what sounds she uttered when she made love.

But she understood the synchronicity of their bodies as Sean carried her down to the pillows with him. The Harem Room seemed to be the least high-tech of all the theme rooms. But she didn't need any special effects to experience the magic of Sean's hands and mouth. Every cell of her body seemed to suddenly recall with vivid clarity each place, each way, he'd touched her.

She clung to his shoulders as the weight of his body pressed into hers, molding to her breasts and settling between the cradle of her thighs, teasing her with the glorious differences between man and woman, reminding her of all the wonderful things he'd taught her about her own body and about pleasure. His mouth grazed along the curve of her shoulder, his hand clutched possessively at the bare skin of her hip.

She was melting. Falling. Wanting.

"Oh." Her breath eased out in a panting sigh. "Oh."

He smiled against her skin. "And then, if I remember my grammar correctly, you top it off with a couple of interjections when you come."

"Interjections?" She struggled to find some oxygen and turn her mind back to the conversation.

Sean rose up on his elbows above her, drawing back from

the languid seduction with a rueful smile. "That is the right term, isn't it? The fact that you're an English teacher makes me a little nervous."

"*I* make *you* nervous?" Right. The pit bull was afraid of the pussycat.

For a moment, his eyes went to a distant place. Then they focused back on her face with their familiar intensity. He stroked his fingers into the hair at her temple.

"You have no idea." He leaned down and kissed her hard, a swift, desperate, punctuated farewell.

In one fluid motion he rolled off of her, climbed to his feet and walked to the secret door. "If I'm not back in thirty minutes, go back to the room. If anyone questions you about me, just play dumb. Pretend you have no idea what I'm up to or why I'm really here. I know that'll be hard for a brainy lady like you. But I have confidence you can play the part."

Caitlin was slower to sit up and process the perfunctory directions. Still rattled by the aching poignancy of that kiss, she hugged a big pillow to herself and tried to find some humor in sending him off to sneak behind enemy lines. "Play dumb, huh? That'd be about halfway between Priscilla Doe and Candy Truitt?"

"That's the idea." He stopped at the opening into the hidden passageway. His piercing green eyes swept over her with a look that was as vivid and skin-tingling as a physical caress. It commanded, it comforted and it offered something more. Something she had neither the intuition nor experience to truly understand. "I'll be back in thirty."

"You'd better." She stood and offered him a game smile. "Be careful."

Caitlin clutched the pillow more tightly and watched him disappear. She stared at the empty space for more than a minute, trying not to place any symbolism on the dark hole or any significance on the sudden trepidation she felt.

But then she roused herself from her self-defeating stupor and went and closed the secret panel as per their plan. She was dependable Caitlin McCormick—a general's daughter, a respected teacher, an all-around good gal. For a few bright, shining hours she'd been more than that. Seductress. Secret agent.

But it was that solid core of strength on which she now drew. She was responsible for keeping Sean safe. Right now that was all that mattered. She wouldn't disappoint him.

She tossed the pillow high into the air. "Whee-ee!"

She surveyed the empty room that had been decorated with bright, colorful silks to resemble a harem tent. Piled on the floor were enough pillows to furnish an entire furniture store.

Caitlin dived into the middle of it all and began to play. "Oh, Sean!" she yelled for the benefit of anyone who might overhear. "You shouldn't!"

And then she hummed and ummed and interjected until she was hoarse.

PLAY DUMB, HUH? Just how did self-respecting women do that?

It was thirty minutes later on the dot, according to her Snoopy watch. Sean was lost inside the maze or being held at gunpoint by Jeffrey and Bert or lying unconscious at the base of one of the island's steep cliffs. And she was just supposed to go back to their room and play dumb?

She had to do something. She had to help.

General Hal McCormick would go straight to the head honcho and demand answers to Sean's whereabouts. Major Ethan McCormick would launch a full-scale investigation. Captain Travis McCormick would go in by stealth of night and come out—guns blazing, if necessary—with a freed hostage by dawn.

What could Ms. Caitlin McCormick do?

She believed Sean to be a man of his word, absolutely. If he wasn't here when he said he would be, then something must have gone wrong.

Caitlin had played this scenario out in her head a dozen times back in the private confines of her car or apartment in Virginia. The grizzled soldier of fortune, who had been kind to the spunky street urchin with the clever mind and heart of gold, was in trouble, and she—intrepid sidekick that she was—would rise to the occasion. With her street smarts and wily ways and secret crush, she'd devise a plan to not only rescue the reluctant hero, but help him see her in a new light. The fantasy always ended with a grand, exultant kiss.

But this wasn't Virginia. She didn't have street smarts. And despite her claim that she wanted nothing more than a naughty weekend fling, she was feeling something considerably more intense than a crush on Sean.

Suddenly, the fantasy wasn't playing out so well. Real fear was twisting in her gut. A man had been murdered. Sean could be in real danger if the killer was here on the island. She'd forgo the final kiss if only she knew that he was safe.

She pushed aside the untouched box of bonbons on the pillow beside her and stood. "What do you do now, McCormick?" She willed the rational side of her brain to kick in. "What do you do?"

If the situation was reversed, Sean would come find her.

She looked over at the secret panel leading into the hidden passageway behind each room. How many times had she demanded a chance to take care of her own problems, and been denied? But no one had ever gotten her on her case for taking care of someone else.

The spunky kid inside her smiled.

Armed with nothing more than her inhaler and some attitude, Caitlin opened the passageway door and slipped into the dark.

CAITLIN COUNTED OFF junction boxes as she passed each room—Harem, Dungeon, Circus, North Pole, Waterworks, Jungle—before taking a deep breath and plunging into the unknown. Sean had surmised that the tunnel ran beneath the main part of the estate and came back up in the west wing.

"Sean?" She descended the rickety wooden stairs down into the darkness and prayed he hadn't fallen and broken his neck. As she diligently followed the stairs up on the other side, she breathed a sigh that was both relief and torture. No Sean, thus far. No Sean.

The passageway floor evened out as she slipped into the far wing of the house. Every shard of light drew her like a moth to the flame—cracks in the walls, natural peepholes carved out by bugs or mice or the decay of time. She peeked through at each opportunity, hoping she wouldn't find Sean tied up—or worse.

The first crack she peered through revealed Ramona Fairchild's boutique. Caitlin next found a bathroom, a boiler room and—bingo!—command central.

She hadn't been following the trail of wires and pipes the way Sean would have done, but with all the electronic hardware and storage cabinets housed in this one teeny space, it had to be the monitor and recording unit for all the microphones and videotapes on the premises.

Sean would have come here to look for a way to get a message off the island. And then what? Exit into the hallway on the opposite side of the room? Follow the passageway on to wherever its destination might be? Get captured?

A good detective would follow the path of the clues. If Sean had gone in there, then so would she. The room was deserted now, and its only light came through an outside window. The door was closed. All she had to do was go in, look around for any signs of Sean, and hightail it back out of there.

Simple enough plan.

Feeling her way around the gear work framing the door, she found the switch and pressed it. It slid open with an alarmingly loud grinding sound. Caitlin pressed back against the cobwebby wall, hiding herself from any curious passersby who might come check it out.

A minute later, she wheezed out a tense sigh. Great. Just great. After her run-in with the cat, her lungs were going to be particularly sensitive to other allergens until her meds worked through her system and she had a chance to rest. She used a puff from her inhaler to quiet her breathing, then sneaked into the room.

It was like a mini television studio. Eight monitors lined one wall, six labeled, as she'd suspected, with the names of the theme rooms. Each of those was turned off. The seventh flashed random pictures from various parts of the estate—the empty dock, the front and back entrances, the foyer. Though it was clearly a security monitor, there didn't seem to be anything to secure. The entire estate looked deserted. She hoped it was a testament of the Fairchilds' hospitality that all the guests and staff were so busy, and not anything more sinister.

She watched the images go past again. No sign of Sean.

Instead of relief, her concern edged up a notch. She pushed the button on the Harem Room monitor to see if he had returned. Her breath rushed out in frustration at the gray screen. Of course, they'd covered the lens to hide their activities. He could be back there and she wouldn't even know it.

"Damn." She borrowed his favorite swear word to ease her growing fear.

Time to move on.

The eighth monitor was hooked up to a VCR. There was an unmarked tape loaded inside. More curious than wise, she glanced over her shoulder to make sure she was alone, and pressed the play button.

Static gave way to a snowy image. Through the snowstorm of interference she could make out movement in the background. But the images were too fuzzy to be distinct. Caitlin almost laughed. If this was the quality of tape being used for blackmail, then it must be a pretty poor business.

The nervous need to laugh vanished when she realized it wasn't the quality of the tape that gave it that snowy look. It was the image recorded on the tape itself. And it wasn't snow.

"Oh, no."

She hugged her arms around her waist. Water. Splashing water. The light in the background gradually brightened and the force of water lessened its intensity, bringing the images into focus. Muscles clenched between her thighs as the erotic silent movie unfolded before her. A broad, muscular back. A nice, tight arch of bare butt. "No." Tawny hair. "Oh, no."

Red shoes.

"Oh, my God!" She couldn't breathe in. It was the tape. Her tape. Sean. Water.

She knocked aside a technical handbook, wires and papers in her haste to push the off button. With her mind working faster than her hands could follow, she upset and righted almost every object on the worktable in her haste to eject the tape and tuck it into the waistband of her pants. Caitlin spent precious, frantic seconds trying to remember where every item had been positioned, then straightening and moving them back into place.

Her breath came in short, quick spurts as the biggest glitch of all stared her right in the face. Would someone notice the tape was missing?

Darting around the room, she opened drawers and cabinets in search of another cassette. She opened up a cabinet directly across from the monitors and froze in shock. She hadn't found one tape. She'd found hundreds. Scads of them, all lined up in meticulous order, all labeled and numbered—10-31, 12-31, 2-14, 5-23, 5-30. Were they dates?

Caitlin's frenzy of panic abated as the import of what she was seeing set in. When she'd agreed to help Sean, she'd never expected she'd actually find evidence. That her quest for a real-life fantasy would include actually helping the FBI solve a case.

She spread her hand across her chest and rubbed gentle circles there, calming her body's tightening reaction. Her father would be so proud. But how could she tell him? It was top secret.

She had to keep everything about this weekend secret. The mission. Sean. Falling in love.

"Oh damn."

Did top secret mean she couldn't see Sean again? After all the trouble she'd caused this weekend, would he even want to see her?

I'm not relationship material.

"Oh damn."

Before the panic flared out of control, she turned her focus back to the task at hand. Replace the tape. Get the hell out of here.

She lifted a sheaf of papers to pick up a tape that lay underneath since it likely wouldn't immediately be noticed if it was out of place. Then the papers themselves caught her eye. The same numbers that were on the tapes had been neatly typed there, and each was followed by a list of names. *12-31, Adams, Bennington, Keeler-Jones, Turner, Vargas.*

"Vargas?" That was the name of Sean's murdered ambassador.

And Turner? Ali Turner?

"I'm not going to fix your damn cameras for you!"

The loud voice echoing in the hall startled her. Caitlin clamped her lips together to keep from crying out.

"Shh." There was a muffled response she couldn't make out, but then, she didn't have time to concentrate. She snatched the tape and closed the cabinet door, then dashed over to the VCR and jammed it in. Hearing footsteps coming closer, she punched off all the monitors and ducked into the passageway.

"I thought I was here to screw my wife this time, not play handyman."

Oh, damn, damn, damn. The security monitor had been on.

Caitlin ran back in and turned it on, toppling that damn handbook again as she did. She hastily tossed it back on top of a stack of papers on the desk, gave the pile two scoots to straighten it up and dove back into the passageway.

She pressed the switch and flashed all kinds of body English to beg the grinding gears to move faster.

Caitlin leaned into the shadows of the passageway and held her breath. The panel slipped into place. The outside door opened.

Too petrified to move for fear of making a sound that would reveal her presence, she unwittingly eavesdropped on the voices inside.

"Look, John." John? As in John Doe? She thought the angry voice had sounded familiar. "It's too good an opportunity to pass up."

That was a woman's voice, too soft-spoken to identify.

John's angry voice carried just fine. "If they're onto you, then give it up. You've got enough money."

The woman kept her voice low and calm. "If it's up for me, it's up for you. Now find out what's wrong with the cameras and fix them."

Was that his wife, Priscilla? Caitlin hadn't seen John with anyone else since boarding the ferry at New Harbor.

The door slammed. Caitlin jumped.

"Bitch." John expressed his fervent opinion, rattled around in the room for about two minutes, then left.

When the door slammed again, Caitlin exhaled.

A hand closed over her mouth and dragged her back into the shadows, and in an instant she was caught in the unyielding vise of two strong arms. Her heart stopped, then exploded. She screamed against the hand and kicked and jabbed and—

"Shush, Caitie. It's me."

Sean's deep, hushed voice whispered with crystalline clarity in her ear.

The blood drained from her head to her toes as overwhelming relief made her light-headed. The second his hold on her eased, she spun around and threw herself into his arms. Clutching him tightly around the neck, she lifted herself up onto her toes and hugged him with her whole body.

"I thought you were hurt." Almost in tears, she sobbed her fears against his ear.

His arms closed around her for precious seconds.

But then she pulled away. She stepped back against his hands and punched his shoulder for scaring her so. "I thought you were hurt."

She heard his sigh. "So, naturally, you went looking for me right under the bad guys' noses." He turned on a tiny flashlight and shined it near her face. "Are you all right?"

She nodded and wondered if the tight lines of strain beside his mouth were caused by anger or something else. "Are you?"

"I'm fine. Let's go."

Well, if he was fine and she was fine, then there was nothing left to hold back the adrenaline rush that was cascading through her body in electric torrents. "Oh, Sean." She snagged the sleeve of his T-shirt to stop him. "I found the tape of us." She patted its cold bulk at her hip. "I took it. I replaced it with another one. There's a list of names in there. Ramon Vargas—"

"You can fill me in on the details later. Let's get back to the room before we're missed."

Without saying or allowing another word, he took her by the hand and pulled her unerringly along in the darkness. With his flashlight to guide them through the intricate darkness, he slowed only for the stairs.

They burst back into the Harem Room and Sean closed the panel behind them. As Caitlin's eyes readjusted to the light, she saw that the triceps of his right arm, from shoulder to elbow, was all scratched up. She rushed to his side and inspected the bloody wound. "You *are* hurt."

He smoothly turned, pulling his arm from her grasp. "It's just a scrape." In the same fluid motion, he patted her butt and urged her toward the door. "Let's turn in the key and get back to our room to clean up so we're not late for dinner."

"What happened?"

"I was hanging from a cliff."

"What?" If that emotionless brute was sugarcoating the pain he'd gone through, just to protect her feelings, then she'd... "Sean." She turned and braced her hands on his shoulders to stop him.

"I found the cellphones stored in Fairchild's office. There

must be some kind of dampening field in the structure of the house—probably on the ferry, too. That's why I couldn't call out. I had to hike out to the north point of the island to get a clear signal.'' The tension that radiated from him like that of a chained wild beast did little to reassure her of his safety. ''Bert came by. I guess it's a routine patrol. I scrambled down beneath an overhanging ledge so he wouldn't see me.''

Caitlin lifted her hand to brush that stray lock of hair off his forehead, soothing him and thanking him for his patience in assuaging her fear. ''Did you get a hold of your partner?''

He nodded. ''Thomas will be here tomorrow with a search warrant and backup. We just have to lie low and not draw any attention to ourselves until then.''

''I thought this would all be fun.'' She pulled her hands back into a protective hug. ''I'm scared, Sean.''

The hardened special agent beast relaxed his guarded stance and folded her in his arms. She wound hers around his waist and held on tight, absorbing every shred of comfort and strength he offered, snuggling closer to offer her own in return.

He kissed her temple and nuzzled his nose beside her ear. ''We got the proof we were looking for. Enough to open up an official investigation of Pleasure Cove Island and Douglas Fairchild. That'll keep Alicia Reyes's kidnapper in jail until he goes to trial, and give us a damn good motive for the Vargas murder.'' Sean pulled back just enough to see her face, and caressed her with the warm, fervent glow of his beautiful green eyes. ''You did great, Agent McCormick. Now all we have to worry about is having some fun.''

DOUGLAS FAIRCHILD WANTED to play another dinner game.

It had been a torturous forty-five minutes already as each person sitting at the table shared a noncommittal report on the past twenty-fours of their stay. Caitlin suspected there were far more stories than the ones Douglas was able to draw out of his guests.

She took another bite of her twice-baked potato and wondered at the wrist brace Les Truitt was wearing. Her cheeks heated at the awkward memory of the dear old boy enjoying his visit—and his wife—with unrestrained enthusiasm.

What would it be like to love someone—to love life—with that no-holds-barred attitude? Now there was a true adventure, an example of life lived to its fullest. What would it be like to be loved so completely? She idly wondered if Candy Truitt knew how lucky she was.

A foot nudged Caitlin's under the table. She glanced up and read the unspoken question in Sean's eyes. He would have noticed her blush and wondered at its cause. But she could do nothing more to share her thoughts than let her eyes angle toward Les. Sean's eyes followed and he smiled, sharing the memory of what they'd witnessed today.

"On each card I have five categories."

Caitlin turned her attention to their host again when she realized Douglas was explaining the rules of the game.

"Romantic getaways, sexual positions, sex words, famous lovers and toys. And I don't mean toy trucks and dolls."

Ali Turner took a sip of her wine. "Douglas, that sounds positively intellectual."

General Whitmore raised his glass in a toast to her. "The brain *is* the real sex organ, Ali."

Ali? When had the two of them gotten so chummy? Caitlin buried her face behind her hand as she felt her cheeks heating up again. She didn't really want to know the answer to that, did she?

"Who wants to go first?" asked Douglas. Tonight he

sported a Hawaiian shirt made of black silk with gold thread. Must be a formal occasion. "John?"

But John wasn't talking, not even to Priscilla. Was she the woman Caitlin had heard him arguing with? The two had barely had their hands off each other the entire visit, and now they were steadfastly avoiding each other's gaze. Was it just a lovers' tiff? Was she jealous that her newlywed husband had been called away by another woman to do some electrical work? Young Priscilla looked too pouty and spoiled and innocent to be running a blackmail ring.

Maybe he'd been arguing with Ramona Fairchild. She'd know her way around the estate.

Denise Fenton? Too quiet and unassuming. Or was that the perfect cover?

And Caitlin had seen Ali Turner's name on two of the tapes. Was she another victim? Or the brains behind this operation?

A second too late, the nudge on her foot registered.

"Caitlin, that leaves you."

"For what?"

Douglas patted her hand and gave her an indulgent smile. "Ladies first, we decided." The pat on the hand became a lingering squeeze. "Get your question right and you get a key."

The sexual trivia game. Oh joy.

"What happens if I get it wrong?"

Douglas laughed, gesturing widely to include everyone. "Then we'll have a marvelous discussion of all the possible answers."

Caitlin set down her fork and braced herself to either look foolish or burn up from embarrassment. She could ace a regular trivia game. But even with all the strides she'd made in her sexual education this weekend, she felt like a novice. "Let's hear it, then."

"Choose a number between one and five."

"Three."

"The category is..." he smacked his lips in suspenseful anticipation "...famous lovers."

Her stomach settled after an appropriate round of oohs and ahhs and a mad brainstorm between Pod and Ali to list as many famous lovers as possible. Douglas read the question.

"How many lovers did Don Juan claim to have seduced? Fewer than one hundred. Hundreds. Thousands."

Dissolute Spanish nobleman. A tragic romantic figure written of in epic poetry and classic drama, and studied by almost every English major in the country. An early favorite in Caitlin's adult fantasy repertoire.

She couldn't help smiling. She and Sean wouldn't have to play this stupid game or spend any more time with this odd assortment of people—at least two of whom were involved in a bawdy blackmail scheme. They could win a key and leave the table.

And have one more beautiful night together.

She let the triumph light her expression as she looked straight at Sean. "Hundreds."

"Choose your key."

15

"YOU COULDN'T WAIT to get out of there, could you."

Sean tossed the key, along with his jacket and tie, onto the table next to the suit of armor that stood beside the door. The Dungeon Room. With its whips and chains and racks and wheels and dark, moody lighting, it lived up to its hedonistic reputation.

Caitlin was already exploring the possibilities. "Who would you rather spend time with—those old fuddy-duddies or me?"

"Is that a trick question?"

They kept up the teasing banter long enough for Sean to pinpoint the camera lens on the back wall. He'd wanted to disable all the cameras this afternoon, but that would have raised too many suspicions. So, for now, he'd stick with plan B. He whipped a leather cape over his shoulders, then let it fall in front of the camera to block its shot of the room.

"Look. There's a first-aid kit next to the basket of condoms. What do you suppose that means?"

"That we have to be very careful."

Sean came up behind her, braced his hands on her hips and nipped at the curve of her bare shoulder. He nibbled featherlight kisses at the nape of her neck, then worked his way across to her other shoulder. She shivered at the caress of heat against her skin, and Sean moved in closer, wrapping his arms around her waist and abdomen and pulling her tight, round bottom into his burgeoning heat. His reaction to her was instantaneous and potent.

Delicate nibbles gave way to wet, openmouthed kisses against the delicate cordons of her neck. He slipped his hand to her breast and kneaded her through the black elastic sheath she called a top. ''Mmm, Sean.''

It was a plea for mercy and a breathless invitation. She stumbled forward and propped her hands against the counter. Sean moved with her, trapping her between the cabinet and his hips. He nudged aside her silky hair, drinking in its subtle, tangy scent while he played with her ear. As she shifted to escape the tickle there, she rotated her hips. Sean groaned against her skin at the unwitting caress and ground his hips into her bottom.

Would it always be like this with her? Fast? Furious? Out of control? Two days ago she'd been an innocent in the arts of seduction. He hadn't been the most creative teacher, but she was a quick study. A prodigy. And now she'd graduated into a living, breathing, combustible siren—a woman whose long-limbed grace was a feast for the eyes, whose body moved and responded as if it had been made just for his. A woman whose quirky personality and stubborn determination shook up his hardened soul.

Needing to claim her as badly as he needed his next breath, Sean turned her and lifted her onto the counter. He spread her legs and walked between them, shoving aside that wild tiger-print skirt and reaching for her panties.

''Sean, wait.''

He tried to slow things down by reaching for a condom. But she didn't make it easy, tangling her fingers in his hair and rubbing her soft cheek against his coarser one. ''Caitie.'' He unbuttoned his shirt and guided her hands to the quaking, needy skin of his chest. ''We don't need any special gadgets to be great.''

"I know." Her hands splayed across his pecs. "Sean." He stole a kiss. "Wait." He stole another. And then she pushed. "I want to try something."

He backed off half a step, giving her the space she'd requested. But her hands stayed on him, rising and falling with each fevered breath. "You mean one of your fantasies?"

"In a way."

That sounded odd. He narrowed his focus, trying to decipher the message in her dark, smoky eyes. Was it the room? "I refuse to whip you or do anything to hurt you, if that's what you're asking."

"I know you wouldn't hurt me. And I don't see any thrill in physically harming you, either."

She brushed a strand of hair off his forehead and stroked his sensitized lips with her fingertips, touching him in ways that seemed much more personal, more emotionally charged than when they'd been physically joined. The tender petting leached through his defenses. It put him on guard. She was going to propose something he wasn't going to like.

"I want to be in control this time."

"In control?"

"I know you know more about this whole lovemaking bit than I do. That you've had real experience where I've had only fantasies."

He tugged down the hem of her skirt to mid-thigh and stroked the soft skin there. She was nervous about this. Now *he* was petting *her*. "You want to try something different?"

"Very different."

His hand stopped at her meaningful pause. "What?"

He might be skeptical but he was listening. Whatever it took to make Caitlin happy, he wanted to do for her. He owed her that much for making his mission a success. He owed her a whole lot more for bringing his body back to the lusty world of the living. He owed her something else, too—something he wasn't sure he could give, something he didn't even want to put a name to because he might end up hurting her.

"You're afraid—" She stroked her fingers across his lips. "I'm sorry. *Afraid* isn't the right word. You're *concerned* that the people you connect with are going to disappoint you. You don't have terribly high expectations of them."

Ouch. Had he really been such a bear and not shown his appreciation to her? "I'm sorry. You've been great. I wasn't sure we could pull this off on a blind date. But you nailed the assignment."

She laughed, easing the misgivings he felt. "I sure did."

"Sorry. Wrong choice of words." She cupped his cheek, stealing the heat of his embarrassment with her soft touch and tender smile. "I've never had a mistress before. I wasn't sure what to expect. I'll have a high standard for anyone else to live up to now."

He meant that—as one of the finest compliments he could give.

"We've connected, haven't we?"

"Yeah." He was being set up for something, but he'd go into it with blinders on for Caitie's sake.

"I need you to trust me."

"I do."

"All the way, Sean." She caught his jaw between her hands. "I think you need to be able to trust someone that much, too."

"What, exactly, are you asking me?"

"We'll do this in baby steps, Agent Maddox. I'm not asking for forever or a year or a month or even a few days. I'm asking that you trust me. Tonight. One night." She swept her fingers though his hair as her eyes searched his face. "Open up that guarded soul of yours and let me show you that you don't always have to control a situation and keep your emotional distance. Surrender your trust to me. Let me make love to you. I promise you won't be disappointed.''

"I know I won't be."

"I want to be in complete control…to prove a point."

"And what's that?"

"That the people you care about aren't always going to hurt you."

He tried to make a joke of it. "What is this? Some kind of junior-high psychology trick?"

But she was serious. He could see it in the moisture that gathered in the corners of her eyes. He could feel it in her firm, supportive touch.

She'd seen through him. Found his weakness. She'd figured out he wasn't such a tough guy, after all.

"Damn." He lifted her off the counter and pulled her into his arms. He needed to be closer to her to talk about this. He buried his nose in her hair. "My father—he loved my mother more than his own life. He wasn't the best husband. He was gone a lot. The attraction between them had been instantaneous. When they met at a USO dance in London, he said he knew. But they were from different social backgrounds." Sean breathed deeply, trying to keep the emotion out of his voice. "He would have done anything for her."

"He trusted her?"

Sean nodded, feeling his parents' betrayals like an old injury that ached whenever the weather changed.

"What happened?" Caitlin asked.

This was hard, this emotional touchy-feely stuff. "My mother was lonely. Even when my father was stationed near home, he traveled." Sean bowed his head to the juncture of her neck and shoulder, taking comfort in the softness of her skin beneath his lips. "She found some companionship."

"Oh, Sean. I'm sorry." Caitlin hugged him tightly, imprinting the swell of her breasts and thighs into his love-starved body.

"More than once. She packed up and left my dad. Then she left the next lover. And the next." Sean slipped his hands beneath the sweet curve of Caitlin's bottom and lifted her so that she'd have to hold on even tighter. "She broke my father's heart."

Caitlin settled into the chair created by his hands, dragging the points of her breasts across his chest, exciting him. Reawakening his body and refilling the well of sorrow and pain and guilt inside him with need and desire. "I'm sorry. I can't imagine what that would have felt like. My parents loved each other until the day Mom died."

Sean teased the corner of Caitlin's mouth, drinking in more of her strength and comfort. "He wasn't any saint, either. He keeps looking for that one woman he can put his faith in. That one relationship that's going to last."

She gave him the kisses he asked for. "And you think you're like your father?" She nibbled his chin. "That you'll fall in love with a woman and she'll leave you?" She kissed his throat. "Why? Because your job is so important to you? Because you turn on that big ol' grizzly bear personality whenever you feel threatened?" She made it sound and feel like those were good things. Acceptable qualities. Traits she liked and admired.

Sean opened his mouth and absorbed the full healing power of her kisses. But she had started something here. She needed to hear the truth.

He pulled his mouth away and leaned his forehead against hers. He rubbed his hands up and down her arms and back. Wanting to hold, afraid to touch.

"I've done just that."

"What?"

"I'm afraid I'll hurt the people who care about me." He was afraid he'd hurt her, too. "I get caught up in my work—hell, no, that's just an excuse." He had to be honest with her. "I push them away."

"Before they can hurt you."

"Pretty noble guy, huh?"

"Pretty human, if you ask me." She made a fist and brushed it across his chin in a playful punch. "Welcome. It's about time you joined us."

"I gotta tell you I'm on mighty shaky ground here." Damn. Was that a nervous tremble in his voice?

"Sean." Caitlin pulled away, robbing him of all body contact except for the reassuring grip of her hand in his. She grabbed a condom and tucked it inside the waistband of her skirt. Interesting. "Have I done anything to disappoint you this weekend?"

"No."

She smiled at that—a deceptively innocent smile that said thanks with her lips, but something much more daring with her eyes. "You asked me to play your mistress. Did I do okay?"

She wanted proof? "Look at my pants."

There was something more erotic than embarrassing in the way her eyes caressed the jutting ridge that tented the zipper of his charcoal slacks. She brushed her fingers across the distended evidence of his desire. He had to close his eyes and breathe deeply to control the urge to buck up into her hand.

When she backed across the room, tugging gently on his fingers, he willingly followed. "You asked me to let you make love to me. Did I?"

"I've never wanted a woman so badly. Yes."

She pushed his shirt off his shoulders and tossed it onto the floor. He reached for her then, but she pushed away. Her hand burned against the skin of his chest. "Not yet."

His lungs swelled, drawing in extra oxygen to combat the urge to take her down to the floor right now and end this crazy torment of talking and teasing and baring his soul.

When she looked overhead, he followed her lead. She'd brought him to an iron bar, suspended from anchor bolts in the ceiling. From that bar hung a long chain with two cuffs at either end.

She lifted his hand just above his head and shackled one cuff around his wrist. The witch. Sean parted his lips, needing to breathe in even deeper as a mix of danger and desire clutched his throat. "Caitie, I don't know about this."

"Let me prove to you that you can trust me." She rubbed her palm in a circle over his heart, steadying the rapid staccato of its drumbeat beneath her exquisitely gentle, provocative touch. "I'll keep you safe. I promise."

Sean ran his tongue around his parched lips and watched with heated fascination as her pupils darted to follow his mouth and then dilated. She took his other arm, raised it and waited.

This was one of the hardest things he'd ever done—surrender his control to Caitlin. Surrender his control, period. Allow her to take care of him and his needs. Allow her to see him for who he really was. And count on her to return all that trust in one piece.

It would be easy to tell her no, to push her away. But he'd done that in the past, and made himself miserable.

He squinted and looked hard into her eyes to read the caring and sincerity there. Something trapped and battered deep inside him was fighting to be heard, struggling to be set free, begging him to take a chance and say yes.

It was his heart.

Sean's breath rushed out in a massive sigh. Then he raised his right hand and slipped it into the cuff at the end of that chain himself.

"Take me."

Caitlin's triumphant smile alone was worth the chance he was taking. Antsy as a chained bear, he paced and turned to keep the wicked little temptress in his sights. And Caitlin played the game well. She untied the scarf from around her neck and tossed it around his. When she tugged at the ends, pulling him closer, he willingly bent his mouth to claim hers.

The kiss was wild, unleashed. Stroking tongues and open, wet mouths.

He tugged at his chains, following the instinctive urge to capture her in his arms. Their torsos touched, and her twin nipples poked into his chest. Basic woman. Basic man.

"I want you." He growled the urgent wish between his teeth and dived after her with seeking lips, catching another quick kiss before she backed out of reach.

"Not yet." She shook her finger at him and ran her tongue around her smiling lips.

His slacks were suddenly way too tight. "Caitie."

"*I'm* in control. Remember?"

The blood was pounding so hard in his ears, her words seemed barely more than a feral moan.

She slinked even farther away, her long, strong thighs moving the tiger stripes of her skirt as if the smooth, graceful coat was real and she was a feline beast.

"You do want me, don't you?" She pulled down her top, freeing her small, taut breasts for his hungry eyes to feast upon.

He took a step toward her, but the chains held him back. "Damn, Caitie. I'm going to embarrass myself."

"No, you won't." The skirt went next. It dropped to the

floor with a swish of sound that skittered across his senses like an actual caress. "I'll take care of you." She stripped off the black lace thong and held it out to him like temptation itself. She dragged it across his chest and he flinched. She rubbed the nubby lace across his flanks and stomach. He closed his eyes, clenched his hands into fists and moaned at the sweet agony of sensation. "I promised to make this good for you, remember."

"It is. Damn. It is."

"It's good for me, too."

She held it up to his chin and he could smell her sweet honey on it. It was an aphrodisiac that went straight to his brain. The chains rattled as he fought against them for release.

"Caitie." He jerked once more against the chains. "Soon."

Her fingers brushed his stomach when she unsnapped his pants. He nearly lost it then. "You don't have to control everything, Sean."

"But I—"

He lost the power to speak when her hand closed around him through his briefs. "Let me do this for you," she commanded in a sweet, husky voice.

Sean's throbbing, aching shaft danced in the air as she pushed his pants and shorts down to the floor around his ankles.

Other than his feet, he was naked. Vulnerable. Chained. Exposed.

Caitie knelt in front of him and gentled him in the most elemental of ways. She pressed her lips against his groin, stroked her hands along his buttocks and thighs. The simple petting tempered his need for only a moment.

Because then she took him in her mouth.

In much the same way he had suckled her beneath the

waterfall, she licked and gently nipped and kissed and sucked. He started to buck as natural urges took control of his body. "Caitie. Damn." He twisted his hips and fought the rush of blood and lust and sanity that flooded his groin. "Caitie."

She pulled away. He heard the rip of paper, smelled the tang of latex, felt the hot, swift sweep of her hands on his penis as she rolled on the condom.

And then she was standing. Too far away. "Caitie?"

"Trust me?"

With his body primed and ready to mate, she was demanding something more from him. With his defenses down, his fears revealed, his heart on the line, he finally crossed over and took that chance.

"I trust you."

When Caitie smiled, the last of his doubts unwound their merciless grip on his heart.

She reached up and grabbed the bar above his hands. Then he could only watch in awe and fascination as she lifted her legs and wrapped them around his hips. She was strong. She was limber. And she was his.

She found him, cradled him, sheathed him in her hot, moist sex. With her eyes boldly locked on his, she linked her feet together and squeezed him tightly.

He kissed her mouth, her neck, whatever he could reach until the need for release grew too powerful to control. He pumped inside her with thrust after forceful thrust, and she held him close every step of the way. He shouted his release and surged inside her with the most explosive orgasm of his life.

And if the word *love* slipped from her lips, he was too far gone in the ecstasy of discovering it for himself to hear it.

"SO, WAS THAT OKAY for you?" Caitlin asked, not daring to look at Sean as she picked up her clothes and began to dress. She still felt too raw, too vulnerable, after what she'd just admitted to risk looking at the bronze man-god chained to the ceiling behind her.

"Try mind-blowing." There was nothing but sincere appreciation in his voice. "Thank God for tall women."

Her arms ached and her body was so spent and sated she could barely stand. But he made her laugh. She tied the skirt around her waist and adjusted her top as she went to the cabinet and picked up the key to his shackles. "I don't know how I would have managed that if I was only five-four."

She returned to him to pull up his briefs and slacks and hook them at his waist. For some reason, she couldn't take her eyes off her work. "That's something you've taught me this weekend. To be content with who I am. To be proud that I'm—"

"An Amazon princess."

She looked up then. Contentment seeped through her veins, calming her doubts about having taken her point too far. "I like that." She stroked his cheek. "You claim you're not a sweet-talker, but it's hard to picture you as a job-obsessed control freak when you say something pretty like that."

"Pretty?" Was that a blush coloring his cheeks? "I thought I was the villain in your fantasies. You're ruining my tough-guy image."

"Only in my fantasies. In reality, I've decided you're my hero."

Caitlin rewarded him with a kiss and Sean gladly accepted his prize.

An abrasive, grinding sound interrupted them.

"Isn't that sweet."

Caitlin whipped around at the intrusion of a husky female voice. Ali Turner, looking chic and polished and wrinkled as a prune with that pissed-off frown on her face, stepped into the room from the hidden passageway. John Doe entered the room behind her, flashing a big black gun.

"What are you doing?" Caitlin gasped. With her family's military background, she'd been around guns before. But she'd never had one pointed at her.

Sean rattled his chains, angling his body to protect her. With him positioned between her and the gun, she couldn't see his expression. But she recognized that deadly, don't-mess-with-me tone in his voice. "Don't point that thing unless you know how to use it."

John scratched his scraggly blond beard and grinned. "What's to know? It's just like a camera. Point and shoot."

Ali's impatient sigh stirred her finely coiffed hair. "John, put that away and try not to act like such an idiot."

"Thanks, Aunt Ali," John sneered. "First you put a crimp in my honeymoon, and now you criticize me."

"You guys are related?" Caitlin asked.

John didn't sound terribly proud of the connection. "My mom's sister. You know, nepotism ain't all it's cracked up to be. Can't really argue that she's got the looks in the family. But now she claims she's got the brains, too. You know, this whole operation wouldn't have gotten off the ground if I hadn't—"

Ali spared her nephew a glance. "Shut. Up."

John got a good look at his aunt's displeased expression and fell silent.

Caitlin clutched the back of Sean's waistband as Ali sauntered toward them. She held up a small white canister between two ruby-tinted fingernails. "Been doing some snooping, have we?"

"My inhaler." Oh God. She must have dropped it in the room with all the monitors when she'd been in such a hurry to escape.

"Douglas likes to keep all his guests accounted for. That way he can assure everyone is enjoying themselves, and no one is infringing on anyone else's privacy." Ali stopped about five feet away, shaking her head in mock confusion. "But you two just don't want to follow the rules, do you? Go get the girl and—" She stopped and snarled again when she realized her nephew hadn't followed her. She pointed to the space beside her on the floor. "John!"

Every muscle in Sean's torso tensed when John jogged across the room with the gun. The chains rattled over their heads and Caitlin realized she hadn't unlocked him. She couldn't very well do that now. If Sean made any threatening move, John might shoot. Sean would be an unarmed target.

Without a second thought, she moved in front of him, slipping the key into his pocket as she went. "Caitie." His voice was gruff with concern.

"It's all right." She tried to calm his anxiety, to soothe the fury in his eyes by reaching up and pushing that stray lock of hair back into place. "Trust me."

"I don't like violence, Caitlin, dear." There was nothing dear in Ali's husky voice. "But I do like getting what I want when I want it. Now move away from him."

Caitie felt a rough hand at her elbow, jerking her away from Sean.

"If you hurt her—"

"Save the dramatic speech, Maddox." John pressed the gun into Caitlin's ribs and dragged her back with him. "She's our insurance. General Whitmore says her daddy's an old-fashioned stick-in-the-mud. If he finds out his little girl's been screwing her brains out all weekend—"

"You son of a bitch." Caitlin saw Sean's anger turn into a desperate look of apology when he glanced at her. But there was nothing but deadly venom in his eyes for John. "When I get my hands on you—"

"Enough." Ali remained unruffled by the combative males. "Your choices are to pay me fifty thousand dollars and forget your little investigation before I show your tape to the Bureau chief and Caitlin's father, or—"

"I'm going to arrest your skinny ass."

"Or…" she paused to emphasize her claim, annoyed by Sean's interruption "…I can dispose of her the way I got rid of the last person who refused to play my game."

"Ramon Vargas?" Sean asked.

"Ramon Vargas." Ali shrugged as if the man's death meant nothing to her. It didn't. "He was too good-looking to be such a lousy lover. But he was rich. When he invited me to his hotel room in D.C., he was supposed to make another payment."

"He refused."

"Don't make the same mistake, Chief Maddox." Ali was beautiful and spoiled and capable of murder. "Or your little concubine here might take a terrible tumble off one of Pleasure Cove's nasty cliffs." She turned to John. "Take her away."

John's fingers dug into Caitlin's arm. She smacked at his bruising hand. "Stop that!" She yelped. John jerked her hard enough to lift her off her feet. "Ow!"

"Caitie!" Sean tugged against his chains, a mighty heave that made the cuffs cut into his wrists, and shook the plaster mounts of the iron bar above him.

John's gun swung over to Sean. Caitlin screamed, "Sean, no."

Sean froze at her command. His beautiful eyes narrowed to slits of intense midnight green. If he were set free, she had no doubt that John would be toast. The exhilaration of

Sean's caring and protection warred with the need to keep him safe, to protect the life of the man she loved. But what should she do? No fantasy adventure had prepared her for this kind of danger.

Or had it?

Without moving her head, she scanned the room. She was surrounded by a fantasy. This whole estate was a testament to one man's gift for making fantasies come true.

A creative rush of adrenaline spread through Caitlin, making her smarter and calmer—and a heck of a better actress— than her red-haired nemesis.

Ali took a few steps closer and flicked her nail beneath Sean's chin, taunting the beast, showing off her power to control him by controlling Caitlin's fate. "Leave him. He can't harm us where he is. Let him stew overnight while we decide the best way to ensure their silence."

She turned toward the hidden sliding panel. Her shoulders rose and fell in an irritated huff. "This exit, idiot. Do you want to draw a crowd with that gun?"

Why not?

The second John opened his mouth to argue with Ali, Caitlin lunged for the suit of armor beside her. The heavy suit was already falling when she grabbed the mace on it— a heavy iron ball covered in spikes—and swung it at John.

Even the glancing blow was enough to knock him to his knees and send the gun flying across the room. "Hey!"

"John!"

John grabbed his injured wrist and staggered to his feet. But Caitlin had already moved on to the rack.

"Stop!" Ali shouted. "Stop this at once!"

It was an easy enough game to get John to give chase. Caitlin toppled tables and tossed chains, dodging his grasp. Other sounds erupted in the room—Ali's screams for order, spiked heels clacking on the stone floor as she chased after the gun, that ear-splitting shriek of metal grinding against metal. Caitlin dived for the cage. John swerved to head her off. She stuck out one long leg and he tripped.

A gunshot thundered through the air.

Caitlin slammed the cage door on John and whirled around. "Sean!"

"Stop this right—" Ali's order gurgled into silence as Sean pulled himself up on the bar the way Caitlin had, and twisted his legs around Ali's neck.

"Drop it." He shook her once and she dropped the gun. He jerked his legs a second time and she put her hands in the air. He swung his gaze around to Caitlin. "Are you all right?"

"I'm fine. Are you?"

He never got a chance to answer. There was a rattle in the lock and the door burst open. Douglas Fairchild threw it wide, and Bert and Jeffrey swept in ahead of him and secured the gun. Ramona Fairchild, Priscilla Doe and every other guest on the island, in various states of costume and undress, flocked in behind him.

There was a beat of dead silence as everyone took in the scene. John in a cage with Caitlin leaning against the door. Sean, naked to the waist and hanging from the ceiling with his legs looped around Ali Turner's neck.

Priscilla Doe broke the silence. She stomped her foot, and in her high-pitched, baby-doll voice, said, "Dang it, John, if you wanted to double up, you should have asked me."

After she turned and stormed out, Caitlin was the first to laugh. Sean's rich baritone soon joined in. Les Truitt added a yee-haw and his wife actually smiled.

Douglas Fairchild raised his arms and hushed everyone into silence. "What's all the commotion about in here?"

Sean released Ali, and Jeffrey took her by the arm. In an incredible move of strength and dexterity, Sean pulled his legs up over the bar. Gravity dropped the key from his pocket into his waiting hand. After unlocking his shackles, he dropped to the floor, a free man.

Then he made quick work of pulling down the chain and locking the cuffs around Ali Turner's wrists. Caitlin took the hint and closed the padlock on John Doe's cage.

Then Sean looked at her from across the room and said, "Come here."

She ran to his side.

"I'm waiting for an answer," Fairchild demanded.

"They broke the rules." Sean tucked Caitlin under his arm and waltzed toward the door. "They didn't ask for permission to join us."

16

"SOLID REPORT, Maddox." Chief Dillon's praise didn't cause Sean's moody frown to waver an iota. "The Reyes case is back on track with the obstruction of justice charge, and the San Isidrans are talking about erecting a monument to Ambassador Vargas."

"It was his death that put us on the trail to Pleasure Cove Island in the first place."

"That's awfully decent of you, Maddox, sharing the credit like that," Dillon exclaimed.

Sean hadn't done the job himself. There was a tall, leggy blonde he hadn't seen in four long days who deserved most of the credit. The chief set the report in front of Sean and rose to straighten his tie. "Ali Turner and John Turner Doe's extortion-murder scheme was your collar all the way. Poor Douglas Fairchild. Here he thought he was doing a favor for all those guests, when underneath his nose, his former lover and her nephew were using his parties as a perfect setup for their con game."

Sean nodded. "At Ali's insistence, Fairchild hired Doe to install what he thought was a security system. If Cai—" He rubbed his jaw wearily as he caught himself. "If I hadn't run across that cache of videotapes, this case would have been dead in the water."

As far as Chief Dillon knew, Caitlin McCormick didn't exist. Sean had given his word about her top-secret adventure. The only way Hal McCormick would find out about his daughter's lusty road trip and fantasy getaway was if she told him herself.

Sean hadn't been able to offer her forever, but he had been able to guarantee her anonymity, even during the upcoming trial. It was the least he could do.

"Good sleuthing, Maddox." Chief Dillon walked to the door, then stopped and turned, a curious expression on his face. "Do you really get whatever you want on that island?"

"Just about."

He'd gotten the bad guys, great sex and a lesson on living that would make his life richer and fuller. It would also be a hell of a lot tougher now that he'd learned to acknowledge his emotions and had found the courage to give them away.

But he hadn't gotten the girl.

"Good night, Maddox. Don't work too late." Sean barely heard the chief leave.

He hadn't gotten the girl.

Thomas and a helicopter full of agents had descended on the island Sunday morning, and he'd had to go to work. Caitlin had thanked him politely for helping make her wildest fantasies come true. She'd given him a kiss, wished him luck and said she hoped he hadn't been disappointed in her performance as his mistress.

Disappointed? No way. He was brave enough to admit that, somewhere along the line, their act had become the real thing.

But two days? Could a man and woman fall in love in just two jam-packed days? His father had courted his mother for a year before he proposed. And they'd ended up unhappy and apart.

Sean wouldn't do that to Caitie. He didn't want to be the man who wound up hurting her. So he hadn't stopped her when she'd said she had to go.

But, damn. He wanted the girl.

With his questionable history with female relationships, he'd really only had one that he'd always been able to count on. Minutes later, he was on the phone to his sister down in Guatemala. They chatted about her work and his, about birthdays and scenery and the weather.

"What's wrong, Sean?" Sabrina had always been one to get straight to the point. "You never call me on a weeknight."

Sean didn't bother to argue. "How do I tell the woman I love that I want her to stay?"

"It's about time," his sister said, and promptly burst into happy tears.

"Bree?" He apologized for making her cry and answered her questions, glossing over the details of his weekend with Caitlin. "I don't know how to make this right."

Sabrina sniffed back her tears. "You just say the words, you big lug."

"You know words aren't my best thing."

"I didn't say it would be easy. But it's worth it." He could hear her laughing now. "Am I going to get a chance to meet this woman who finally cracked my big brother's heart?"

"I hope so, Bree. I hope I can convince her to put up with me for good."

After hanging up, Sean looked up Caitlin's number. Hell. He'd never even asked her out on a proper date. And now he wanted to ask her about—dare he say it out loud?—commitment.

Long-term. Exclusive. Permanent.

His hand hesitated on the phone. He should do this in person. Maybe he should just surprise her. He could pick up flowers. A bottle of wine. No. That sounded too damn heroic. Caitlin liked—

Sean's office door burst open. He jumped to his feet and braced to defend himself. With a quick glance at the intruders, he realized his reckoning had come sooner than he'd expected.

He didn't need to be a rocket scientist to identify the three men who had stormed in and surrounded him—one at the door and one at either side of his desk, blocking an easy escape. Each man was tall—well over six feet. Each man had some shade of blond hair. And two of them wore Marine Corps uniforms—one khaki dress, the other camouflage fatigues.

"You must be the McCormicks." Inside him a ripple of unease mixed with a tiny light of hope. "I'm Sean Maddox. I assume you're here to set me straight about Caitie."

CAITLIN PACED IMPATIENTLY, waiting for the elevator door to open. Of all the stupid, pigheaded…

One heartfelt conversation with her father and the whole thing had gotten blown way out of proportion. Hal McCormick hadn't heard much of anything beyond, "I spent my weekend with a man." The "Dad, I think I love him" got lost in the rapid-fire questions about time and place and condoms and a Porsche.

Caitlin was trying to push the door open as the elevator dinged. And then she was running down the hall. She'd made good time from Alexandria to Quantico. But without a military pass, it had taken a frantic woman considerably longer to gain access up to the third floor of FBI headquarters. She hadn't taken time to put on makeup after crying or to change out of her jeans.

After getting calls from both Ethan and Travis in one night, she'd grabbed her purse and ran. If any of them hurt Sean… Oh damn. She'd promised she'd keep him safe.

"Is Caitie all right?" Thank God. That was Sean's voice. They hadn't shot him yet.

She heard the cocky intonation of Travis's voice next. "If you call hanging out in her room crying for the past four days all right, then, hell, yeah, she's fine."

"Crying?" Oh no. Sean would beat himself up over that one.

Caitlin closed in on the sound of the voices and flung open the door to Sean's office. "I was not crying all that time. I was thinking. I was trying to figure a way out of this mess that would keep everybody happy. I was giving Sean time to figure out what *he* wants."

She looked past her father's shoulder and drowned in the heat of Sean's green eyes. He needed a shave. He needed some sleep.

He needed to know that she trusted him to love her.

Walking away from him on Pleasure Cove Island had been the hardest thing she'd ever done. She'd promised no strings on their relationship. A trio of overprotective family members demanding a shotgun wedding were definite strings.

She'd wanted to play his mistress, have her adventure. And though she wanted their fantasy weekend to have a happy ending, she was prepared to handle the consequences of her choices. If she wanted to be treated as a grown, independent woman, she intended to act like one. He'd come a long way when it came to trust and it was up to her to help him keep the faith.

He needed to know she wasn't going to let him down.

But her father caught her first. "Honey, we just want *you* to be happy. If this jackass has done something to hurt you, then what he wants doesn't matter."

As her brothers advanced, Caitlin ran around the desks and threw herself in front of Sean. "Yes, it does. He didn't hurt me, Dad. He loves me.'' She sensed the sudden stillness in the man behind her. He didn't think she knew his secret. He might not have even admitted it to himself yet. But she'd protect him even if he denied the truth. ''He saved my life.''

Her father's cheeks flushed with ruddy color, then went pale. ''Just what were you doing that you needed saving?''

She started to explain, but Sean's hands closed around her shoulders and scooted her to one side. With all the snap of a recruit reporting to a superior officer, he picked up a folder and handed it to her father. ''Preliminary report, sir. We took down two perps who were allegedly conducting an extortion scheme with international implications. I can't share all the particulars. Top secret, you understand.''

''Top secret?'' Hal swore. ''You got my daughter mixed up with this?''

''She helped bring them in, sir. We expect to go to trial by the end of the year.''

''What?''

Travis grinned. ''Go, Caitie.''

Ethan, her quiet brother, was less ebullient. ''You said she was in danger?''

''I did my best to—''

''He saved my life, Dad. I've always been safe with him.'' She turned and looked into those questing green eyes so he could understand she meant her heart as well as her life. ''Always.''

But her father wasn't convinced yet. ''So you recruited her—a civilian—to work an undercover operation for the Bureau?''

''No, Dad.'' Caitlin answered for herself. ''I volunteered. You three aren't the only McCormicks who want to serve their country.''

Hal looked at Ethan. He looked at Travis. When he finally looked at Caitlin, she knew he was going to be okay with this. "What are your intentions toward my girl?" he asked Sean.

"My intentions?"

"Dad. Let me handle this part of the conversation. Please?" She circled the desk, gave her father a kiss and hugged him around his neck. "I love you, Dad. I'm gonna be okay."

She dismissed Ethan and Travis with a kiss and a hug each, and finally she was alone with Sean.

"Now I really feel like the villain."

He sat on his side of the desk and she lingered on hers.

"You shouldn't. You're the hero of all my fantasies, Sean." She looked him straight in the eye. She needed him to hear this and see that it was true. "I love you."

Then he was coming around the desk. He stopped in front of her. Caitlin held her breath. "I guess you figured out how I feel. I'm crazy in love with you, Caitie. And I want to give this relationship thing a shot. Take you out to dinner. Spend some time with your family. Meet your kids at school." He reached out and tucked a curl behind her ear. "I want you and me to work—for a hell of a lot longer than just one weekend."

"Me, too." She lifted the hair that had fallen across his brow and brushed it back into place. "I feel like I'm going backward on this, though. Where should we start?"

Minutes later they were in the parking garage, falling into the back seat of his Porsche. In a greedy flurry of touches and kisses, he had his hands in her shirt and her pants undone.

This was the bad-ass bad guy she was so crazy about.

In another few minutes they were joined together and happy in love.

"Umm, Sean?" she gasped as he opened his mouth against her throat.

"What is it, sweetheart?"

She wrapped her arms around his shoulders. "From now until forever, I promise that in all my fantasies my hero will be named Sean."

"Fantasy, nothing." He kissed her soundly and drove himself home. "I'm the real thing."

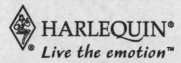

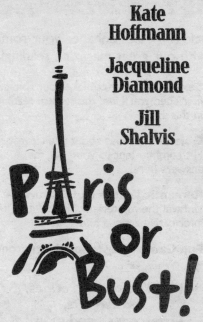

eHARLEQUIN.com

Sit back, relax and enhance your romance
with our great magazine reading!

- **Sex and Romance!** Like your romance
  hot? Then you'll *love* the sensual reading
  in this area.

- **Quizzes!** Curious about your lovestyle?
  His commitment to you? Get the
  answers here!

- **Romantic Guides and Features!**
  Unravel the mysteries of love with
  informative articles and advice!

- **Fun Games!** Play to your heart's content....

**Plus...romantic recipes,
top ten lists,
Lovescopes...and more!**

**Enjoy our online magazine today—
visit www.eHarlequin.com!**